praise fo

"A charming story about love least expected."

—USA TODAY RITA AWARD-WINNING
BESTSELLING AUTHOR SUSAN MAY WARREN

"Rachel D. Russell has crafted a deep, heartfelt
romance that brings home not just the courage love takes,
but the courage it takes to trust God when life is scary.
This beautiful romance had me smiling, laughing, and
wishing it would never end."

—JESSICA WAKEFIELD, AUTHOR OF THE CHRISTMAS BOX

"This is the perfect book to curl up with and be swept up
on the story. You get romance and some thought
provoking truths intertwined into this delightful story."

—NICOLE, GOODREADS

"Deep Haven is one of my favorite fictional towns to visit.
Did I mention there were a lot of horses in this book?
swoon I laughed, gasped, and cried. Then I got the
warm fuzzies at the end. Another five-star read by an
author I know will deliver."

—SHARON H., GOODREADS

it's your love

A Deep Haven Novel

Fox Family ✻ Book Two

rachel d. russell

Edited by
susan may warren

sunrise
PUBLISHING

In memory of Mom and Dad.
I miss you both, yet rejoice in your salvation.

The LORD himself goes before you and will be
with you; he will never leave you nor forsake you.
Do not be afraid; do not be discouraged.
Deuteronomy 31:8

one

· · ·

KIDS WERE GOING TO DIE ON THESE HORSES. AND IT WOULD BE ALL his fault.

The mare beneath Grayson Fox let out a grunt. Dust rose from the Trinity Horse Camp corral, a flurry of hooves, bucks, and squeals slicing through Minnesota's North Shore and its late May heat wave.

"I asked you to bring me camp horses." The deep voice rumbled across the din. Grayson's audience of one, camp director Noah Standing Bear, stood outside the corral, a grim press to his lips. That hurt more than the whiplash his body was taking.

Grayson's torso snapped forward and back with each jump and kick of the buckskin mare. He rode it out, mad at himself for hopping on without doing the proper groundwork.

He'd known it didn't bode well when he'd set the saddle on her. The ears pinned back. The muscles flinchy. Her feet had danced, and her black tail had swished back and forth.

But he'd kept pushing through and swung into the stirrups.

Please, Lord, please answer this one prayer.

Another buck nearly dislodged him.

Nope. Maybe God still wasn't listening.

Grayson looked past the weathered top rail, beyond the arena, to where several cross-fenced paddocks held the camp horses in knee-high grass. Deep, three-sided run-in sheds provided shade and shelter from the elements. It would have been a pastoral view if not for the unhappy mount beneath him.

He urged the mare forward on loose reins. The bucks had turned to crow hops after a few more NFR-worthy launches into the air. She slowed with fatigue and moved around the pen, first at a broken lope, then slowing to a jog and walk.

Her nostrils flared with puffs of breath, and her golden sides heaved.

Poor girl. He wasn't the kind of horseman who'd put an animal into this position—that's exactly why Oregon's Three Sisters Ranch had hired him nearly twelve years ago.

Good thing those clients couldn't see him now.

He waited for her to settle, then rubbed her quivering shoulder. Watched her eyes, her face. The softening—a little give.

Noah stood, a silent, incredulous six-foot-three wall.

Grayson dismounted, swift and quiet, glad to have his feet, *and* the buckskin's, all on the ground. The smell of horse and sweat and leather permeated the stifling heat of the day.

He lifted his Stetson, wiped his sleeve across his brow, and resettled his hat.

The mare's entire body balled up again, ready for another round of bucking, but she remained standing, tight and tense. "Easy, girl. I'm sorry. How about we take that tack off for today, huh?" He waited for her head to lower and the press of her lips to release before loosening the latigo hitch on the cinch.

She pinned her ears.

"You're okay, Tally." Tally. Aptly named—probably for the number of riders she'd dislodged, unseated, and dumped. He slid the saddle and pad off, pulling them away when the mare grunted and kicked out.

His chest constricted, the burden of his actions pressing in. He knew better. Horses were his life. All he'd wanted was to return to Deep Haven with an offering. Something good for the camp that had changed his life after his parents' deaths. A way to be helpful.

Well, he could handle this. If there was one thing he knew, it was how to dig in and get things done.

He braced the cantle on his hip and let out the lead line until he reached the corral side, then hoisted the saddle over the panel.

When he turned back to the mare, her ears moved back and forth, listening. She was stocky, with powerful muscling that had coiled and burst beneath him. Far too many times. A few scratches and old scars marred her forelegs and rump. Unnatural white patches of hair marked her withers where ill-fitted saddles had chafed.

Her legs trembled when he drew the line back in. "Easy," he said, hoping the encouragement would keep her still. He removed the bridle, glad he'd left the halter on underneath, and slung it over his shoulder, then untied the throatlatch knot and slid the rope halter off.

Tally threw her head back, the whites of her eyes bright against her gold coat. She turned, bolted to the far side of the corral, and nickered to the two other horses he'd bought with her.

They answered from the small paddock nearby. She drew in another breath and let out a poignant holler that shook her whole body.

He tried to rub away the pressure in his chest with his palm. So much for his demo ride. Even though Noah had arranged the buy, Grayson should have checked them out before he'd loaded them up.

All three of them had probably been bound for the auction yard when he pulled up with his truck and trailer to complete Noah's purchase. He'd thought it was an easy favor for the camp that had introduced him to horses when he was a distraught ten-year-old.

He climbed over the top rail and jumped to the soft grass below, then took off his Stetson and ran his hand over his hair. Watched the dust lift off the corral footing.

Noah blew out a breath and lifted his hands toward the corral. "What am I going to do with them? Are they all like that?"

Noah Standing Bear. A name as impressive as the man who wielded it. He'd started Wilderness Challenge camp on the shores of Mink Lake right around when Grayson turned ten. It hadn't taken long to branch out and add the horse camp a couple years later.

"Apparently they were drugged when I picked them up." Disgust edged Grayson's voice. Hopefully not all three. He shoved his Stetson back on his head. How many livestock sales had he been to over the years? He wasn't some green rancher wannabe.

"Or could be some rough stock from the rodeo?" Noah asked. By the press of his jaws, he was probably asking a serious question.

Grayson should have known better than to have been lured by their lackluster energy and listless attention. To have chalked it up to their so-called babysitter status—the kind of horse that someone could plop a kid on, point down the trail, and not worry about.

These horses—at least Miss Tally—were anything but safe.

Noah's hand landed on Grayson's chest with a heavy smack, but his dark eyes held a smile. "Good thing you're here for summer." His brow arched with a dubious lift, and he nodded toward Tally. "Let's not put that one in the string."

Grayson blew out a breath. "To be fair, you're the one that said you needed me to pick up three camp horses in North Dakota." He let out a wry laugh. "I did what I was asked. These are the horses the guy had for you."

"Okay, Horse Whisperer, but I thought you'd give them a look-see before you hauled them here. I asked you to come fill in as camp wrangler to help me out—not to create more work." He crossed his arms and leaned against one of the tall birch trees that shaded the barnyard.

"Funny. And also probably fair. But look at her—other than me being an oaf getting on her like that, odds are, we saved her life," Grayson said. And okay, Grayson was a sucker for an animal in need. An aged horse that wasn't rideable didn't have good prospects. "Let's give them time to settle down. Then I'll see what we've got." He sure hoped he'd have something to work with, because he'd come to Deep Haven to sell his parents' vacant lot, fill in as Noah's camp wrangler for summer, and leave town with all the cash he needed to put a down payment on his own ranch in Oregon and secure his loan. "She'll be okay."

Noah rubbed a hand across his chin, his eyes on the buckskin standing in the corral. "I'm not the horse expert around here, but I have doubts."

Yeah. Grayson didn't blame him. "It's okay. I've got this." Because he would. He always did. He had to.

Noah narrowed his gaze. "You heading into town?"

"At some point," Grayson said.

"I'll be frank—I wasn't sure you'd say yes. It's been, what, six years since you've been home for a visit?"

Home. He didn't think of Deep Haven as home anymore. "Work's kept me busy—lots of horses coming through the training barn at Three Sisters. But as it turns out, I have an opportunity to buy my own place." Oh, and here was the hard part. "And, I, uh, suddenly found myself in want of employment."

Noah stood upright, his jaw slack. "You were fired?"

"Not exactly. Let's just say the new head trainer and I agreed to disagree about training techniques—and since he's the ranch owner's brother..." Grayson wasn't keen on reliving that barn aisle showdown. "Turns out twelve years of loyalty isn't a match for a blood relation."

"Ah." Noah crossed his arms again. "But he didn't know you already? Didn't know you'd take issue with his style?"

Grayson shook his head. "He'd been working at a big outfit in Texas. Decided to take the vacant job at Three Sisters working for his brother when the spot opened up." Grayson lifted his hands. "So when you called to say your wrangler was out of commission with a broken leg, how could I say no?"

Noah nodded. "God has a way of working things out. Tell me about this place you want to buy."

Grayson wasn't sure God had anything to do with it. "One of the other local trainers I've gotten to know over the years is retiring. He's ready to downsize, move into town. Travel." The thought of Vincent Tucker's place caused a swell in his chest. The way the unpretentious, small cabin stood against the backdrop of ponderosa trees and the Cascade Mountain Range. The rich, green growth of the irrigated pasture, and the location—backed right up to thousands of acres of federal land. "I had this idea that maybe I could open the place up to youth."

"A camp?" Noah asked.

"Yeah. Something like Trinity." Because even though Grayson had been dropped off at that first camp season as an unwilling participant, all it had taken was one hour with the horses to change his mind—and his life.

Noah's brows rose. "Wow. That's a big undertaking."

Grayson's heart sank. "I know. It's crazy, but I can't stop thinking about it. About the kids out there who are just like I was. Kids who need that kind of opportunity." Grayson watched a butterfly pass between them. "But it's...not cheap." He gestured toward the arena and paddocks, where horses of every color swished flies and dozed in the rising heat.

Noah rubbed his chin. "No, it isn't. But you can find a way, like I did." He set his booted foot onto a rock and leaned forward. "Can you believe it's been twenty years since that first season?"

"I was a scrawny preteen back then."

Noah waved him off. "You were fine." He tugged a handkerchief from his pocket and wiped the sweat from his brow. "Your grandma must have been glad you lost your job in Oregon, though. Got you back to Deep Haven."

"They don't know. I think they assumed I took the summer off to help out." Grayson toed a patch of bare ground. "I didn't want them getting ideas about me coming back here to stay."

"Do they know about the place you want to buy?"

"Not yet."

He lingered at the side of the pen, putting off the inevitable, and tried to buoy his confidence. He listened to the *kvik-kvik* chatter and song of the barn swallows for a moment, and then walked back to the horse trailer he'd left open. He'd known returning to Deep Haven would be hard. Still, the full force of driving in on Highway 61 had rattled him harder than landing flat out from a bull's buck. The fleeting thought of a U-turn straight back out of town had been crushed by the heavy rumble of his Ram's diesel engine, the loaded three-horse trailer in tow.

Nope. There'd been no turning his rig around. Especially with the Memorial Day weekend crowd caravanning into Deep Haven right behind him.

He swung the back door on the trailer closed and latched it. Stared at the camp's faded red barn.

The sight of the hitching posts, corral, and outdoor arena settled over him like the melody of crickets on a summer night. Curious nickers from the new horses were met with a chorus of whinnies from the nearby pastures.

Noah turned from the corral and walked across the gravel. Lines creased his brow. He paced for a few minutes, as if thinking.

Grayson leaned back against the trailer. The breeze through the white pine and spruce didn't ease the heat that flared from his neck upward. "Your new wrangler, Jesse, broke his leg—but what happened to Walter?" Walter Kreder...the Sam Elliott lookalike who'd let Grayson tag along while he cared for all the camp horses.

"He retired about five years ago. Jesse Schmidt—he's the one I told you about—broke his leg in a car accident in March. Let me tell you, I'm glad you're here, because we're a bit behind on the summer schedule." Noah placed a hand on Grayson's shoulder. "The barn apartment is ready for you." He gave a tap before stepping away. "Get cleaned up, and then you probably should head into town."

"What about the horses?"

Noah glanced back at the paddock. "We'll deal with them later."

"I can stick around to keep an eye on them." He tipped his face to the deep-blue sky. "It's a hot day." He knew with enough time he could work it out with those animals. Even Tally.

A nod from Noah. "They've made it this far. I don't think you staring at them through the fence is going to change much." He gave him a wry smile. "They've got water, shade, and hay. They'll be fine."

Grayson let out a laugh. "Right." He didn't move.

Noah scratched his beard. "It's been a long time—we've missed seeing you around Deep Haven."

A tightness coiled around Grayson's throat. Made it hard to swallow. He nodded and turned away. Everywhere his eyes landed, the past stood with stalwart reminders. The four-stall barn with its gabled roof and hayloft, built of local lumber. The horse paddocks, tall with spring growth.

A few rough-hewn log benches tugged a smile from his lips. Because it wasn't all bad.

S'mores and songs and the smell of sweat from a hard day of playing in the outdoors.

But he had his reasons for staying away.

Noah stared at him for a moment, his lips pressed together. "Well, you better get into town. You can't hide out here."

"Oh, I'm not hiding." His voice didn't even convince himself.

"You drove across the country, brought me three drugged-up horses, and hauled them to camp instead of driving straight to see your family, whom you haven't seen in…years." Noah leveled Grayson an expression that said every part of *I don't believe you* that it could.

Grayson shrugged. "It's too hot a day to leave the horses in the trailer." He wiped sweat from his brow again, just to make his point. And horses were his work.

"Yeah. Then you unloaded said animals. Felt the need to tack up. Ride." Noah laughed. "And let's be honest—we could have sold tickets for that rodeo."

Grayson held up his hands. "Okay, point taken."

"I can't imagine it's easy, but family matters often aren't."

"It's been so long." He rolled his shoulders like he could rid himself of the knots that were coiling. It didn't help.

"Gone so long you didn't quite know how to come back?"

Grayson shifted his weight.

Noah walked toward his truck, stopped, and turned. "I'm sure you had your reasons for staying away, but you're here now. Clean up. Head into town." He dug into his pocket and tossed a key to Grayson. "You'll need this. There're fresh linens on the bed. Meet me back here at five and I'll walk you through the horses' feeding routine."

With the departing crunch of Noah's truck on the graveled drive, Grayson hauled the saddle back to the tack room, grabbed his duffel from his rig, and walked into the barn. Everything in him still wanted to flee.

Because he was the guy who'd run away, as far from Deep Haven as he could, almost before his graduation cap even hit the ground. Buried himself in work and spent late nights at Rowdy's bar, finding comfort with any number of women on the dance floor. Darts. A few games of pool. He hadn't needed alcohol.

Just something to occupy his mind at the end of the day. Enjoy the attention, then go home. Alone.

Never getting attached.

Even that had cost him. Memories of Harper Pennington's bright smile and blue eyes wheedled into Grayson's consciousness, followed by the sharp sting of reality. She'd deserved better.

Even now, after finding his tentative way back to faith, shame and regret dogged him. And not even a shower in Trinity's barn apartment could wash that away.

***

"You're dead. Stop moving," Vivien called out.

Beth Strauss grimaced at the black-painted ceiling, the cold floor seeping through her thin summer T-shirt and a spreading pool of corn-syrup blood probably turning her light-brown hair auburn. Yep. The sum of all things in her life led to being a corpse on the floor of the Deep Haven playhouse.

But how could she have said no to Vivien?

She scratched at the tickle on her nose. Wondered if she'd remembered to put Dad's laundry into the dryer.

Vivien Buckam cleared her throat. "I saw that." She tucked a lock of dark hair behind her ear, looking retro-stylish even in her maternity blouse and crop pants. Not that she was showing much yet. "I do think that's the perfect recipe for the blood." Vivie pinched her lips together. "Hmm...I hope that was the non-staining one."

"Really?" Beth groaned, rolled to her side. "I'd rather not have to exfoliate half my head to remove it."

Her assailant, known under the alias Courtney Wallace in real life, stood nearby and shoved her fake gun into the waistband of her shorts. "Come on, Beth. We're almost done and I'm starving." She pulled her strawberry-blonde hair back, took a hair band off her wrist, and made a quick messy bun.

"Et tu, Courtney?" Beth frowned. "I don't know why the

detective gets shot. She's the best character in the whole show." She wiggled around, trying to find a comfortable position on the hard floor.

Being dead was so disagreeable.

"It's in the script—that's why it's a called a *murder*-mystery comedy." Vivien paced the front of the stage.

"Don't you think that's an oxymoron?" Beth asked.

"You're just a stand-in. You don't get a vote." Vivien winked and flashed a smile.

Stand-in. Yeah, that was about right. In the theater. In life. But not even her fake role was real.

Well, not once she secured the camp assistant director spot. Then, maybe—just maybe—she'd find her path to independence. Perhaps even move out of her dad's house permanently and prove Lyle Fredrickson wrong.

Lyle. The name had the full-on effect of being at the bottom of a lake, the surface too far above, running out of air.

The burning ache, the panic. The crushing pressure.

Nine months had passed, and yet she could still see him standing there in front of Licks and Stuff, his hand outstretched, asking for the ring back. Telling her she had to choose.

Marry him and go to Texas, or stay with her dad in Deep Haven.

How could she choose between two people she loved? How could she choose him if it meant abandoning her dad?

Lyle *was* wrong. Dependable didn't mean afraid. He didn't understand that sometimes—most of the time—the needs of others trumped her own.

She sat up. "You can practice without me. I'm not actually doing anything."

"Of course you are—you're filling the space. Giving everyone else the opportunity to be their best. To shine. And we love you for that."

Right. Because she was the one who showed up.

Vivien looked at her watch and clapped her hands. "Okay,

cast and crew," she shouted, "let's take lunch. Be back in your places in forty-five minutes." She rubbed the tiny curve of her abdomen. "I'm ravenous. All the time."

Footsteps scuffled behind the set pieces, and a remarkable number of backstage crew and actors swarmed from the set, vacating faster than the kids called for KP duty at the camp kitchen.

Beth took the towel Courtney offered and wiped the smudges of blood from her hair and face. She checked the clock on the theater wall. "I need to head out. I have a shift at the library."

Vivien furrowed her brow. "You're going to miss out on the chase scene this afternoon. It's hysterical."

"Isn't this character dead?"

Vivien held up a finger. "Ah-ha! That's what the audience thinks—which is why the scene is so funny."

Beth frowned. "I'm sorry. I can't. I promised Joyce I'd help with a new summer reading program thing. I'm not sure what it is, but she sounded desperate."

Vivien let out a breath. "Fine." She touched the back of her hand to her brow. "I don't know how we'll get on without you."

"That might be a little thick, Vivie." Courtney laughed and picked up her lunch bag. "It's true, though. I think half this town runs because of Beth."

"That's preposterous." So what if she had four Volunteer of the Year plaques on her wall and two honorable mentions. They'd never made her feel truly wanted. Once the leftovers were packed up at every awards banquet, everyone went home with their Tupperware, and she looked for the next thing to fill the void.

"What about tomorrow?" Vivien put her palms together like she was praying. "Ella will still be finishing up that big rush order at her soap shop. She can't be back until Monday."

Beth grimaced. "I have to be at Trinity." She contemplated offering tomorrow night.

"Oh, that's right." Vivien lifted her arms toward Beth and

turned to Courtney. "Did you hear? You're looking at Noah's new assistant camp director."

"What?" Courtney gasped. "That's fantastic news—why didn't you tell me?"

Beth held up a hand. "Interim. I'm just the interim assistant." Despite her best efforts to convince Noah otherwise. "Noah said he's had a lot of interest in the position. Apparently, everyone in the Cities thinks a paid position on the North Shore is all the rage." She fluttered jazz hands.

Courtney unzipped her lunch cooler. "We do have World's Best Donuts, Java Cup, and the Footstep of Heaven Bookstore."

"I hear the kayak instructors are amazing at Wild Harbor," Vivien said. She placed a hand over her heart.

"We are fairly awesome," Beth conceded with a smile and winked at Courtney, who'd recently joined their Wild Harbor team.

How many kids had Beth taught to kayak on the waters of Lake Superior and smaller lakes?

"So, when do you get the job for real? It seems like you've been volunteering there for ages." Courtney pulled a sandwich and chips from her cooler. "Hey—does this mean you'll be cutting back your lessons at Wild Harbor?"

"I am—I'm already off the schedule."

"How does it feel to be stepping into your first full-time job?"

"Ask me in a few weeks. Noah's having me run some of the camp start-ups for the season through June." She grimaced. "I have to make sure everything at Trinity is ready to go. He focuses on Wilderness Challenge. Officially, I go full-time on Tuesday." She stood. "Pray for smooth operations. I'm also helping him with the family camp."

"At the end of June, the job will be yours?" Vivien asked. "You'll be the official ACD, right?" She pulled a bag of apple slices, cheese, and cracker rounds from her lunch sack.

"Barring any disasters. Since my resume is lacking on management experience, Noah needs me to show I can do it."

Beth sighed. "I get it, though, why he needs me to prove myself. It's a substantial job. Lots of responsibilities." All she'd ever been was the summer kayak instructor at the camp, camp counselor, and camp gofer—most of which had been volunteer spots. "It's kind of intimidating. I'm responsible for a bunch of funding that Trinity relies on. Grants and accounting and the scholarships."

"You can do it," Courtney said. "Just like when you got that lead role in Vivie's show a couple years ago. You surprised everyone."

Yeah, she had—because like everything else in her life, she'd always been on the periphery, backstage, or sidelines. Organizing, making things happen, but never truly belonging in her own place.

Until now. Now she hoped to secure the job—one where she'd finally find fulfillment without being scattered across the county with a portfolio of part-time positions, paid and volunteer.

Courtney took a bite of her sandwich and chewed. "Are you running the trail rides?"

"If by *running* you mean I take all the camper registrations and waivers, greet them, and wave to Jesse as he heads down the trail with all those happy kids, yes. Absolutely." Beth grabbed her water bottle and took a long drink.

"It might be good for you to get out on one of those trail rides yourself," Courtney said. She brushed several crumbs off her T-shirt and shorts. "You never do anything for yourself."

Beth shifted. The very thought of riding made her palms sweat. "You know I can't do that."

"You really should." Vivien paused halfway through eating an apple slice, dropped her hand, and studied Beth. "Do you ever miss riding?"

The question made Beth itch like she had hay down her shirt. "My riding days are long, long over." She'd packed away her 4-H ribbons and shoveled every last remnant of barrel racing from her life before she'd even finished high school. A galloping face-plant would do that.

"You were outstanding." Courtney swallowed a bite of sandwich. "I was so jealous. You were…fearless."

"I was a kid." A kid who could live life undaunted. Before enough years had passed that reality had sunk in. Mom was never coming back.

"You loved it, though, didn't you?" Vivien asked.

Yeah, she used to love a lot of things. "Things change." She had her dad to care for and, well, riding had been her thing with her mom.

And she wasn't like her mom.

But camp presented her with a choose-your-own-adventure. A chance to move out of her dad's house for the summer. To find her own path. To see what it might be like without the long-term commitment.

"Is Eli going to camp?"

The mention of her ten-year-old nephew touched a soft spot in her heart.

Beth nodded. "Yeah. Dylan thinks it will be good for him. He's been a little withdrawn since Marie's diagnosis."

Courtney shook her head. "That's so scary. I can't imagine being diagnosed with breast cancer at our age."

Her sister-in-law's breast cancer diagnosis had shaken Beth too. Which was exactly why she needed this camp job.

Because thirty was only two years away, and she hoped this job would finally give her the sense of being someone instead of being the one who helped everyone else achieve their own dreams—and she'd still be close to home for Dad.

Beth took an apple slice offered from Vivien. "I think it'll be good for Eli to get out of the house and keep his mind busy. Marie doesn't want him worrying about her."

Vivien smiled. "I think it'll be really good for you to get out of your house. Get out of your comfort zone. Worry less about your dad."

"It's possible you might be doing a little too much for him." Courtney set down her sandwich.

"I don't do too much," Beth answered. She couldn't keep the defensiveness out of her tone, because no. She didn't do too much. A lot was different than *too much*.

"Does he actually know you're moving to the camp?"

Beth blew out a breath. "He's still trying to talk me into commuting."

"Of course he is—he'll be lonely." Courtney crunched a potato chip. "He'll get through it, though."

She was going to be lonely too.

Guilt sliced through Beth's heart. But she still had a promise to keep.

I'll never leave you.

Sure, the words had been spoken as a child, but they'd settled into the fertile soil of her wounded heart. Because no, she'd never, ever be like her mom, who'd abandoned them.

"Maybe this is what you both need. A little space," Vivien reasoned.

Right. "You know how my attempt to leave for college went." Well, the truth was, she'd been as reluctant to leave as Dad was hesitant of her going. It hadn't taken much for her to withdraw her commitment to the University of Wisconsin. To say goodbye to plans for an environmental education and recreation degree when her dad had asked if she really wanted to go.

Vivien pressed her lips together. "He's afraid."

"I'm...afraid," Beth whispered. "I've never not lived there. Every breakfast. The pad of his slippers down the hall. Reading the paper. Cooking dinner."

"It's well past time, though," Courtney said.

"I never meant for it to happen—to end up approaching thirty and still be Daddy's girl. But I am—and it's all I know." Beth lifted her hands. Dropped them.

Courtney blotted her lips with a napkin. "Change is hard."

The tight coils of guilt wove around Beth and clamped down.

"I assured him I'm not going far." Most of her stuff would be staying right there, in her childhood bedroom.

Comfortable. Steady. Safe.

"This might be the best thing for both of you." Vivie gave Beth's arm a little squeeze. "What's the verse in Deuteronomy? About the Lord goes before you? He will never leave you or forsake you?"

Except sometimes, that's exactly what it felt like. Mom had forsaken her. Possibly God had too.

"I don't think that applies to me," Beth answered. "But I'm going to figure this out. I might not have my degree, but I can still have the career I wanted." And never be far from home.

Vivie twisted her lips, studied Beth.

"What?"

"What was your plan for being married when you were engaged to Lyle?"

"What do you mean?"

"Before Lyle announced he was moving to Texas. Did you expect Lyle would move right into your dad's house with you after the wedding?"

"Of course not," Beth said. Except, well, she hadn't ever thought that far ahead. Which should have been a red flag about their relationship. If she were honest with herself, maybe she hadn't loved him like she thought she had.

Beth checked her watch. "Oh no! I'm late. I gotta go." She gave them a wave and sprinted out the door of the theater.

Her day could only get better after starting it out as a corpse.

two

· · ·

NOT EVEN THE SMELL OF FRESH-BAKED BREAD BROUGHT COMFORT TO Grayson, despite the cavernous ache in his stomach when he entered Fox Bakery an hour later. He rubbed his knuckles against his chest to try to ease the constriction and squeezed his other hand around the handle of the gift bag he carried.

The sights and smells of the shop snapped him back to his youth, adding power and velocity to his nervous energy.

He removed his hat and looked over the changes since his last visit.

Bistro furniture had been added to the floor space, the upholstery and finish crisp and unscuffed. The Fox Bakery mural still took up a substantial chunk of the wall, looking out over the few patrons sitting and talking.

The family business enveloped him with both the familiar and the foreign. The same long display case. But through the swinging kitchen doors behind his sister, Robin, a shiny new oven gleamed.

Her auburn hair was pulled back, and she wore a bright white apron embroidered with the Fox logo. The sight of her made his heart ache and turned his mouth pasty.

She stood at the counter, her face turned down as she

scribbled on the notepad in front of her. When the door rattled closed, she glanced up at her would-be customer.

"Grayson." His name left her lips, soft and faint, like he was a specter. She set down her pen and wiped her hands on a towel. "Man, it's been too long!"

"Hey. Yeah." His answer sounded lame, even to himself.

"When did you get to town?" She walked right up to him. A small hesitation, then she threw her arms around him.

He felt like the Grinch. Like his heart grew three sizes in her embrace. The pressure in his chest didn't ease.

Longing—a deep ache in his soul for the open spaces of central Oregon—collided with the unfamiliar weight of seeing his sister again.

She drew away, her eyes glassy.

Aw, Robin.

"I thought you might slug me."

"Tempting," she answered.

He shook his head. His nerves still coiled his gut. "I got in this morning. Had some horses to deliver for Noah."

He sidestepped out of a customer's way and rubbed the edge of the Stetson he still held in his fingertips.

His hat. His boots. He didn't exactly blend into Deep Haven, where the customer apparel was all summer tees with flip-flops or logger plaid with work boots.

He shifted his weight. He stood out like a Black Angus in a herd of Herefords.

"I'll bet Noah's excited to have them." She shoved her hands into her back pockets.

Oh yeah. So excited. Maybe if he were running a rodeo instead of a children's camp.

Several beats passed between them.

"I brought you something." He held up the gift bag.

She smiled. "You didn't have to do that."

"I know how much you like being spoiled."

"Ha-ha." Robin lifted the tissue paper from the bag, peeked

inside. A smile spread across her face, and she drew the silver-and-turquoise necklace out. "It's beautiful. Thank you."

"You're welcome." He cleared the awkwardness from his throat. "It's from a local artist in Oregon." He shifted, rubbed the edge of his hat, and fought the sense that the bakery would implode on him.

She latched the necklace around her neck and set the turquoise pendant to the center.

A big football-player-sized man walked in. He set his eyes on Robin, smiled.

"Hey, Sammy," she said.

Ah, yes. Grandma had mentioned Robin's new boyfriend. He remembered Sammy from school.

"Good to see you, Grayson." Sammy extended a hand.

He returned the handshake. "You too."

Sammy turned back to Robin. "Do you have the cake Megan called about?"

She nodded. "It's in the cooler, boxed up." She patted his arm. "Thanks for delivering it."

"No problem. I'll catch you later." He leaned in and gave Robin a discreet kiss on the cheek before heading through the kitchen.

Robin gave Grayson a soft smile, her face still glowy from Sammy's interruption.

Huh. He didn't suppose he had too much room to talk as her big brother after being gone so long, but that didn't stop him. "He's a good guy?"

"Stop—of course he is." She shook away his question. "Hungry?"

A chair scraped across the floor, and a customer stood at a nearby table. Grayson shifted out of the way. Then two more customers came through the door.

"No, it's okay—you're busy."

She moved back to the counter to serve her new patrons but

held up a finger to him to wait. Then she disappeared into the kitchen for several minutes.

When she came back, she smiled. "Here, you have to have one of these." She drew out an oversized cinnamon roll from the bakery case and plunked it onto a plate with a napkin-wrapped utensil.

His stomach won out over his nerves. He lifted the offering, his mouth watering before his fork reached his lips, and took a bite.

Oh man, it was good. The sweetness of the glaze landed on his tongue with the gooey, double-filled cinnamon roll.

He'd forgotten what home-baked tasted like.

"Take a seat—I'll be over when I can." She waved him off with a tentative smile.

He slid into a chair at the front window. Took another bite. He couldn't remember the last time he'd had anything so delicious. The kind of taste that left him craving more.

Robin finished with the last customer and dropped onto the chair across from him. "Do you like it?" She set a cup of coffee in front of him. "I didn't know…if you still drink it black."

"I do, yeah—and this is amazing." He chewed. "I remember when you were a kid, we'd end up with crunchy brownies."

She laughed. "Don't even bring that up—I didn't realize those egg shells had fallen in."

"Seriously, though"—he raised another bite—"this is award-winning."

"I think I'm done with contests for a while. I've got lots to do here." She smoothed her apron. "And I hear you'll be busy at the camp."

"Yeah."

"I'm a little surprised—I didn't think anything would get you back here."

"Me either." He rubbed his arm, a sudden itch crawling on his skin.

"What gives?" She put a hand on her hip. "Why'd you come all this way to work at the camp?"

Yep. She was on to him.

He toed his boot against the slick tile floor. "I'm buying my own place. My own little ranch."

Robin's eyes got big. She blinked. "Wow, Grayson, that's amazing—but can you afford to be gone all summer? I can't imagine Noah pays as much as you were already earning."

Here it goes... "I had to part ways with Three Sisters." He held up his hand to her gaped mouth. "No—it's okay. It was the push I needed to move on and take a risk on my own place."

"Wow. Okay." She pressed her lips together, as if processing the news. "That's big news and seems so...permanent."

What could he say to that? He shoved his hands into his jean pockets.

"You're staying at the camp?"

"Yeah. There's an apartment in the barn. Makes feeding and caring for the horses easier." He lifted a shoulder. "And, you know—it's what I'm used to."

"Right. Sticking to your comfort zone. Dusty boots and manure?"

Deep Haven was nowhere near his comfort zone. "Exactly."

The door opened behind him. Closed. He could tell by the way Robin's eyes went from him to the arrivals—a smile creasing her face—it was *them*. Her brows rose and she fluttered her hands at him. "I'll talk to you later," she said, then walked back up to the counter.

He stood and turned.

Grandma approached with confidence and threw her arms around him. "I'm so happy you came." She had tied a pink scarf in her silvery hair and wore bright white linen pants with a floral top. Stylish as ever.

The pressure cinched down on him like a dallied lariat. Yep. He felt like a ten-year-old kid again. The one who'd wholly and completely destroyed their family. "Hi, Grandma." He gave her an awkward hug in return.

"You!" She held him at arm's length, tears filling her blue eyes, and squeezed his arms. "A strong one, huh?" She winked, but the shine in her eyes swelled the thickness in his throat. "That ranch life is treating you well."

He gave her a half laugh. "Thanks." She still had the power to embarrass him.

She sniffed, nodded, and blinked.

As soon as she released him, Grandpa stepped up and gave Grayson a handshake and a half hug. "Glad you came." He'd lost weight since his heart attack and looked healthier. "Good drive?" His dark-gray hair had thinned a little more on top, but he sported a tan under the Hawaiian-print button-up he wore. "I heard they'd already started some construction projects through Grand Rapids."

Small talk. Always awkward. "Yeah. Long," Grayson said. The chitchat made his skin itch. "Is everything okay?"

"Yes—certainly." Grandma gestured toward the bistro table where Grayson's coffee sat. "Let's sit down."

He took his seat, and each of them slid into the empty chairs.

"Here you go." Robin placed two more cups of coffee on the table.

Grandpa settled in. "Working at the camp, huh?" He nodded. "That's good. Very good."

Grayson sipped his coffee. Let the hot, bitter fluid scald his throat.

Grandma shuffled through her tote bag and pulled out a manila envelope. She slid it across the table to him. "Here. This is yours."

He looked up at her and wiped his hands on the napkin. He was pretty sure he knew what was in the envelope, but oh, now he didn't want to see it, even if he needed it.

Robin watched from the bakery counter. Grayson tugged the

metal tabs up and lifted the flap, then drew out the stack of papers inside. Thumbed through them.

A lot line map. A quitclaim deed. His name. Wow. They'd given him Mom and Dad's vacant lot.

The one with the lake view where they'd planned to build their family home.

He swiped a hand over his face. Oh boy. This was going to be harder than he'd thought.

Robin walked over and slid into the empty seat at the table, her brows drawn tight. She stared at the deed, her eyes skimming down it. "You're giving him the lot?" The lilt in her voice said the gears were churning. "Were you pulling my leg about the place in Oregon? Are you actually here to stay?"

Grandma looked at him, her lips twisted and brows creased. "Why would he stay?"

"He doesn't have a job in Oregon—"

"You lost your job?" Grandpa joined the fray.

Grayson held up his hand. "I'm buying my own place." He looked at Robin. "In Oregon. One of the trainers I know is closing his business—offered me a good deal."

"But you're working at Trinity. You could build on this lot. Stay." Robin tapped her finger on the lot map.

"I can't." And no, he wasn't excited to sell it. To part with that dream. Unfortunately, he didn't know any other way he'd be able to buy Vincent's place.

Oh boy. Grayson fought to speak through the slew of emotions that pinched his throat. "I'm helping Noah out for the summer. That's it. My life is in Oregon."

Robin crossed her arms. "It doesn't have to be."

"At my own place, I can run some youth programs. There isn't a camp like Trinity there."

Grandpa tapped the paperwork. "Selling this lot will go a long way toward that goal."

"You can't sell their lot, Grayson," Robin said, her voice pinched. Begging.

He couldn't look at her. Couldn't see the hurt on her face.

"The bakery is yours," Grandma said, lifting her hands to display the remodeled bakery. "Look at all you've done with it."

Grayson ventured a glance up at Robin, which turned out to be a big mistake. Her eyes had glossed over with unshed tears. "I didn't know you didn't know about the lot," he said.

"That's our fault." Grandpa straightened the stack of paperwork on top of the envelope. "We've been so busy making plans for the move." He put a hand on Robin's arm. "It wasn't intentional."

Grayson looked at Grandpa. "You're moving?" Apparently, Robin wasn't the only one out of the loop.

Grandpa took Grandma's hand across the table. "We took that trip to Florida after my heart attack, and let me tell you, coming back to a late Minnesota snow brought a few things into clarity for us."

"I got to spend time with my sister, and we had sunshine—it was glorious," Grandma said. "So we decided—why not move?"

Grayson sat back in his chair. "You're moving to Florida? Permanently?"

"We are. You kids are grown and...off on your own." Grandpa said it without accusation. "Quite frankly, I've been too old to be running this bakery for a while."

"Don't even get them started on our winters," Robin said. She let out a breath. "I mean, I knew you were moving, but I don't know—I guess I thought everything would somehow stay the same."

Grayson ran his fingers over the envelope. "You're really giving this to me?"

Grandma closed her eyes, opened them, and continued. "Like Robin said—when we spoke at Christmas, you mentioned hoping to finally buy a piece of land in Oregon, have your own ranch." She offered him a sad smile. "And since then, your friend seems to be moving forward with his intent to sell. It's the perfect solution as we prepare for the move."

He stared at the map. Swallowed. No, the last thing he wanted to do was sell that lot of land. That would be saying goodbye to every dream his parents had had. It wasn't the perfect solution. But it was a solution.

And it wasn't something he'd ever thought he could do.

"If you want to get it listed while you're here, we have a few real estate agents we can refer you to."

He studied the pair and looked at Robin.

She looked away.

He shook his head. "Let's talk about it later."

Grandpa put a hand on Robin's shoulder. "It'll all work out."

Movement across the intersection caught Grayson's eye. Outside the library, a two-legged—what?

Book?

Yep. A person-sized book wandered along the sidewalk, zigzagging like his cattle dog searching for scent. Petite arms protruded from the costume, the oversized book covers something akin to the mascots he'd seen at Mariners baseball games in Seattle.

Except those were the Mariner Moose mascot and assorted costumed cohorts, including a hot dog, ketchup bottle, and relish jar racing down the warning track. But a book? Complete with a tasseled bookmark sticking out the top?

Wow.

"Looks like the library has a new release." Grandma pointed past Grayson's truck toward the library.

Robin joined them at the window, her distress forgotten. "Oh—"

The book faltered, paused, staggered.

"Oh dear."

"Who *is* that?" Grayson asked.

Robin leaned closer to the glass like she was deciding which éclair to select. "Based on the size of the book—more novella than epic tome—I'd guess that's Beth."

"Beth Strauss? Dylan's sister?" He tried to tamp down a

sweep of nostalgia filled with Friday night football games spent with his best friend and the tagalong little sister.

Beth—the girl he never should have kissed in high school. Nothing had ever been the same after that night.

He shook away the memories of those bygone days.

He hadn't come back to Deep Haven to stir up the past.

This little trip to Deep Haven had put him on an emotional bull ride, and he wasn't sure how he was going to last until the buzzer.

"Yeah, of course." She shook her head at his silly question.

"Why is she wearing that horrendous costume?" Even he had never expected that the nerdy girl he'd dubbed Bookworm Bethy would be wandering the streets of Deep Haven dressed as an actual...book.

"She works and volunteers at the library." Robin squinted at the signage on the sidewalk next to Beth. "Looks like she's promoting the children's summer reading program."

Beth, however, staggered around in the full sun.

"She's going to overheat in that thing." Grayson caught sight of two loose dogs farther down the block. Both had zoned in on the mysterious book bait, their focus now sharp and their pace quickening. Their barks split the otherwise still afternoon.

"Oh no," Grandma said, her eyes also on the disaster unfolding before them.

A buzz rattled through the bakery, an oven timer calling for attention. Robin let out a breath. "I need to grab those loaves." She tossed one last concerned glance over her shoulder before running to the kitchen.

Grayson shoved his hat on his head. Every dog he'd ever known loved to chew on a good book, and he'd venture a guess that by the excited barking and raised hackles blasting toward the library, the dancing book was their next target.

"I'll be back," he said. "Excuse me."

He pressed the door open and broke into a run. His boots

clomped on the sidewalk in his sprint toward the teetering novel.

🐾 🐾 🐾

SOMEONE WAS GOING TO PAY FOR THIS.

Beth shifted in the oversized costume, her head pounding and steam rising around her. When they'd said "unseasonably hot" on the news, she hadn't been thinking near nineties.

She stumbled along the sidewalk in front of the library, her vision impaired by the fact that the eyeholes had been set too far apart.

A dog's whine cut through the din in Beth's head. She turned, squinting through one of the screened eyeholes of her costume like a desperate cyclops. No luck.

One bark. Two.

Ehh…lots of barking. Growing closer.

Please, God, help.

Rivulets of sweat streamed down her face. Her back.

She spun in a circle, hoping to zero in on the dogs' location and go the opposite direction. The tassel on the bookmark flopped forward. Nothing. She could see absolutely nothing. She swung an arm to swipe at it, but the firm frame of the book cover prevented her arms from doing more than flopping wildly.

Why couldn't she have been a paperback?

She tried to toss it backward by flipping her head.

Oh, mistake. Her balance faltered.

Mayday! Mayday!

Her foot hooked the hard edge of something—maybe the sidewalk? She crashed to the ground, the bright light of the eyeholes turning dark with furry bodies. Barks loomed over her with a cacophony of yaps and excited growls. Paws pounced onto her, and for the first time, she was grateful for the rigid frame.

She'd landed flat on her back. She kicked her legs and tried to roll over, with no success. Based on the rhythmic tugging, at least one set of canine jaws had locked on to the costume. The gloomy world inside the book costume started swirling, caught in a mental eddy that spurred a wave of nausea.

She should have said no. Walked away. Let the library find someone else to advertise the summer reading program.

But an hour earlier, and on paper, this had seemed like such a bright idea—and far better than playing the part of a corpse on the community theater floor. She loved kids. She loved books. What could possibly go wrong?

If only the word *no* were part of her vocabulary.

Well, she'd have to say no after Tuesday, when she was living at the camp full-time.

But Joyce had handed her the costume she'd said she'd spent three months making—although, in examining the ghastly ensemble, it had looked more like three days. Maybe three hours.

Crafting wasn't Joyce's jam.

But Beth had committed to three hours of dancing around on the sidewalk outside the library. Dressed as a book. A book—complete with a bound spine on one side and a cover that said Venture into Adventure!

The vibration in her head took on a staccato pulse.

Tugging. Growling. They'd probably bury her in the yard when they were done.

"No!" Her shout came out hollow, tinny to her own ears and likely never reaching beyond the costume fabric. She tried again. "Bad…dog!"

She was pulled one direction, then the other, as if they'd started a game of tug-of-war. Weight smashed into her. Nails—two pawfuls, by the feel of it—skidded across her exposed sleeves.

She clamped her eyes against the sting of sweat rivulets searing her vision. She was dressed as a book, for goodness' sake. Locked inside a tropical casket.

"No!" A deep voice commanded. "Quit." The pressure released from her right arm, followed by the left. "Go home." A hand wrapped around hers, slightly rough, manly, strong. "Go on." He softened his tone. "You go on home," he finished.

Whoever this man was, she'd buy him every last pastry in Robin Fox's display case.

Not Casper Christiansen, Boone Buckam, or Cole B...Ba... What was his last name?

She discontinued her Deep Haven roster, her thoughts foggy and incomplete.

"They're gone now." The hand gave her a little tug. "Let's get you up. Are you okay, Beth?"

"I—I think so? Thank you." He knew her name, which was kind of nice. She tried to pull herself up with the hand holding her own, but wobbled. Her body was plucked off the ground, costume and all, and she was set back down onto her feet. Then he released her hand.

Oh. Okay. So, her hero was strong too.

The earth swayed. Or it was her?

Hands steadied her.

Why were a million cicadas buzzing in her ears?

"Whoa, let's get you out of that. It's got to be a hundred and twenty degrees in there." A pause. "How do I get you out of there?"

"Zipper. Starts at the bottom...goes up...side." Goosebumps prickled her skin.

"You're...uh...dressed?"

Movement. Pressure. Dizziness.

"Of course I'm dressed." They weren't pretty, but she had clothes on.

Queasy?

"Oh my goodness!" Joyce, the librarian. Beth could hear her

thick high heels clogging nearer. Like a jackhammer through Beth's skull. "Are you okay?"

She swallowed, tried to stamp out the tidal wave of nausea that threatened to further ruin her day.

A cool breeze blasted her skin as the costume opened up and was lifted off her sticky body. She blinked against the bright afternoon sunshine.

Focus. Focus. Find an anchor point. "I don't feel so well," she whispered, still trying to get her eyes to open in the light. She blinked again, and the world came into hazy focus. Joyce stood, holding the costume. Next to her, boots. Jeans. A cowboy hat?

No one in Deep Haven wore a cowboy hat.

Her brain tried to make sense of the apparition—a larger-than-life champion. Right from the pages of a Louis L'Amour novel or the television show *Heartland*.

He had a strong, clean-shaven jawline, and a dark-blond wisp of hair strayed from his hat brim. Green eyes. And the arms that had rescued her? Tan with a generous curve of muscle under the cuffs of his T-shirt sleeves.

And she was standing there in bright blue tights and shorts, her ratty T-shirt, dark with sweat, clinging to her. More beads of sweat dripped off her nose. She scrubbed her palms across her eyes.

She had to be hallucinating.

"Beth?" Joyce's voice, closer now, tried to reach through the fading dream to her.

She shook her head, fighting for clarity.

The man. Those green eyes met hers. "Beth?"

Oddly familiar. The eyes...the voice... A jab of awareness pierced her.

Everything dimmed to black. Anyone, anyone but *him*. Not Grayson Alexander Fox. She was pretty sure they called it a teenage crush because he'd done just that. Crushed her heart.

She groaned.

Not that he knew anything about annihilating her tender heart the night of the high-school pit party.

He sucked in a breath. "You're bleeding." He drew her close.

She fought the darkness. "No—wait." She rubbed her head with her hand, drew it away, red. Sticky. "It's not—it's from Vivien."

Joyce gasped. "Vivien did that?"

"No—it's not—" Beth closed her eyes. "I'm fine. Please." She tried to pull away, stumbled.

"You're not fine." Grayson held her firm.

"How did Vivien do that?" Joyce asked again, her voice somewhere behind them.

"No," Beth squeaked. "It's stage blood." She wiped her reddened palm on her shirt. "I didn't get hurt."

Joyce squeezed into Beth's line of sight. "I called for an ambulance." She hoisted the costume and towed it across the grass back to the library.

"I'm fine." She wriggled from Grayson. "I don't need your help." The flush to her face wasn't only from the heat.

"What were you doing in that ridiculous costume?" Grayson gestured toward Joyce and the abominable book carcass she was toting away.

"Oh, you know, just going for a Friday afternoon jaunt."

He pressed his lips together. "You're going to be like that?"

"I'm not like anything, Grayson." She swiped the sweat from her eyes and bobbled.

His hand shot out to steady her.

Fine. She'd play nice-ish. "Volunteering for the summer library program."

"So, you're still doing too many things for other people, huh?"

"What are you even talking about? You don't know me."

"You should have told her no. You couldn't even bend your arms, and by the looks of it, you couldn't see, either."

No, she couldn't, but he didn't need to know that. "I don't

need you looking out for me," she snapped. "We both know how that turned out the last time." Her head thundered. Why, oh why had she brought that up?

His Adam's apple bobbed, like maybe she'd actually hurt him. "That was a long time ago. You were drunk. I was trying to help."

She didn't remember all of it, but she remembered enough. Showing up at the pit party at sixteen and being handed a drink. Then two. Maybe three? Music and dancing until Grayson showed up and practically dragged her to the car.

"I was fine." She closed her eyes to block out the swirling grass and sky. She'd been fine that night until she'd given in to that crush. Kissed him.

His jaw flexed. "I never should have kissed you back."

She remembered the touch of his lips, soft and sweet on hers, and then being pushed away. Rejected. "You humiliated me." The spinning wouldn't stop. She took a staggered step. "I don't feel well."

"Beth, I—"

A siren screamed on approach. Her legs gave way, and arms—Grayson's arms—lifted her. Carried her.

He smelled like soap and fresh cotton, and in a moment of weakness, she let herself succumb to the safety of his arms before the darkness.

three

. . .

GRAYSON SHOULD HAVE GONE WITH HIS FIRST INSTINCT TO FLEE FROM town. Instead, he found himself pacing the emergency room waiting room twenty minutes later, waiting for Beth's brother to arrive. If only Noah didn't need him as much as he needed the camp income.

He wished he could rewind the day—the past two days, even.

A nurse in animal-print scrubs rushed by with a lab cart, vials clattering down the small hospital's corridor.

At least he'd been able to assure Dylan over the phone that Beth was doing fine now. She'd had him worried when she'd gone limp in his arms.

Man, he hadn't even seen her the last time he'd come through town, so it had been…what? Eight years?

He'd tried to give her space, not knowing exactly how to bridge the gap between them. How to make amends for trying to do the right thing and having it go completely sideways.

One more reason he didn't belong in Deep Haven.

She'd grown out her light-brown hair so it fell past her shoulders. Petite, athletic build, with soft green eyes that could still pierce his soul.

Still in Deep Haven.

Still living with her dad, from what Dylan said.

He'd always expected Dylan's tree-climbing, book-toting sister to have had a full-ride scholarship to the college of her choice.

Grayson sat down on a vinyl seat and picked through four-month-old magazines strewn across the side table. He thumbed the pages, scanning the articles.

Pretty potluck pies, retro-eighties home decorating on a budget, or the beginner's guide to quilt making.

No, no, and definitely not.

He tossed them back onto the table and set his hat down on the seat next to him.

The intercom crackled to page a doctor.

He rested his head in his hands. The camp, the horses, the lot. Robin. His grandparents. Beth. Too much for him to process.

He hadn't even remembered to give Grandma the earrings he'd brought or Grandpa the silver belt buckle.

It was a stretch for Deep Haven style, but for Florida? Oh boy. He'd have to warn Grandpa not to wear it with his island-print shirts, or Grandma would never forgive Grayson.

The automatic doors whooshed open, and he lifted his head. Dylan Strauss, Beth's brother and his former best friend, rushed in. A few new wrinkles and maybe an extra pound or two, but overall, the man hadn't changed much. Just the same as always in a blue T-shirt and gray cargo shorts.

"Hey—thanks for calling me." Dylan put his hand into Grayson's, then pulled him forward into a man hug. Smacked his back. "It's been a long time."

"Of course," Grayson answered. "Glad I was there—I was sitting in the bakery and saw…her." He didn't even know how to describe the mascot Olympics he'd witnessed. "How's Marie doing?" Robin had told him about the cancer diagnosis Dylan's wife had been hit with.

"She's doing good," Dylan answered. "Thanks for asking. The treatment makes her sick, but she's strong. She's got grit."

Grayson didn't even know how a man handled his wife being diagnosed with cancer at thirty.

Which was exactly why Grayson kept his life free of any such attachments. He helped horses—and yeah, he'd had a few horses break his heart with inoperable colic or an all-night labor that ended with a stillborn foal.

Those were hard enough.

But he'd found he could just dig in deeper to the work. Help more horses.

"I'll bet she does," Grayson said. He gave his friend a light smack to the chest. "She needs to, dealing with you." As soon as the words left his lips, he held his breath, not sure how they'd land.

Dylan laughed, full and satisfied. "That she does." He nodded. "She says I need to get out of the house. I start driving her crazy after a few days—maybe hovering." Dylan shook his head. "We'll have to get some fishing in while you're here. She'll welcome the break."

The nostalgia of summers in the north woods poured over Grayson, causing an ache in his stomach. Fireflies and friends and fishing.

The scent of lilacs and honeysuckle from his mom's garden.

All the reminders that kept him out of Deep Haven. Because he didn't need to be lured into the complacency of comfort. That's how people got hurt.

But he hadn't expected an invitation from Dylan. Not when they'd left things like they had. Grayson fidgeted. "I want you to know, what happened between Beth and me was never what you thought it was. That night of the pit party? I was trying to help." He shook his head. "I could have done it a lot better than I did. I'm sorry."

He'd carried her into her bedroom after driving her home. Brushed her hair off her face and watched her sleep for a few minutes, replaying their kiss. The one he never should have let happen.

He'd realized then how much he'd wanted her to be sober. Wondering all the what-ifs because the pesky little sister of his best friend had grown into a beautiful young woman, and he hadn't even noticed until that night. She'd shed her baggy sweats and her dad's oversized shirts. Instead, she'd worn cut-off shorts and a T-shirt that her dad would have said was a little too tight and six inches too short. But he'd gone to a weekend men's retreat, and Dylan had been out with his girlfriend.

Grayson hadn't heard their front door open, but he remembered the steel in Dylan's eyes when he'd found Grayson tucking Beth into bed.

Don't ever look at my sister like that again.

"Hey," Dylan said. His voice snapped Grayson back to the hospital corridor. He pressed his lips together. Nodded. "It's history, okay? That was a long time ago." He placed a hand on Grayson's shoulder. "It was a knee-jerk response for me. I could have handled it better too."

Grayson nodded, wishing the weight on his chest would lift with Dylan's words. "Don't worry about it."

"I still can't believe you're here—when you called about Beth, it took a minute to put it all together." Dylan drew his hand across his mouth. "It didn't all connect right away." He smiled. "Seriously, it's good to see you, even if you do look like you're dressed for Western Days at the elementary school."

Grayson took the well-deserved cheap shot. "Thanks." He picked up his hat. "Are you still in construction?"

"Yep. Working for Seth Turnquist—best custom log homes on the North Shore," Dylan added. "I heard some news this morning about you now being the owner of a lot."

"I'm not building a home here." Despite owning that prime piece of real estate.

Dylan stepped back. "Okay. I felt I should mention it." He smiled. "Gotta do my part for business."

"How did you hear about the lot? Robin didn't even know until today."

"Ouch." Dylan cringed. "News travels. Eli's Sunday school teacher was in the bakery this morning and told a woman named Janet, who happened to have told Dad, who told me."

"Of course."

"I suppose I should wander down to check in on Beth," Dylan said. "I told Dad not to come down. She doesn't need him creating a scene." Dylan cringed. "He's still a wee bit protective."

Like father, like son.

"I haven't seen her since they brought her in. She's in room three. They were cooling her down and had her on IV fluids in the ambulance."

"Come on, let's go," Dylan said.

"I should head ba—" Grayson turned to find Dylan several strides away, walking down the corridor. He hustled to catch up.

"Nonsense. I haven't seen you in how many years? Besides, you've always been an expert at pressing Beth's buttons. She probably needs a little rousing to get back on her feet. What was that nickname you used to call her?"

Oh, that. "I doubt she wants me in there."

"She was always tagging along, and you could always get rid of her when we were tired of babysitting." Dylan stopped mid-stride. "Bookworm, right?"

Grayson cringed at the silly moniker.

"Yeah." He'd coined her hot-button nickname by luck one day. She'd been toting along her usual stack of books, dragging them into the tree house while wearing her dad's flannel shirt and sweats.

He'd chided her.

"I'll never forget her face when you called her Bookworm Bethy that first time. Her mouth dropped into an O, and I was sure she'd slug you."

Grayson had known she wouldn't. She'd been too sweet to do that. "I was such a jerk."

"It worked though. You could get rid of her every time we wanted to."

"What happened to being the protector?"

"Oh, that came with age. When she was a pesky elementary school tagalong, we were supposed to ditch her."

"Right." Grayson's fingers tightened on his hat brim. He needed to steer clear of the past, or he might just sink in it.

"Name calling didn't fall into my best moments." His voice came out roughened by shame.

"You probably owe her an apology."

No doubt. For more than the teasing.

They turned the corner of the hospital corridor, their footsteps clicking on the hard linoleum floor.

Today, outside the library, she'd looked up at him, gratitude and admiration in her dazed eyes—and a little piece of him wanted to be the man she thought she saw. The man who could show up instead of hide away.

Until she'd realized who he was.

Her face had fallen, and her already crimson cheeks had blushed darker.

Dylan checked in with a nearby nurse, who nodded and pointed toward room three.

Grayson stayed at the threshold of the patient room while Dylan walked inside.

"Hey, how are you?" Dylan asked.

"Oh my goodness, Dylan—you wouldn't believe who—" Her eyes landed on Grayson.

She lifted a hand to her hair and tried to smooth the tangled tresses. "Hey." She sat up on the bed. "You didn't have to come to the hospital." Her words were flat.

"I wanted to make sure Dylan got here."

Her green eyes met his, more lucid now, swirling with curiosity.

Her color had returned to an outdoorsy tan, though she looked positively small in the hospital bed.

"What did the doctor say?" Dylan asked. "Whoa—is that blood on your head?"

"No, it's not." She rubbed her temple. "It's only heat exhaustion. They put me on fluids. Can you cut me loose?"

Dylan held up his hands. "Slow down. Heat exhaustion? Is that serious?"

"I'm fine, but I need a ride home." Her eyes stayed on the hospital blanket. She swallowed and looked up at Grayson. "Thank you."

"Sure."

She opened her mouth as if to say more, but her phone buzzed inside her purse. She drew it out of her bag, hit the button, and stared at it a moment. Then her mouth dropped into that same little O like when they were kids. "No way."

"Did you make the front-page news?" Dylan asked. He sat in the guest chair near the bed.

"It's a message from Noah," she said. She thumbed a message on her phone. "Wait, what?" She groaned. "He says…" She continued scrolling what was either *Moby Dick* or the world's longest text message. "He says the new camp wrangler has arrived and brought the three camp horses he'd bought, and there isn't an assistant wrangler because, in Jesse's absence, it was forgotten."

She frantically typed back. "What is he talking about a new camp wrangler? Jesse is supposed to be back this coming week." She looked up from her phone, a deep furrow cutting her brow. "This can't be happening." Her phone buzzed again, and she looked down at it. "Great. He says Jesse had complications and he forgot to tell me he'd made other arrangements." She put her fingers to her lips, tapping them as she waited for his next message. "And the three new horses are of questionable use for the camp." She tossed her phone down. "He used the word *wild.*" She pressed both palms over her eyes before slumping against the pillows.

Grayson's heart sank. This was bad. Oh so very, very bad. He shifted, a new level of unease twining through him. "Why's he telling you?"

Dylan scooted forward in the chair. "Beth's the new assistant camp director."

"Interim," she said, sitting back up and folding her arms across her chest.

Grayson closed his eyes. Oh boy. Noah had failed to tell him that little tidbit.

"I'm the interim assistant camp director. I've got to earn the permanent slot." She sat back up and adjusted the blankets. "And at this rate, I won't have a job even doing that." She looked back to the phone. "Wild horses? No assistant? And now, some new camp wrangler?"

Grayson peeled his tongue from the dry roof of his mouth. "It's me." He cleared his throat.

"What's you?" Beth asked.

"I'm the wrangler he hired for the summer." He swallowed and braved a look at Beth.

The color drained from her face. She opened her mouth. Closed it. Looked at Dylan.

Her brother shrugged his shoulder. "Don't look at me. How would I have known that?"

Grayson held up his hands. Jobless and homeless for the moment, he didn't have a lot of options. "Let's table it for now. We can talk to Noah."

Beth scrubbed her hands over her face. "What am I going to do?"

"What is there for you to do?" Dylan Grabbed a pack of crackers off the tray table next to the bed.

Beth looked Grayson up and down like he was the last sad beast at the auction. And she wasn't buying.

He resisted the urge to squirm.

"I can't work with him."

"We don't have to actually work together. You do your thing, I'll do mine."

Dylan shifted. "He's right. You're both grown-ups, and Noah needs you both." He unwrapped the crackers. "*Eli* needs you both—he's been waiting months for this camp."

Grayson pictured the spunky blond kid he'd seen the last time he'd come to town. The boy had only been around four.

Beth lifted the phone again, her eyes skimming across a new message.

She gave a pointed look at Grayson, her green eyes meeting his. "What about the three maniacal mares to deal with now?"

Oh, that. Grayson held out his hands. "They'll be fine—and only one is a mare. I'll be working with them, no matter what."

Beth held up both hands. "I'm sure we can get this all sorted out."

Dylan gestured toward Grayson. "Noah's already hired him." He took a bite of cracker, chewed, and turned to Grayson. "Do you actually work with kids? I mean, didn't I hear some crazy story about an ambulance being called to your children's program at your church?"

Beth gasped.

"I don't know what you heard, but that wasn't my fault." Grayson held up his hands. "I was convinced to help out with a children's program at church. It just happened that four kids ended up crying, one kid bleeding, and possibly there were seven very angry parents." Heat crept up his neck. "There may have been an ambulance, out of an abundance of caution."

Beth's brows lifted. "Did Noah even do a background check on you?"

Grayson's jaw dropped. "Hey, it wasn't criminal. They were little maniacs."

Beth folded her arms and looked him up and down. "And you—big, strong cowboy—couldn't handle a few little children?"

Her words and the way her eyes flicked to his arms sent another warming flush up his neck. Um—

"Give him a chance, Beth." Dylan crunched his cracker.

He knew Dylan didn't give the plea lightly. Not with the history Grayson and Beth shared. And he wasn't going to put their renewed friendship in jeopardy.

"Like I said, we can talk to Noah." Grayson didn't want to walk on the broken glass of memories any more than necessary. "I've got my family lot to sell, anyway. My plans were camp and getting the lot sold."

She tilted her head. "You're selling your parents' lot?"

"That's the plan. Get in, do the job, and get out."

"Just here for the T-shirt?" Beth asked. "How touristy of you."

At that, he smiled.

She was right, though. Except most of the tourists had visited Deep Haven more often than he had.

Dylan leaned back in his chair. "Don't forget—I know a builder."

"We still don't have an assistant wrangler."

A phone alarm buzzed. "That's me." Dylan sat forward and silenced his phone. "I need to run home. Marie has an appointment."

"Don't tell Eli about the camp situation. He'll be crushed if he thinks there are any issues—and that kid has enough to worry about," Beth said. She touched Dylan's arm. "I'll talk to Noah." She stared at Grayson. "I guess find this guy an assistant so the trail rides can still run. I'm going to find a way."

He recognized that set to her jaw. She had grit too.

This summer was setting up to be anything but the slam-dunk path to owning his own ranch.

BETH HAD COMPLETELY LOST HER MIND.

With the morning sunlight promising another warm day, she grabbed her book from the tiny end table and curled up in the living room recliner with her coffee.

If only the sun could burn off the residual memories of Grayson Fox from the day before.

"How are you?" Courtney asked, sliding onto the couch facing Beth. She wore her faded jean shorts and a navy-blue T-shirt that said "North Shore nights" in silver sparkle across the front.

"I can't believe you were rescued yesterday by a real-life cowboy." Vivien placed a hand over her heart. "That's kind of swoony."

The book fell from Beth's hands, landing with a thunk on the floor. "It wasn't a cowboy. It was Grayson Fox. And I'm thinking I puked in front of him." Beth covered her face in her hands, a long guttural moan rolling from her lips. "Oh no. I puked." Oh, and then there was the whole camp wrangler thing.

"Details, details." Vivien waved her hand, dismissing the unsuitable, indisputable facts. "Let's not overlook the rescue portion of that story." She pointed her finger at Beth. "That's the part that has blockbuster quality. I watched him scoop you up and carry you to the ambulance." She clutched her hands to her chest.

Courtney gave Beth a side-eyed glance with a lift of her brows. "And he *is* a cowboy. Wranglers. Boots. Hat. I heard from Robin he even brought horses with him."

Horses. The camp. Grayson. Beth wasn't sure if it was the fog from the heat exhaustion or the fear of not getting the permanent camp position, but Grayson? The camp wrangler?

She wasn't sure how Noah would sort anything out. Jesse was out of commission. Walter, the retired wrangler, was out of state.

They still needed an assistant.

And let's be real—it wasn't like there was a horseman on every corner in Deep Haven.

Really, she just wanted to forget everything that had happened the day before. From the costume to the dogs to passing out and coming to with paramedic Jensen Atwood staring down at her.

And puking. There was that.

And you—big, strong cowboy—couldn't handle a few little children?

She let out an audible groan. Big, strong cowboy? What had she even been thinking?

Grayson was the kind of guy who never got too attached. Ask the many girls he'd dated in high school. From what Dylan had said, things hadn't changed when he moved to Oregon.

So yeah, she knew better. Even if she'd always been captivated by his easy charm and hard work so many years ago.

The telltale sound of Dad's slippers scuffling down the hall drew her attention. His round frame filled the doorway. He wore his favorite navy track pants and faded Fish Pic T-shirt.

"Good morning," he said and grabbed the cup of coffee she'd poured for him and the stack of mail she'd left on the peninsula.

Just like every morning, their easy routine was as comfortable as those slippers on his feet.

"Hey, Dad." She smiled.

"Vivien. Courtney. Good to see you, ladies."

"Good morning," Vivien and Courtney answered in unison.

"Hey, sweetie, how are you doing?" He snugged his ball cap over his short, graying hair and flipped through several pieces of mail. "You had me worried—maybe you shouldn't be moving up to Trinity quite so soon."

"I won't be far, Dad—right out Gunflint Trail."

Maybe this is what you both need.

Okay, yeah, Vivien was probably right. But that didn't make it easier. Not when she'd seen what her mom's betrayal had cost him. Had cost them.

Not when she'd made her promise a life mantra. *I'll never leave you.*

She could still see him sitting in his recliner. Sobbing.

All Mom had left behind was a letter. She hadn't even had the guts to tell them goodbye.

So, yeah—Beth had given up her shot at college. Turned down Lyle's offer. Her roots were in Deep Haven.

Courtney stood. "We brought a few groceries over—we're going to grab those from the car."

Beth nodded and waited until Courtney and Vivien closed the door behind themselves.

She took a sip of her coffee. "I'm doing okay. I feel silly about the whole catastrophe."

"I'm glad you're okay." He shuffled through several more pieces of mail. "Huh." He opened an envelope and unfolded the letter inside.

"What is it?"

"A class reunion…thing." He adjusted his glasses. "A Rhine River cruise."

"Wow." Beth sat up in the recliner. "Like, the whole class is going?"

He flipped the paper over. Beth could see a bright yellow Post-it Note stuck to the front of the letter but couldn't read the words.

Her dad finished reading the back page and picked up the slick brochure, read it, and stuffed it all back into the envelope. "It's just a small group from high school." He started to toss it into the recycle can. Paused. Set it back in the stack of mail. Pulled it out and looked at the contents again, then shoved them back into the envelope.

Huh.

The side door opened.

Her dad stepped out of the way to let Courtney and Vivien back in, grocery bags in tow. They plopped the bags unceremoniously onto the kitchen island while he exchanged his slippers for shoes.

"I'll leave you girls to it." He stood and tapped his hand on the stack of mail, as if his thoughts still lingered inside that envelope. "I'll see you later. I'm off to a meeting."

The door clicked shut behind him.

Beth would have thought Grayson pure imagination except that, from her vantage point on the gurney, she'd seen Robin step out of the bakery. She'd waved to her brother as he headed back to his truck while paramedic Jensen Atwood closed the doors of the ambulance. Grayson Fox, the man who'd left town in a cloud of dust, had driven away. Again.

Except, then he'd come to the hospital.

"So, back to this Lone Ranger rescue." Courtney pulled a loaf of fresh bread from one of the bags.

"So handsome too." Vivien rubbed her hands across her barely showing baby abdomen. "A six-foot dark-blond. Green eyes. Muscles."

"Wait—when did you see him?" Beth asked.

"I was on my way home from the theater, and I saw him getting into his truck when the ambulance was pulling away. Of course, I didn't know the whole story until you helped me put the pieces together." Vivien winked and tapped her index finger on her lips. "He's the complete opposite of Ly—"

Courtney clamped her hand over Vivien's mouth.

Beth pressed her hands to her temples, the blade of a headache jabbing her skull behind her eyeballs. "Please don't bring him up." His name still made her chest ache a little. The last thing she wanted to discuss was her failed engagement to Lyle Fredrickson or how handsome Grayson Fox was.

Vivien pried Courtney's fingers from her face, and three shades of realization transitioned across it.

Oh no. Beth groaned.

Vivien sucked in a breath. "You *liked* him."

Beth waved her off. "I more than liked him—I was engaged to him!" She flung her arms wide. "I loved him."

"Not Lyle." Vivien set her hands on her hips. "Grayson." She lifted a perfect brow. "How did I never see it before?"

"What?" Heat crept up Beth's neck. She hadn't been friends with Vivien in high school. Of course she wouldn't know their history. Unless she'd heard the rumors. But Beth doubted it. Vivien would not have resisted the mention of it.

Vivien leaned in. "Methinks the lady doth protest too much."

Beth rubbed her temples again. The pain had grown to an iron bar wedged through her temples.

Courtney and Vivien stood side by side, their heads slightly tilted in the same direction like puppy dogs.

"It was kind of romantic," Courtney offered. "Joyce said he caught you when you passed out."

"She told me he caught her *and* carried her."

Courtney let out a long *mmmm*.

"Is there anything or anyone Joyce didn't share this with? And you say *I* read too many novels." Beth scooped her tome from the floor and waved it in the air. "Let's not forget, he's a cowboy. I've already told you I'm not getting on a horse again."

Vivien held up her hands. "Just because he's a cowboy doesn't mean horses have to be involved."

"Do you even listen to yourself sometimes?" Beth shook her head. "Let it go. He's not only a wrangler–ranch hand. He's a horse trainer. Lives and breathes everything equine—and lives in Oregon."

"I'm just saying. We're talking about the man, not his transportation." Viven narrowed her gaze. "You seem to know a lot about him."

"I hear things." Beth swallowed. "And he stopped by the hospital."

Vivie's blue eyes rounded. "Oh?"

"Let's not forget that I was a mess—by the way, that wasn't your non-staining fake blood. I had to use an exfoliator scrub five times to get it off." Beth had cringed when she'd finally seen herself in the hospital room mirror. Still red-faced, even if turning more pinkish, and her hair had clung to her skull, dark with sweat. And losing her lunch… Yeah. Super romantic.

Not that she cared. She wasn't a starry-eyed teen anymore.

"Sorry about that." Vivien rubbed her hands together, ideas knitting her brows into a fine line.

Beth held a hand. "No. Stop. I know what you're thinking."

"What am I thinking?" Vivien threw her hands in the air like the innocent party in a dispute.

"You're thinking of polishing off your matchmaker manual. I can see it in your eyes." Beth put a hand on her hip. "And let's be honest—the last time you tried to set me up with someone, *you* ended up marrying him."

Courtney sputtered a laugh before coughing and clearing her throat. "She's got you there."

"Not that I mind. I mean, you and Boone are perfect together, but you are zero-for-one."

"Okay, so noted." Vivien paced the floor of the living room. "But that should not disqualify me from future matchmaking. If anything, it's given me much greater clarity."

"Well, then, for your recordkeeping, I will give you three reasons why that is a preposterous proposition." Beth held up her index finger. "One, he's Dylan's friend, and that would be weird." She held up a second finger. "Two, he lives in Oregon and I live in Deep Haven, so it's a dead end." She lifted a third finger. "And three—I'm done with dating for a very, very long time."

Fourth, she wasn't ready to admit—her teenage heart had already experienced the sting of adoring Grayson Fox.

"But it's been more than nine months since Lyle left. You need an adventure."

Beth picked up her journal. The one where she wrote all the things she dreamed of doing. "Adventure doesn't require me living—how many is it?—six states away. Or a man. But this camp position? It's my dream job. A real career in outdoor recreation and education."

"Can't beat that."

"That reminds me—" Beth stood and went to the peninsula, shuffled through the mail. She pulled out the envelope. "My dad got an invite for a European river cruise."

"Oh, that sounds like fun!"

Beth opened the envelope and pulled out the letter. The Post-it on the front page was handwritten.

It's been a long time.
I'd love to have you join us.
Janet

She turned the page around to Vivien and Courtney.

"Who's Janet?" Courtney asked. "Is that Janet who recently joined the church?"

Beth nodded. "She was his high-school sweetheart. Before he met Mom."

"Oh?"

"Her husband died five years ago. She moved back to Deep Haven last summer."

"Oh." Vivien rubbed her hands together. "He should totally go on that river cruise with Janet."

"He hasn't traveled anywhere since Mom left except for that one conference in Canada he had to attend for work." Beth studied the Rhine River cruise pamphlet. "Look at these castles!"

"He needs to rip off the Band-Aid. It's time." Courtney pointed to the brochure.

"It's also time for brunch." Vivien pointed to the Fox Bakery bag she carried. "We brought you fresh cinnamon rolls—and they're still warm." Vivien carried the bag to the kitchen and pulled three plates from the cabinet. "And French bread for later."

"They smell delicious." Beth hadn't eaten much since she'd tossed her lunch on the library's lawn yesterday.

Vivien carried the plates over and handed them out, followed by forks and napkins. "Now, we need to figure out how to get your dad on that cruise."

"Do you think he'd go?" Courtney asked. She took a bite of her cinnamon roll.

"I don't know," Beth answered. She tried to picture her homebody dad as a world traveler.

The sweet smell of sugar glaze and cinnamon filled the room. Beth took another sip of coffee and then a bite of roll.

One of the phones on the coffee table buzzed. Courtney leaned forward and glanced at the trio of cells on the table. "That's yours, Beth. Looks like it's Noah," Courtney said, speaking around a mouthful.

Vivien scooped up the phone. "You keep eating. I've got this." She clicked the button. "Hi, Noah, this is Vivien for Beth." She winked at Beth across the coffee table. "...Oh, yeah, she's fine, we're just having a little girls' brunch together... No, I didn't realize that..." Vivien pinned Beth with a sharp look.

Uh-oh. Beth braced herself.

"Right... Grayson Fox?" Vivien's eyes rounded and her mouth dropped open before she mouthed *Why didn't you tell me?* and then gripped Courtney's arm with her free hand. "...Yeah, sure. I'll let her know. If she has any questions, she'll give you a call."

Vivien disconnected and pointed at Beth with the phone. "Girl, you've got some explaining to do."

"What just happened?" Courtney asked.

Vivien set the phone down onto the table and stood, put her hands on her hips. "Well, Noah Standing Bear informed me that Grayson mentioned you had concerns about him being the camp wrangler."

"What?" Courtney wiped her mouth with a napkin.

Beth grimaced and set her plate down on the table.

Vivien threw a palm out. "But wait—there's more."

So much more. Beth fidgeted in her seat.

Vivie tilted her head. "He was calling to find out what issues his interim assistant camp director has with the new wrangler. He said to let him know the status because if camp has to be canceled, then he'll help you make the calls." She paused, shifted position, and crossed her arms. "He said there's also the issue of the assistant wrangler to discuss."

"What?"

"Beth! If you don't have a wrangler, you won't have that job. Noah can run Wilderness Challenge by himself."

"What's wrong with Grayson?" Courtney asked.

"Nothing. Absolutely nothing," Vivien said, waggling her eyebrows.

"Like you even know—you haven't seen him or talked to him in years."

"I saw him in town. He's capable. Strong. Dressed for the part." Vivien grabbed a second plate with a cinnamon roll. "And he's not a man afraid to jump into action. I love those qualities in Boone." She took a bite of her roll.

Right. "He said his last attempt working with children apparently involved an ambulance."

"Oh dear." Courtney cringed. "Who else can ride?" She stole a hunk of cinnamon roll from Vivien's plate.

"Beth can," Vivien said.

"Already been there—and I'm the interim ACD. Not a wrangler."

Courtney tapped her lips with her finger. "I don't think your case against Grayson will stand. Noah's not going to fire him because you have personal issues."

The energy seeped out of Beth. "I know," she whispered. Once all the indigence had faded away, her case against Grayson stood on the sole fact that she'd been humiliated by him.

Twelve years prior.

And no, Noah wasn't going to risk his camp over that, and neither could she.

"But you do still need an assistant, right?" Vivien asked. "What about Walter? He was the wrangler forever."

"He's out of state visiting family until after the Fourth of July," Courtney said, "but there is Johnny Lane. He used to work there as an assistant, right?"

Beth shook her head. "I called him last night when I got home. He works in Duluth now."

"Who did Jesse have slated to help him?"

"Usually there are a few high schoolers interested, but the last two moved away for college in the fall. Neither one is coming back for summer." Beth groaned. "With Jesse being on medical leave, it hadn't occurred to him to put feelers out for new staffing."

"So Grayson's doing it himself?"

"You did point out how capable he is." Beth took three glasses from the cupboard and poured milk in all three, then passed them out.

"Thanks," Courtney answered. "Wouldn't he be better than none? What's the big deal with him? Assuming he didn't actually cause a bunch of kids to get hurt...it seems like your beef is a little more...personal."

She couldn't argue with Courtney's point. "We have a history." Beth slumped. She might as well tell them now.

"Oh?" Vivien and Courtney perked up, leaning forward.

"From before we all were friends. High school." Beth looked down, collected herself, then met their expectant gazes. "It was an incredibly stupid thing."

Courtney took a drink. "Okay. Spill."

"Did either of you ever go to a pit party?"

Vivien wiped her fingers on a napkin. "You mean those teen parties just outside of town with underage drinking and excessive stupidity?"

"Never," Courtney answered. "Never, not ever."

"I'll take that as a yes," Beth said. "For both of you." She blew out a breath. Swallowed. "When I was a sophomore, my dad went out of town for a men's retreat. These girls I'd been hanging out with invited me." She shook her head. "It was a dumb thing to do."

Courtney wiped her fingers on a napkin. "We all learn that at some point."

"Yeah, well, I was so naive. The punch was spiked, and I'd had way too much. I remember dancing on the hood of someone's car."

"Oh." Vivien's eyes were round. "I'm having a hard time picturing that. I mean, you were...you—and I mean that in the best way possible. Sweet. Responsible. Maybe a little sheltered."

Beth closed her eyes. "Yeah. Well, Grayson showed up at some point and saw me."

"What was he—a senior?"

"Yep. And Dylan's best friend." Beth tucked a loose lock of hair behind her ear. "I mean, we'd known each other for years, but the summer before that school year, he grew up. Filled out." Beth could still see him that night.

White T-shirt. Blue jeans. Fresh haircut.

And those eyes that turned her teen self into a puddle anytime he came near.

"So, you did like him."

Beth forced a nod. "He got me down off the car. At first, I thought he'd dance with me. Instead, he practically dragged me back to his car."

Vivien put down her cinnamon roll. "That's probably the best thing you could have had happen to you that night, Beth."

"I can see that now—but not then." She swallowed. "He forced me into the car and said he was taking me home. I was drunk. I...uh...kissed him."

Vivie gasped. "What? How did we not know this?"

"You can't stop there," Courtney said. "Then what?"

Beth lifted a shoulder. "He dodged my first attempt, but on the second one, he kissed me back."

"Oh." Vivien's mouth gaped open, and she looked at Courtney. "While you were drunk?"

"Don't worry—then he pushed me away. Told me he didn't want to kiss me. I was mortified."

Vivien put a hand on Beth's arm. "He was looking out for you."

"I don't remember much else. He took me home. I don't even know what stupid, idiotic things I might have said to him. I was embarrassed and humiliated. Then Dylan showed up at the house and saw us. I didn't tell him it was my fault. He was furious. Grayson and I stayed away from each other after that." She rubbed her fingertips in the fog on her glass. "He and Dylan didn't hang out much from that night on. Then graduation—and he was gone."

"Oh, Beth," Courtney said. "I mean, I get that was awful back then, but you see it differently now, don't you?"

She stared at the floor. "I felt so...rejected. Rejected by my mom. Rejected by Grayson. I didn't want to face him again. And now he's back and he's standing between me and this job. What am I going to do?"

"I think you know what you need to do," Courtney said. "You need to find a way to overcome the past."

"You don't have a real choice," Vivien said. "You've been talking about working at that camp since you started doing kayak lessons and volunteering there." She picked at her cinnamon roll. "You've wanted this job more than I've ever seen you want anything else."

Beth met Vivien's bright blue gaze, and she let the words settle over her. She could do this—she could do her job and let Grayson do his. And by the end of summer, he'd go on his way, and she'd have secured her position at the camp permanently.

four

. . .

THE INSTANT GRAYSON'S EYES OPENED THAT MORNING, BETH'S words prodded him. *I'm going to find a way.*

Grayson stared at the ceiling of the barn apartment, as he had most of the night. How had he only been in Deep Haven twenty-four hours? And how was he suddenly tangled up in all this mess?

He'd been caught off guard the day before, but he shouldn't have to give up his summer job—and subsequently, his future ranch—because he'd be working with her.

Like Dylan said, they were adults. They could steer clear of each other. She didn't have to find a way. They already had one.

He scrambled from the bed to the bare wood floor. The mattress sat on a rustic log bed built into the end wall. The studio apartment included a kitchenette with a two-burner stove.

Before diving into his day, he needed coffee, because he had a full morning figuring out exactly what the story was on the buckskin bronc, Tally, the gentle bay, Remington, and the sorrel powerhouse, Maverick. He tugged on his jeans, T-shirt, and boots.

He checked his phone for any new messages from the bank.

Nothing. He knew he shouldn't expect anything over a holiday weekend, but all the possibilities had sprouted an unexpected hope inside him. He needed to know he was pre-approved for the loan.

A quick search through the cupboards revealed a few food staples. He set up the four-cup coffeepot and hit the button, hoping that was enough to fuel his day.

"Knock, knock." The words preceded a light tap on the door. Noah.

"Come in," Grayson answered. He pulled a second cup from the cupboard. "You're just in time." He filled both cups and handed one to Noah. "I hope you like it black. It's all I've got."

Noah smiled. "This is good." He took a sip. "Beth is on board."

Grayson nearly choked on his coffee. "Really?"

"I know you were concerned with her feelings about the two of you working together, but when pressed, she said it'd be fine."

Fine. Oh, he knew what that meant. It meant she'd work the camp with him, and he'd need his winter jacket for the chill whenever she came near.

"Great." He drowned the word with another swig.

"We've hit a little snag, though," he said.

"Beyond the fact that she was ready to fire me?"

Noah shrugged. "Technically, I'm your boss, and I'd do the firing—but we still don't have an assistant for you."

"I can't take the kids out by myself."

"The regular wrangler usually hires them. We've got a couple younger guys who've been on repeat for a few summers, but neither one is available."

Grayson held up a hand. "I'm going to need more coffee before I can process that. Let me feed the horses, check out the three I brought in for you." See what part of his summer plan he could salvage. "Do you have any ideas?"

Noah shook his head. "Neither did Beth. I don't want to have to shut the horse camp down." He took another drink. "The kids need this. I know you know that."

Grayson closed his eyes. Nodded. He did know. "I still can't believe Walter let me follow him around all day long, even when camp was over." Who would he even be if he hadn't become the unofficial horse camp volunteer after his parents died? The horses had saved him from a dark road. No, it hadn't been without wrong turns, but he still remembered how lost he'd been as a child.

How much the grief and regret had overtaken him. How the horses had given him a purpose.

"He used to repeat some phrase—Churchill, I think. About the outside of a horse."

Grayson nodded. "'Is good for the inside of a man.'" He wondered if Walter knew how much he'd redirected Grayson's life. He'd never even touched a horse before that first day of camp. "One ride and I was hooked. I'd completely forgotten how much I hadn't wanted to come."

"I remember." Noah finished his coffee. "And you weren't the last. Sure, some kids just come and go—it's a fun activity for them. But others, I see it plant seeds in their lives. Change their trajectory."

Grayson let Noah's words settle over him and took a swig of the brew. The acid seared his gut. Maybe he could still make something of the trajectory of his own life.

"How did it go with your family?"

Grayson let out a sharp laugh. "Fine—Robin's a little sore at me." He tapped his fingers on his mug.

Noah raised a brow. "How's that?"

"She doesn't want me to sell the lot."

"Oh. That's tough." He rubbed his beard. "She could buy it from you."

"Oh, that would go over real well when I tell her that. She'd want me to give it to her." Grayson shook his head. "Our parents had planned to build their dream home on that lot. They'd scraped and saved for it. It's tough. I get where she's coming from." He set down his mug. "Selling that lot is like…"

Noah's eyes softened. "Like letting them go."

Grayson nodded. "It's easy to imagine and make plans for it—much harder to follow through."

"It's not, though. Not letting them go. They'd want you to use it to pursue your plans." Noah stared into his mug. "That land's worth quite a bit of money now. It could take a chunk out of any loan you need for the place in Oregon."

Grayson nodded. "Exactly." When the numbers were crunched, no bank could offer him an affordable loan without the funds from the sale.

Noah finished his coffee and took his cup to the sink, washed it out, and set it on a folded towel. "Thank you for the coffee and for feeding the horses."

"No problem."

"I'll check in with Beth later. If she wants this job, she'll have to figure out an assistant wrangler hire." Noah tucked his chair back in. "Unfortunately, I've got too much going on at Wilderness Challenge to deal with it." He walked to the door, opened it.

"She'll do great with it. Beth's always been the one who's everywhere, making sure things get done."

"Sometimes to her own detriment." Noah shook his head. "It's an important position. I do hope it works out for her—and you."

Noah's parting words needled Grayson on his way through the barn.

His apartment was adjacent to an office space. The tack room door, a stall, and a storage bay filled out the rest of that side of the barn aisle.

Opposite, three stalls were bookended by hay storage and a tractor bay.

A heavy, wooden ladder in the end bay leaned against the loft, where several tons of hay were stored.

He hefted a bale into the double-wheeled hay cart, just like Noah had shown him the night before. He paused at the first empty stall and wiped away several cobwebs. The barn was still only used for quarantine and injury treatment. It wasn't cost effective to keep nearly thirty horses stalled.

He pulled the cart out the back door of the barn toward the paddocks, where the entire herd lifted their heads and a chorus of nickers greeted him.

Yeah, they were all happier to spend their time outside too.

Noah's words churned inside him.

It had to work out. For him and Beth. He just didn't know how.

Sunshine filled the space, a few clouds of gnats swarming along the path. Cool morning air filled his lungs and swept him back to the many camp mornings when he'd walked the same path. He'd tagged along behind Walter and sought every opportunity to reach through the fence wire to run his hands along the sleek summer coats of the horses.

Especially his favorite. A bay gelding named Mr. Pickles. Of all things, who named a horse Mr. Pickles?

The memory lit a spark in Grayson's heart. Picky, as he'd dubbed him, had known a few things about boys. Most notably, that boys like Grayson needed a friend. Someone who listened without judgment. Someone who loved without limits. Someone who could pull him out of the dark, lonely place inside himself after his parents died. Picky knew how to start out slow and then turn on the speed.

Grayson set his hand on a fence post, now weathered and worn. Chew marks interrupted the hewn log's surface where a nervous horse had gnawed at it. Tufts of long gray and black mane hair caught the breeze, marking its use as a scratching post.

Tally watched him through the wire. He hoped to work with several of the horses. The forecast called for a cooler day, topping out in the seventies. That would make it more comfortable for arena work.

If he ran the camp, he'd be giving up time to get things squared away at the new place. Not to mention getting his boots dirty in all this Deep Haven business.

But if he didn't, there wouldn't be a camp for Eli. Whose mom was battling breast cancer. And Beth would be out of a job.

Grayson shook the rattling thoughts away and pushed the hay cart. He tossed hay into all the camp paddocks and returned to the first one, where Remington and Maverick joined him. He scratched their necks and withers. Each one leaned into the attention, and Maverick stuck his muzzle against Grayson's chest, content to chew his hay while having his face rubbed.

Tally watched from a distance.

After ten minutes, he'd picked up all four feet on both horses and run his hands over their bodies. So far, so good.

He ventured back into the tack room and looked for a saddle wide enough for Maverick's broad, copper-red back, then collected brushes, a pad, and bridle.

This time, he'd do it right. He brought Maverick into the round pen.

Grayson took his time, letting Maverick get to know him and watching for signs it was too much pressure. He worked him at liberty first, changing directions, bringing the horse in to him.

Like he should have done with Tally.

He put on the rope halter, and Mav stood like a true ranch horse, unflappable even when Grayson moved to sacking him out. The heavy muscling rounding the gelding's chest and the width of his chest were reminiscent of some of the American Quarter Horse Association's most famous sires.

Enviable conformation for any quarter horse.

Grayson had tied a plastic bag to the end of a whip he'd found in the barn and moved it around the horse, rubbed it on him, smacked the ground with it, testing the horse's reactivity.

Maverick turned an ear. Moved his mouth in licking and

chewing motions, showing signs of ease and relaxation. Interest without fear.

"Nice. You're the real deal, huh?" Satisfaction lifted Grayson's spirits. This was the work that kept his spirit humming throughout each day.

By the time he tacked up and swung onto Mav's back, he had no doubt Maverick would do well.

The horse had a buttery-smooth canter. In fact, the horse was soft and responsive—maybe a little rusty, but he'd stepped right into lead changes and responded to the lightest cues. He'd done some high-level work, and Grayson ventured he must've been the camp wrangler's horse.

Putting a kid on him would be like setting a sixteen-year-old into a Ferrari to drive.

Two hours later, he'd just finished riding Remington when a gray Dodge Durango pulled up and parked beneath the black spruce. At least he was two out of three on the horses. Finally, a glimmer of redemption. Remington was an honest horse, probably near twenty. Patient and well-mannered.

A slender boy bailed from the back seat and scrambled up the side of the corral, and Dylan followed from the SUV.

Remington lifted his head but kept his feet still. Grayson reached down and rubbed the sleek, warm coat.

"Can I pet him?" the boy asked.

"Eli, you can't climb on things without asking." Dylan stepped up to the rail next to Eli.

"I asked to pet the horse."

Dylan laughed. "Not what I meant—you climbed the fence. You probably don't remember Grayson. The last time you saw him, I think you were around four."

Eli shook his head. "I was too young back then. I'm ten now."

Grayson laughed. The kid said it like he was a college student now. He had Dylan's blue-green eyes and Marie's light-blonde hair. Well, if she hadn't lost it all. "You like horses?"

Eli nodded. "I'm coming here to camp next week. I signed up to do the trail rides every single day."

"Oh, you are, huh?" Grayson gave Dylan a glance.

In return, he got a shrug. "That's the plan. As long as camp is running."

The boy's face fell and he turned toward his dad. "You registered for it, right?"

Dylan nodded. "I did, but Aunt Beth's working out the details."

Grayson stepped down from the horse and led Remington over to them. "He likes having his face rubbed right here." Grayson demonstrated by giving a good rub to the broad spot on the bay's forehead. Remington dropped his head into it and pressed against it.

"So, what are you doing out here? Gearing up for next week?" Dylan asked, nodding toward the horse.

"You're ruthless and relentless," Grayson answered. "These are the maniacal horses your sister mentioned." He patted Remy's neck. "As you can see, I didn't go all wrong. Two out of three isn't bad." At least, that's the story he was telling himself.

"What's his name?" Eli asked.

"This one's name is Remington—sometimes I call him Remy."

"Hi, Remy." Eli put his small hand where Grayson's had been. "My mom likes horses. She has cancer."

Grayson braced against the memory of his own mom, the emotions threatening to capsize him. How she'd loved animals of all kinds. How Eli's small voice captured the uncertainty of the future in those three words. "Your dad told me that. I'm sorry about your mom's cancer. I think horses are pretty special too."

"Me too. Can I ride Remy today?" Eli waved when an older blue Honda Pilot parked next to the Durango. Beth exited the vehicle. She wore jeans and hiking boots, her light-brown hair loose around her shoulders. She gave a tentative smile and walked toward them, her hands full with a stack of file folders, binders, and pens.

Eli turned his attention back to Grayson when Beth walked their way.

"I can't let you ride Remy today, but you can help me take all this tack off of him and brush him. How does that sound? If it's okay with your dad."

Dylan checked his watch. "Sure, we have a few minutes."

"Yes!" Eli pumped his arm.

He climbed off the panel and followed Grayson to the hitching post. With each piece of tack removed, he obediently followed directions. Dylan and Beth sat on the weather-worn bench nearby, their conversation swallowed by Eli's chatter and questions.

"That's all," Grayson said, dropping the brushes Eli handed him into the grooming bucket. "Time for this guy to head back to the pasture."

Dylan and Beth stood, waiting with Eli while Grayson turned Remington loose. The horse gave a robust shake and wandered off to graze.

"Bye, Aunt Beth." Eli waved, giving her only a spare glance. "Bye, Mr. Grayson."

Beth stepped up next to him, still carrying her stack of paperwork. "I thought you said you were bad with kids."

"What? *You* said I was bad with kids." Grayson adjusted his hat.

"You're exaggerating, but by the looks of it, you have been granted hero status."

He couldn't help but smile at Eli.

He pressed his fingertips into his temples and tried to rub the tight creases from his brow.

"I think we can both be professionals about this." Beth leaned her back against the hitching post. "I'll keep to my work. You keep to yours."

Grayson let Beth's statement float on the heat of the day. "You should know I'm not singing camp songs."

"Fine."

"Good."

"It's remarkable that you're not allergic to anyone under the age of thirteen."

He shot her a toothy grin. "Ha."

"The bad news is you're going to have to run the trail rides by yourself. I'll keep looking for an assistant."

"You must still be affected by your mishap in the book costume." He picked up a curry comb that had fallen from the grooming bucket. "There's no way one person can run the rides."

"Sure you can. You're capable." She said it with a smirk and rolled her eyes. "Of course, I'll keep looking for someone."

The dust settled from Dylan's Durango heading down the drive, and Grayson wagered he was about to make one of the worst mistakes of his life.

He faced Beth. "You've got to do it."

Beth looked away, looked back at him. "Do what?" She started to step away from him.

"You can help with the trail rides." Grayson stepped in front of her. "Noah said there won't be a horse camp without two of us. It's a safety issue." And not only his ranch was riding on this. Every time he thought of Eli and his mom's cancer, he thought of himself at that age. No kid should have to face the potential loss of a parent.

"I'll find someone."

"Really? Who are you going to get? Because Noah told me the two of you had already exhausted everyone you knew."

Beth looked up at him, her lips rounded into an O.

Man, she had pretty green eyes. He'd never noticed the gold flecks. Or the way the sun had kissed freckles across her nose and cheeks. None of which he should notice, because Dylan would kill him. "You need this and so do I. You've got to help."

BETH CHARGED INTO THE CAMP OFFICE, FLEEING FROM GRAYSON'S demand. She didn't like how she wanted to say yes to him, like she was under his spell again.

The very idea of it was preposterous.

She dropped the schedules, grant files, and waivers onto her desk—the desk, quite unfortunately, housed in the office that sat between the barn apartment and the tack room.

Hello—she had a lot of work to do already.

No way could she get back on a horse.

Nope. There had to be some other solution. Some other way she could help make this happen for both of them.

And okay, yes, maybe she should have sucked up her pride in high school and just been grateful he'd hauled her home from that pit party—but he'd still rejected her.

And that *still* stung.

His footsteps followed and his form filled the doorframe. "Come on, Beth—you already said you need this camp to run. You need me—and I need you."

She wished he wouldn't word it like that. It made her pulse whoosh in her skull.

"I'm already the ACD. That's a full-time job." She pointed to the paperwork on her desk.

He gave her a look.

You don't have a real choice. Vivien's counsel rolled over Beth.

And yeah, okay, she was right about that. She patted fingers against her temples. "You don't understand." A little hitch of loss ached in her chest, a raw memory filled with the noise and motion of running the barrels in 4-H.

Yeah, well, kids were fearless. Then they grew up. Particularly fast after being dumped on the head.

How could she admit it to Grayson?

She closed her eyes. Just the thought of admitting it caused heat to flare across her face.

"Are we going to do this or what?" Grayson asked. "You know the camp needs us. And Eli—he needs this. So, are we going to make this happen or not?"

His plea caught her off guard with its palpable need and the raw scrape in his voice.

Like it mattered to him.

She shook her head. Blinked back tears. Why had she let Dad talk her out of getting back on? "I haven't—I stopped—I fe—" Her words stumbled over themselves. "I just can't."

His jaw went slack and he leaned back against the nearest stall after looking out the back barn door, toward the horse paddocks. "What is it?"

"I stopped..." She turned away. "...riding." And now she sounded pitiful. Just like in childhood when she'd begged Dylan and Grayson to let her tag along.

"Beth?" His voice was soft this time. She didn't speak. His Adam's apple bobbed, then he looked at her.

She'd fallen off. That didn't do the catastrophic somersault off her horse at a gallop any kind of justice. She'd been a human lawn dart.

Knocked unconscious.

She stepped away from the desk. "I don't know why I ever thought I could do this job."

He held out his hands as if he could prevent her from stampeding straight out the door with sheer hope. "Please?"

"I'll find someone else to help you." Even as she said it, she knew she'd already exhausted her call-down list. "I can't." Her voice made a silly, squeaky crack. "I kept riding after my mom..." *Left.* Why was it so hard to just say it? She shook out the nerves. "Then I had a bad wreck on the barrels."

"I don't remember that."

"It was an out-of-town gaming event," she answered. "I was mortified."

"Everyone has a bad fall. Or five. You get back on."

She shook her head.

"You didn't get back on?"

"No. Literally. Not once." And now those stupid tears again. Fast-blink, fast-blink. "Dad wasn't into horses or 4-H or any of that stuff, but he supported me after Mom left because he knew I loved it." She smoothed out a crumpled note on the desk. "We'd come out of the last barrel, hit top speed, and Chase tripped. I went flying off him."

"Ouch."

She swallowed. Nodded. "I came to, lying there in the dirt. The arena had gone silent. Chase was long gone. He'd tumbled, rebalanced, and run straight out the chute." She shrugged. "Mom wasn't there to dust me off and plop me back up there like when I was little."

"I'm sorry," he said.

"The worst part was Dad's face. Complete terror. He packed me up, took me home. Terminated the lease agreement for Chase. That was that."

"I thought back then that you'd just outgrown it or something." He offered a teasing smile. "Grew up and got more interested in boys than horses."

"As if." But he'd pulled her mind out of that dusty arena dirt. She took a deep breath. "I never told Dylan at the time. He was at a youth retreat." She shrugged. "By the time he even asked about it, it was all a done deal. I'd moved on to theater and kayaking."

He nodded, his green eyes on her.

"I didn't tell him the whole story until the summer after I graduated high school, when I turned down—of all things—a horse camp position. I still love them—still think they're incredibly beautiful. I just can't ride anymore."

He nodded, scrubbed his hands over his face. "What do you want to do?" His shoulders hung. His voice faltered. "I—I can't do this alone. Is there anyone else you can call?"

She shook her head. "I haven't found anyone yet."

"I think the kids need this." His raw voice scraped Beth's resolve.

She had the sense Grayson wasn't a guy who asked for help. Ever. "The kids need this—I need this. This is my opportunity to have a real career—something I'm passionate about—but I don't know how," she whispered. If she didn't find a way to make camp happen, she'd watch her dream job slip away. "I don't know how to overcome the past."

She lifted her shoulders and dropped them, shaking out the tension and nodding like she was about ready to take on a kayak relay. She tried to still her trembling hands.

"Come on." He held out a hand to her in invitation.

She hesitated. She could hear Vivien's words of encouragement. *Get out of your comfort zone.*

He lifted two halters from a hook near the storage bay. "You okay?"

You were...fearless.

"I'm not afraid of being near them." She wrinkled her nose. "I just don't get on them anymore."

"Well, that's something." His green eyes landed softly on her, just like they had on the horse he'd been working with. "You can do this." He had the nerve to wink at her. "It's like riding a bike."

"Because bikes have brains and free will and flight instincts." She crossed her arms.

"Well—"

A crash from behind the barn interrupted him.

Without a word, they both took off running for the paddocks.

five

. . .

GRAYSON REACHED THE PASTURE GATE WITHIN MOMENTS OF THE crash. His heart sank as Tally limped midfield, looped strands of wire fence loose across the tall grass.

The other horses scattered in the paddock, fleeing the disruption, then resettled.

The mare stopped, her left hind leg contracted off the ground.

Beth pulled up next to him. "Oh no!"

He unlatched the gate. "That's one of the new horses—"

She hung back when he entered the paddock. "One of the wild ones?"

"She's been mistreated. She's not wild." But she was unpredictable—not that he blamed her. And he'd done zero to earn her trust.

Grayson looked at Tally. Beth. Tally.

He held back the groan that swelled inside his lungs. Beth was the last person he'd have help him with the buckskin.

He closed his eyes. Swallowed. "In the barn, outside the tack room, is a metal can. Inside is a bag of horse treats. Grab a handful." Maybe with a little bribery, Tally would cooperate.

Beth nodded and ran for the barn.

He carried the halter through the paddock, zigzagging his way closer to Tally and hoping not to disrupt her.

Footsteps brushed through the field. Beth jogged back and took a wide loop through the tall grass, meeting him on his final approach to the horse. She held the long hem of her T-shirt up in a sling with a mountain of horse treats piled inside.

"I said a handful, not a stockpile."

"I can take them back." She raised a brow and slapped two horse cookies into his open hand.

"It's fine. Thank you." He offered one of the treats to Tally with an outstretched arm and stepped toward her. "Hey there."

The horse backed away with a stumble and a grunt.

Beth let out a little sound, like a cry of distress. "You have to catch her. She's going to make it worse." A line creased her brow, and she worried her lower lip between her teeth.

Unfortunately, he was the last person Tally wanted to pal around with.

He'd need Beth's help. There was no getting around it.

Tally stretched her nose toward Beth, who smelled like a five-foot equine goody bag with the cache she was hauling in her shirt.

"Her name is Tally," Grayson said. "I'm not her favorite person right now."

"Oh, girl." Beth smirked and turned to the horse. "I get it. This guy?" She nodded toward Grayson. The mare's ears swiveled. "He's trouble."

"Really?" Grayson shook his head. "You're going to do that now?"

"I'm finding common ground with her. That's Camp Counseling 101. Relating to someone in distress." She reached out her hand to the horse.

Tally took a hobble toward Beth, who let out a little moan with each step the horse took.

The sound unwound every scrap of good sense he had in him.

"Can you put on the halter? Are you comfortable with that?"

She nodded. "Like I said, I still like them. I just don't ride them." She snugged her shirt fabric tight and drew it into a knot around the treats, freeing her hands.

Grayson walked around behind her and handed off one of the halters. It wasn't Tally's, but it would fit.

Taking two tentative steps forward, Beth carried a treat in one hand and the halter in another. Tally leaned in and lipped the treat from her palm. Beth placed a hand on the horse's neck, testing out her behavior.

Okay, she wasn't green at this. She still remembered.

Another treat, then she slid the halter over Tally's nose, buckled it. Fed her another treat.

"Don't give her colic."

Beth cut him a look.

He held up his hands. "Easy." He approached the horse's hind leg. The gaping slice didn't have much blood, but the clean edges had curled back from the front of her hock joint. "You got her?" he asked.

Beth nodded.

He leaned in for a closer look, one hand on the mare's hip.

Tally swished her tail, slapping Grayson in the face, and stepped away from him.

"Should I call the vet?" Beth asked.

"Do you have the number?"

"She's a friend of mine—you remember Lena Larson?"

He nodded. Their families had grown up next door to each other.

Beth fished her phone out of her pocket and dialed. After a quick conversation with Lena, she disconnected. "She's on her way."

An hour later, Beth still stood at Tally's head in the barn aisle. They'd brought her from the pasture into the barn with slow steps, letting the horse set the pace.

Tally hadn't been keen on leaving Remington and Maverick behind. She'd heaved several loud whinnies, calling out to them. Remington had answered several times.

Grayson watched Lena finish wrapping the wound. Every so often, the mare lifted her leg as if to kick, but he couldn't tell if it was from pain or fear.

"The antibiotic will hopefully stave off any infection." Lena tossed a leftover roll of tape into her vet kit and rechecked her crisscross bandaging over and under Tally's hock joint. "That should hold if she doesn't get rowdy in here."

Beth reached for Tally's forehead, but the horse tossed her head up. "Poor girl."

"The good news is that it doesn't look like she ruptured the tendon. Only the tendon sheath. I tell you, a breath farther, and we'd be dealing with a much more serious injury."

It still didn't sound like very good news to Grayson.

"I don't know that she's going to come out of this a ridable horse." Lena stood and gestured toward the leg. "Even though only the tendon sheath's been breached, that's still a dangerous injury."

Beth pressed her lips together in a frown and rubbed the horse's neck.

"Watch for any signs of infection. If you see any swelling, redness, call me right away—day or night." She wiped her hands on her utility coveralls.

Grayson nodded. "Will do."

She handed him a bottle of pills. "Here are some antibiotics to give her once a day when you feed. Mix them in some applesauce. Obviously, I couldn't stitch it due to the location."

"How often do we need to rewrap it?" Beth asked.

We? Huh. She probably meant it as in "we at the camp," not the two of them specifically. Except, they were the two at the horse camp, so there was that. And he wasn't sure what to do with the realization.

"You'll need to change out the Telfa pad daily. Because the sheath is breached, there's going to be fluid loss. The less movement, the better right now."

"We'll have to keep her on stall rest," Beth said.

"Once we're done here, I'll bring in one of the other horses to keep her company," Grayson said.

Lena nodded. "Do all that and the rest is up to nature." She pulled a medication tube from her kit. "You can give her bute once a day for pain, one to two grams. The local anesthesia will wear off over the next hour."

He took the tube of anti-inflammatory medication from Lena and slid open the stall door. "Do you want me to take her?"

"I can do it." Beth led Tally step-by-step into the stall kept bedded for emergencies, then removed the halter. Tally threw back her head.

This would be fun.

"I feel so badly for her," Beth said. She closed the stall door and went straight to prepping the stall across the aisle for a second horse.

"Sorry to run." Lena handed Grayson a stack of Telfa pads and rolls of self-adhesive bandage wraps. "I have another call. You guys take care."

"Sure. Thanks," Grayson said.

"See you tomorrow." Beth grabbed the wheelbarrow and shoveled fresh shavings into it.

Lena packed up her vet kit and headed out to her truck while Grayson grabbed Remington from the pasture.

Beth had already spread the shavings in the stall facing Tally's by the time he returned. The gelding didn't complain about having his own stall. He went straight to the flakes of hay Beth had also dropped in.

She walked back to Tally's stall. "She has to be okay," Beth said. "Look at her—she looks like she's been used, abused, and abandoned. Scars and fear and old saddle sores." She swallowed. Blinked. "And now this. She doesn't even want to let me pet her." She closed her eyes. "I just want to let her know it'll be okay. That we'll take care of her."

Oh man. He got it. Because as much as he saw a bit of himself in Tally with her standoffish attitude, Beth had to see so much more of herself.

He didn't know how a mother left her children any more than he knew how a loving God turned His back on the prayers of a child.

Beth swiped the back of her hand across her eyes.

And shoot, he just wanted to reach out and hug her. Comfort her. "We'll do everything we can."

We, again. Because somehow, they were in this together.

She nodded but didn't move.

He rubbed his chest. After everything they'd been through this afternoon, he'd forgotten the strain that had hung between them.

"I'm sorry, Beth."

She looked up at him. Blinked.

"For calling you Bookworm Bethy when we were kids. For the night of the pit party." He leaned against the stall wall. "I was trying to do the right thing that night, and I totally botched it."

A warm breeze swept through the barn aisle, sending loose hay tumbling past them.

The silence was filled only by the birds outside and the horses moving around their stalls, chewing their hay.

He shifted, opened and closed his fists, then met her eyes. "Are you going to say something?"

"I...I don't remember much about that night." She wrinkled her nose. "I didn't intend to drink alcohol—I know that sounds stupid, because what else do kids go to those parties for, right? I should have guessed the drinks were spiked."

He lifted a shoulder. He wasn't one to judge. "I'd gone

looking for Oliver." He'd expected to find his brother drunk, not Beth. His brother who'd decided coping was found at the bottom of a bottle. Grayson had lost his mind a little bit when he'd seen Beth dancing on the car.

Okay, a lot. He'd totally freaked and hauled her to his truck despite her protests.

"I could have handled it better too. I was just so embarrassed." She toed the floor with her hiking boot. "First"— she held out a hand—"don't take this wrong, but I had a little crush on you—which was totally stupid, but I did."

"Wait—why was that stupid?"

Beth shook her head. "Stop." She huffed out a breath. "When I..." She let out a groan. "When I kissed you, and then you kissed me, for that moment I felt...I don't know. Seen. Special. I was drunk and it was dumb. And then you rejected me."

Ouch. He closed his eyes and lowered his head. "You were special—you are special."

"I don't need a sympathy vote."

He looked back up. "I shouldn't have kissed you, Beth. You were drunk and you weren't in control of yourself. It was wrong. I just wanted to get you home safely." He kneaded the tight muscles of his neck. "There were guys at that party who could have taken advantage of you." Unfortunately, he'd made himself look like one of them.

"I get that now," she said, her words soft and distant. "But at school that Monday, everyone was talking about it. Rumors were all over the place about how you'd dragged me off to your truck." Her face flushed. "What we'd supposedly done. And all I could think about was how I was not only rejected but my reputation was trashed." She ran her hand along the top rail of the stall door.

He scrubbed his hands over his face. "I'm sorry."

"I held on to that rejection and bitterness for a long time. After that, I barely saw you. Then your graduation—and you were gone."

She swept several horse-treat crumbs from her T-shirt. "I know you lost your closest friend that night too."

Dylan. "We've made some progress over the years." He offered her a half smile. "And he did ask me if I'd go fishing with him this summer."

"That is progress." She gave him a wistful look. "Still, if I hadn't done what I did—and if I'd been sober enough to know that you'd done nothing wrong—I would have spoken up. I would have taken the blame that was mine." She looked up, her green eyes bright and clear. "I'm sorry too."

He wasn't prepared for the way her forgiveness washed over him. How the burden of responsibility had dogged him. "Thank you."

She nodded and turned toward Tally's stall. "I'm afraid to leave her. What if she pulls off the bandage?"

He wasn't keen on leaving her unattended just yet either. "Cards?"

She narrowed her gaze.

"There's a deck of cards in the tack room. How about a few rounds of Crazy Eights?"

She laughed, something light and sweet—and a little dangerous, because she stood up and looked him in the eye. "You're on."

He pulled two folding chairs from the tack room and handed her the deck. Let her shuffle and deal while he set the chairs up in the aisle outside Tally's stall and stacked two hay bales into place as their table.

"What exactly do you do in Oregon?" she asked. She flipped over the top card from the deck to begin play.

"I've been working at a ranch, mostly training horses." He placed a five of clubs on the five of spades.

"I know that much." She perused her cards and dropped a seven of spades. "But, I guess, why Trinity for the summer? What's the tie-in?"

No sense hiding the truth now. "I was let go. Difference of

opinion on horse care and training techniques." He added another card to the upward-facing stack.

Beth placed another card. She pressed her lips together, as if in thought. "But you're not staying here in Deep Haven?"

"I'm hoping to buy my own place. A guy I know is downsizing." He swallowed and placed a crazy-eight card down. "Diamonds." He declared the new card suit. "I'd actually like to open my own place for youth."

Beth held her card mid-placement. "Really? Like, a camp?" He didn't miss the incredulous tone in her question.

"Yeah. I mean, it'll take a while to be able to buy or train enough kid-safe horses."

Beth placed her card. "You, running your own camp?"

He laughed. "I know. It's an idea I haven't been able to shake."

"I didn't see that coming." Beth drew a card. Then another. "You surprise me. I was picturing you riding the range. Chasing cows. Rodeos and roundups." She set down a jack of clubs. "Not working with youth."

"I used to do all that at Three Sisters. I love working with the horses. That's where my time's been focused." He swept loose pieces of hay from the makeshift table. "But you know, I've always carried with me what this camp meant to me."

"And Oregon?"

"Winter is an actual season, not a badge of courage we endure for nine months." He laughed. "Where I live, we get decent snow, but not like here. And we have the mountains, the sandy beaches." He stared at his cards. "Sunrise, when the light hits the snow-capped peaks, or the sun dipping into the ocean." He lifted a shoulder. "Whatever scenery I want, I can find it there."

"Hmm. Sounds pretty." She reorganized her cards and cleared her throat. "And the...sisters? What are they like?"

"Cold."

She lifted a brow. "Like…standoffish? Or mean?"

He placed a card, realizing her misunderstanding. "They're mountains, not people. Faith, Hope, and Charity."

She sat up. "Mountains?" A little flush crept up her neck.

They kept placing their cards and making draws.

"Yes, ma'am. And Three Sisters Ranch is owned by a husband and wife—the Rutherfords. They're good people, and I could have fought harder for the job, but I didn't want to create family friction."

"Maybe it was time for you to move on."

He drew several cards, finally finding a two of spades to play. "You're probably right."

She placed a two of hearts on the two of spades. "I won!"

Well, okay.

Beth looked over to Tally, then back to him. "Another round?"

"I need to feed first." He returned the rest of his cards to the deck and gave them a shuffle. "Want to help?"

They worked in tandem, dropping several bales of hay down from the loft, loading the hay cart, and feeding the entire herd before filling the outdoor water troughs.

Ordinary, mundane tasks he'd done hundreds of times at Three Sisters.

And it didn't go unnoticed how well Beth worked with him. But he should be in Oregon. Working on the ranch. Training horses. Alone.

Instead of whatever this was. Because he didn't like how easily a guy could fall into the comfort of having someone to help him out. Someone to laugh with. Someone to catch his eye across the room.

Nope. He didn't need or want any of that.

Thirty minutes later, he parked the hay cart in the barn, and Beth stopped at Tally's stall. The buckskin backed away, and Beth let out a sigh, then turned. "Ready for another round?"

"You sure? It's getting late."

"I still don't want to leave her."

"You know, my apartment is right there." He pointed to the apartment door at the front end of the barn. "I can keep an eye on her."

"That's not the same."

She wasn't leaving. At least, not for now. "Okay, maybe Go Fish this time." He laughed. "I haven't played cards since I don't even know when."

They drew up their chairs and he dealt the cards.

"You're really going to sell the lot?" she asked.

"I have to." He blew out a breath. "Robin doesn't want me to, and I get that. It's a piece of our past. Feels a little like letting go of their plans. Permanently. Does that make sense?"

Her green eyes met his. "I kept a jade horse necklace my mom gave me. It's broken, but it represents what was meant to be." She let out a sharp laugh. "And I suppose it being broken is symbolic, huh?"

"Dylan said you guys never hear from her."

Beth shook her head. "Nope—but still remember the day she left." Beth picked at a seed head sticking out of a bale they'd been using as a table. "Every crazy detail like it's tattooed on my soul. I used to think the worst part was her leaving. But it wasn't. It was what it did to my dad."

She paused. Busied herself organizing her cards.

He waited.

"She drove off. Not even a goodbye." She cleared her throat. "Dad was sitting in his recliner late that night after he thought I was in bed." She reorganized her cards a second time and set them face down. "I'd gone to the kitchen to get a glass of water. That's when I heard him." She rubbed her hands together. "Weeping. I mean weeping from the depths of his soul." She looked over at Tally's stall, then back to Grayson.

"I climbed into his lap with a box of tissues, and I promised him I'd never leave him."

Oh, Beth. "I don't think he took your promise literally," Grayson said. "You were, what, nine?"

She nodded and looked up at him. "It sticks with a child, you know?"

Yeah. He knew. And her honesty peeled away so many layers of life he'd buffered his relationships with. "So you've stayed all these years, keeping your promise?"

"I have. I mean, I do love it here." She wrinkled her nose. "I got engaged last year. Give me all your sevens."

Oh?

He glanced at her bare left hand and surrendered a seven of diamonds. Hoped he'd kept some kind of poker face. "But you're not now."

"Nope. Kings?"

"Go fish." He waited for her to finish her draw. "What happened? Give me all your eights."

"Go fish."

He drew a card.

"Give me all your fours," she said. "He picked a job in Texas over me."

"You didn't want to go?" Grayson dropped a couple cards onto the table for her.

"I made that promise to my dad. Lyle knew that, but he still expected me to choose." She rubbed the back of her neck. "Queens?"

"Go fish."

She drew a card. "If things with this camp job fall apart, it'll be one more way he was right—that I'll never be my own person."

Lyle. Suddenly his least favorite name.

"Give me all your aces."

Beth handed over three cards, and he placed the set down.

Grayson tidied the stack. Swallowed. Beth could so easily prove that jerk wrong. "How about I take you riding tomorrow?"

"How about you don't."

"Just give it a try? We both need this camp running in a week." He rubbed his hand over his face. "There's no one else around who can fill in."

"I'm sure we can find someone."

He cut her a look. "Really? Didn't you say you'd already exhausted your call list?"

She worried her lower lip, her eyes on Tally. "I don't know that I can."

Somehow, the words tumbled out of his mouth. "Trust me. You can do it."

She swallowed and took a deep breath. "Okay. I'll try."

Nope. Beth wasn't the worst company one could have all evening, and that little fact needled at Grayson when he finally lay down for a few hours of sleep. He wasn't a guy who needed friends, right?

Or seventy games of Go Fish, Crazy Eights, and Slapjack.

Oh, who was he kidding? If he was being honest, he'd found himself leaning in to her company. The fact that she'd trusted him with her story kept him restless until dawn.

BETH HAD MADE A GRIEVOUS MISTAKE. SHE STOOD IN THE PASTURE beside Grayson, the dew sparkling with the early Sunday morning light, and the chatter of birds mocking her for agreeing to show up to ride.

She'd said too much the night before. Just blabbered on about her parents. Her dad. Lyle.

Beth could remember the smell of Old Spice and flannel on her dad the night Mom left. She'd burrowed her head against her dad's neck. Clung to him, terrified of losing him too.

I don't think he took your promise literally. The rich tones of Grayson's voice had been a balm to the heartache she carried.

Maybe.

But in the light of day, she wasn't sure he'd get her in the saddle. Even if he did look so competent and capable. He wore jeans and boots and a navy T-shirt that had a smudge of dust across the chest where he'd received a nuzzle from the red horse in front of him.

He smiled at her. "I was afraid you wouldn't come." He rubbed the horse's neck. "I'm glad you're here."

Oh boy. "I shouldn't be." He'd suckered her in, getting her to open up about her past. Just like he'd somehow talked her into this. Was she actually going to get on a horse again?

Eh…

He adjusted his hat—he'd swapped his felt Stetson for a molded straw one. Much more practical for the summer heat. Somehow, she'd gotten used to his cowboy look—despite the fact that it was completely not Deep Haven, it suited him.

And yeah, okay, he was handsome. Incredibly handsome— broader and taller and most definitely stronger than when he was a teen.

"I think you're where you should be."

The memory of last night's card games tugged a smile from her lips. There'd been something wholly comforting in Grayson's company. His apology had surprised her.

Then she'd dragged a few details out of him about his life in Oregon. The horses he trained. His plans for the future.

And even after she'd embarrassed herself thinking the Three Sisters were women, not mountains, he'd made the conversation easy. Comfortable.

Like an old pair of boots.

Yeah, stress and fatigue had overtaken her good senses.

He haltered the sorrel horse. "This is Maverick, who's kind of, possibly, the nicest horse I've ever ridden. He's a little out of conditioning, but the training's all there."

"Oh?" She let the horse sniff her hand before she reached to pet the bright white blaze down his face. Sleek and soft.

"Yeah—like, he's advanced, and it's odd that he was at that camp. He takes a very light touch."

"Interesting." Beth let her fingers glide across the horse's muscular shoulder. "So there's a mystery there." On his left hip, a hairless and indistinct brand marked his hide.

"Maybe. If only he could talk." Grayson pointed to the brand. "That might be a research project there, looking through the brand registries." He handed the lead rope to Beth and haltered a second horse, a dark bay. "And this one is Rex. He's apparently one of the camp rock stars, based on all the thank-you notes that were left in the barn by dozens of kids who've been toted around by him." He held out his arm, ushering her back toward the barn.

Her stupid feet followed him—a compulsion, like when she was a kid following him anywhere.

He tied both horses to the hitching post. "We'll start at the beginning." He scratched the sorrel horse's withers. "This is a horse."

"Funny." She socked him in the kidney, enough to zing him without hurting him. "Just because I landed on my head…"

"Okay, fine. What you're saying is that I can fast-forward through the easy stuff?"

He grabbed a saddle pad and handed it to her. "Tack up." He gestured to Rex, who stood like a royal guard at Buckingham Palace. "Do you remember how?"

She took the pad. Ran her hand down the bay's neck. He leaned into it. His sleek coat had warmed in the sun, and she inhaled the sweet scent. She'd forgotten how much she loved that smell. "We'll see."

She set the pad into place while Grayson picked up a footstool and set it on the ground next to Rex. She adjusted the placement a half inch.

Yeah. She remembered this.

"Pop up there."

She stepped up on the stool, and he handed her a western saddle with tooling that had been worn flat along the fenders and skirt. She hefted it up, then dropped the cinch on the far side before returning to thread the latigo through.

She let out a breath. "I remember."

She could do this.

Grayson set a saddle on Maverick and fastened the cinch, then picked up two bridles from the hook. "Where are your boots?"

She took the bridle he offered. "Dad rehomed those with Chase." Add a shopping trip to Duluth to her to-do list. She'd be able to convince Vivie to go.

Beth checked the tightness of her cinch between Rex's front legs and put the bridle on. She could feel Grayson's eyes watching while he finished tacking up Maverick.

Was she actually, really, totally going to do this?

"Follow me." Just like that, Grayson snagged Maverick's lead and waved for her to follow.

Rex followed her like a puppy dog out to the arena. Grayson stood next to a mounting block.

"Nervous?"

Beth's fingers blanched against the leather reins, but she nodded. "It's only been—what? Uh…fourteen years?" Oh boy.

Don't cry. Cowgirls don't cry.

This had sounded like a much better idea when she'd been tired and caught up in the whirlwind of Tally's injury, the aftermath. Her anger at Lyle. Cards with Grayson.

Now? She couldn't muster the courage to get on. Somewhere in the tangle of nerves, her voice formed the words. "I'm afraid."

His eyes held hers, gentle and filled with certainty. "I won't let you get hurt. Rex here"—he rubbed the horse's face—"he's my favorite. He'll take good care of you."

And how could a girl not buy into that?

She climbed the dusty steps, and he handed her the reins. She set her foot into the stirrup.

Froze.

Except for her shaking left hand, holding the reins on the horse's neck.

Nope.

Grayson stepped closer and placed his hand over hers. "You can do this, Beth." Her eyes met his, and the warmth of his body heated her. He smelled richly masculine—a heady mixture of aftershave, soap, and summer.

Why was he still so stupid-handsome?

His hand gave hers a squeeze, then he rested it against Rex's neck. "Up and over. I'm right here."

"Right." She shook her head. "Why didn't I think of that?"

"You can do this. Today, though. Before the sun goes down and Mav and Rex want dinner."

"Funny." She drew in a breath, released it, then hoisted her other leg over the top of Rex's back. Settled.

Oh boy. She was on a horse again. A living, breathing, perhaps not-God-fearing horse.

"Hey—you've gotta breathe. You can't pass out twice in one week." And there he went again, giving her a crooked smile that transformed him into the boy she used to know.

"Right." She attempted the breathing technique Vivien had taught her, drawing air slowly into her lungs, holding, and releasing. This time, the rhythmic thunder in her ears slowed with each breath.

"Let me adjust your stirrups one more notch." She moved her legs forward while he shortened the stirrups on each side. "There, try that."

She slipped her feet back into the stirrups. "Yeah." Her hiking boots were a little clunky in the stirrups.

He gave her a kind smile that felt like a pat on her head.

Rex swished at a fly. The movement made her clutch the horn like she was digging into the pocket on the third barrel.

"Ready to go? You've got this." And the absolute belief in Grayson's eyes gave her the courage to try.

"Sure." Liar.

He stepped away, his hands out like she was a house of cards he was afraid might topple. "Ask him forward."

She nudged Rex, her balance a little wobbly on the first steps.

"You're stiff. Let the horse's motion move your body—relax. You know how to do this. I've seen you on barrels."

He remembered her running the barrels?

Heat flashed up her neck.

She tried to let her weight float forward like she would in the kayak. Let the squeak of the leather—both familiar and new—calm her. She followed the side-to-side movement of the horse's barrel beneath her. Listened to the steady thud of each footfall.

Grayson swung up onto Maverick and circled behind her.

Beth leaned down and rubbed Rex's shoulder.

She was riding a horse again, and it filled her with a wild swirl of wonder.

"You're pretty good at this whole teaching thing." She glanced over at him and would have smiled—except she already was. She couldn't stop herself. The memories of galloping on Chase, the wind, the thrill. The joy.

It all bubbled out of her with every stride Rex took.

"It's you. You've always been a good rider."

And why did that observation make her feel all Jell-O-y and mushy inside?

Grayson rode alongside her, let her explore the feel of Rex's body moving beneath her. And yeah, maybe it was a little like riding a bike, because after five laps around the arena, she nudged Rex into a trot.

She bounced a little. Grabbed the horn.

It wasn't the smoothest, but it was big and rhythmic, and the motion settled into her soul after several strides. She drew in a breath and let go of the horn.

How had she stayed away so long? How had she let fear rule her?

Grayson had let her ride ahead, setting the pace, and when she started a figure eight and passed him, the big, broad smile on his face made her feel giddy.

"See? That's all there is to it," Grayson said. "I knew you could do it."

She slowed Rex back to a walk. Her cheeks hurt from smiling.

"You want to lope. I can see it in your eyes." Grayson pulled up Maverick next to her and Rex.

"I don't know." She did, but then—she didn't want to fall.

"If you can ride his trot, you can ride his lope. I know you know that."

"Really?" Butterflies tickled her stomach. "I'm so rusty. I feel like I need a seat belt."

"He's a camp horse. Not your barrel horse. Trust him."

The familiar buzz filled her veins, and before she could stop herself, she moved off with Rex and pressed her lips together, made a kissing sound, and nudged him with her outside leg into a lope.

Her heart soared with every stride.

Two hours later, she turned Rex loose in his paddock. "The dust and sweat on my body have their own layers of dust and sweat." She still wasn't sure her feet had touched the ground.

Grayson looked across the gate at her. Smiled, something satisfied and thoughtful. "It's a good look. Once you got those jitters out, you were fine. I knew you would be."

There went those butterflies again. Twice he'd told her that— he believed in her. A girl could get used to a cowboy looking at her like that. And she'd be lying if she didn't admit that Grayson, standing there in those Wranglers and boots, eyes on her, didn't make her feel all warm inside. She checked her watch. One hour to make it to the church service. It'd be tight. "I'll see you at church?"

"Umm…" He rubbed his hand across his neck. "Sure. I mean, yes."

There went more of those flutters in her stomach again. *Rein it in.* He'd be leaving. And she wasn't. This was all business.

Oh boy. The horses weren't the most dangerous part of the job.

six

. . .

THE AFTER-CHURCH POTLUCK CAME WITH OVERSIZED PANS OF homemade macaroni and cheese, fried chicken, casseroles, and a heart-stopping number of other high-calorie treats.

But Grandma hadn't given him a choice when she'd thrust the basket of croissants at him and ushered him toward the food table.

He'd planned on a low-key Sunday after his early ride with Beth. Family brunch so he could head back to Trinity to check in on Tally.

The little mare had heart and some serious trust issues—and she probably needed a chiropractor too. Her body and behavior told a story. The white marks over her shoulders, scars and scabs on her legs. Someone had ridden her hard, and she wasn't so sure she wanted to be close to anyone anymore.

It had only caused her pain.

Oh, he got that.

He rubbed the tightness in his chest. He hadn't been hurt by others, but he knew the excruciating kind of pain that came from getting close. Trusting everything could be okay.

Even today's sermon on James couldn't convince Grayson to

consider it pure joy to face trials. Nope. He had plenty of perseverance, thank you very much.

Still, the words challenged him.

Pastor Dan's words rattled around in Grayson's head.

Genuine faith perseveres in trials. Roots itself in steadfastness.

Maybe his faith was less firm than he'd hoped.

He wove through the fellowship hall, delivered the croissants like a Pony Express rider, and kept moving until he found a quiet spot at the far wall. He leaned against it and closed his eyes.

That was probably a mistake, because all he could see was Beth's face during their ride. The bright sparks in her eyes and smile on her lips when she'd finally brought Rex down to a walk and she rode beside Grayson and Maverick, cooling the horses out.

She may have been away from riding for a very long time, but anyone watching could tell how much she loved it. The eagerness, the smile that never faded. The satisfied sigh when she finally slid to the ground.

Quiet Beth had a fire inside her—and he didn't even think she knew it.

He'd searched for her during church but had only caught a glimpse of her on the other side of the sanctuary during the service.

"Are you going to get in line for food or hold up the wall?" Dylan's voice intruded into Grayson's thoughts.

He opened his eyes. Dylan, Marie, and Eli stood in front of him. Marie's pale blonde hair had been cut short. Super short. She'd lost a bit of weight, but her blue eyes still landed on him with a bright smile that creased the corners.

"Probably the wall," Grayson answered.

Marie shook her head, still smiling. "Hey, you. It's been a long time." She handed a glass dish of potato salad to Dylan and wrapped her arms around Grayson.

So many hugs in this town.

"How are you doing?" he asked when she released him. She wore a dark-blue wrap dress, cinched tight around her narrow waist. She'd always been slender, but she looked a little worn. A little frail.

He wasn't the only one who struggled with trials.

She let out a groan. "I'll be glad when this is all behind me." She gestured toward her cropped hair. "But I'm doing okay. Today's sermon was a timely reminder for me."

Oh. The words dug into Grayson's heart.

His face must have spoken louder than his silence.

She let out a soft laugh. "I assure you, I've had lengthy conversations with God—and it's scary. Cancer is scary. But I have to look at the kind of faith I can have, the person I can be. I can let it separate me from God, or I can let Him use it to draw me near. To deepen my faith. God is good. I can trust Him."

Grayson chewed on her words. Silenced.

"I'm going to camp next week," Eli announced, "and Mr. Grayson and Aunt Beth are going to let me ride."

Marie ruffled Eli's hair. "I know. Pretty awesome, huh?"

Eli nodded. "Only eight more days!" He grinned, then headed straight for the growing spread of dishes on the buffet table without another word.

"I heard you got Beth riding this morning," Dylan said. "Wow—I'm surprised."

Marie laughed. "It was all she talked about when she sat down in the pew. She said she planned to drag Vivien to Duluth to go shopping for new boots."

There went that ache in his chest again. *Dad rehomed those with Chase.*

"Once she got past her fear, she did fine," Grayson said.

Dylan lifted his shoulder. "But none of us ever expected her to get past that."

"And if you couldn't tell, Eli's so excited. He's got a calendar and has been marking off each day as a countdown," Marie said.

"Hi, everyone." Beth joined the group.

Unlike the ponytail and old jeans she'd worn to ride, she now wore her ashy waves loose, brushing past her shoulders. She'd changed into a jade green, summery dress with a fitted top and swishy skirt that hit right above her knees. It highlighted her...everything.

Grayson pulled his eyes away, meeting Dylan's raised brows. The man pinned Grayson with a look, then his glance shifted to Beth, back to Grayson.

Oh. He knew that look.

Don't ever look at my sister like that again.

Nope. No girl was worth putting a friendship at risk again. Especially since his romantic relationships had never been the kind that lasted.

Harper Pennington's face flashed in his mind. Her easy smile. The way she'd run up and grab his hand. Drag him onto the dance floor.

Whatever might have been, cut short by tragedy—so, yeah. Still not the kind that lasted.

He rubbed the knot in his chest.

"Are you contemplating the beef stroganoff or the spicy meatballs?" Beth asked.

Grayson shook his head to clear away the debris field Harper's memory left. He returned his focus to Beth. "Hi. How's it going?"

She met his eyes. Smiled. "I'm a little sore from our ride."

Marie laughed. "I bet! But oh my goodness, how cute you look!"

"Thanks." A rosy blush crept up Beth's cheeks.

Dylan leaned forward and lifted the bowl he still held. "We should get in line. Eli's going to be on his second trip through before we even get our potato salad on the table."

"Sure." Marie placed a hand on Grayson's arm. "Nice to see you."

"Thanks," Grayson answered.

They wandered away, but Marie's words lingered.

I can let it separate me from God, or I can let Him use it to draw me near.

Beth faced him, waiting. "Are you eating?"

"I need to get back to the barn." His growling stomach betrayed him with a loud rumble. "It does smell good."

"You'll need some calories if you're going to be able to keep up with the hefty to-do list I've got for you."

"Seriously? I thought I was pointing kids down the trail. And I need to work with Tally."

"This is the part where you help me help you help me."

Grayson's jaw went slack. Um— "What?"

She shook her head. "Just trust me—it isn't that bad. It's hay and farrier and a manure pile. Complete some tack repairs. Unless you want the hard stuff. Accounting, fundraisers—Do you know anything about grants? Because I have a big grant renewal and new grant applications to complete."

He held up his hands. "Oh, no thanks to that."

Eli ran up with an oversized fudge brownie on a napkin. "I brought this for you, Aunt Beth. Mom said she didn't feel up to eating it."

"Thanks, sweetie." Beth took the brownie. "I guess I'm starting with dessert."

Grayson shook his head and watched Eli's retreat. "Fine. Bring the list by the barn."

She smiled. "Thank you."

He followed her across the room, weaving around the tables.

Grandma waved them over to her table. "I have something for you, Grayson," she said when they reached her. "Here's a list of those real estate agents." She handed him a note with three names and numbers listed. "That lot will sell fast. It's one of the last lots in town, and it has that beautiful view of the harbor and lake."

Oh, yeah. The lot. He'd been so busy at the camp it had dropped off his radar. "I'm not ready yet."

Grandpa stopped with his fork halfway to his mouth.

Dropped his hand. "You haven't talked to a real estate agent?" He dabbed his mouth with a napkin.

"I've got to talk to Robin."

Grandpa stood and put his hand on Grayson's shoulder. "It's up to you, but you don't have to keep it."

"You could always build on it," Grandma offered, a smile curving her lips.

He laughed at the ridiculous idea. "Uh, yeah? I guess I could."

Beth smiled. "You'd be right next door to our place." She shifted. "Well, Dad's place. I need to move to the camp tomorrow."

Yeah, he knew that. Hadn't actually considered it because he wasn't going to build on that lot. Was he?

No—that was crazy. He had a life and a plan and even a church, all back in Oregon. It was his home, even if it was a little quieter than Deep Haven and even if lacking in…something he hadn't quite figured out.

He folded the note from his grandma. "We're going to grab some food." He followed Beth to the food line. "Which cabin?" He spooned macaroni and cheese onto his plate.

Beth picked a bean salad. "It's on the north side of Trinity— along the tree line. There's a little drive on the left end of the barnyard."

He nodded. He'd ridden past the small bungalows. Each one had a quaint front porch, and several had decks on the back side. A few of them were under renovation.

They each added more sides to their plates.

"I need to go over the camp schedule and fill out my planner with due dates," Beth said. "Besides the huge grant renewal application, I track which waivers and payments we're still waiting on and put out an advertisement for a summer assistant wrangler."

"It sounds like a lot of work."

She lifted a shoulder. "It isn't work if you love it, right?" She smiled at her use of his own words.

He nodded and followed Beth toward an empty table.

Noah leaned back in his chair as they passed by. "Before you leave, stop by our table. I have a few files to hand off to you."

"Sure," Beth answered. She took a few more steps, drew in a breath, and leaned toward Grayson. "Hey, go see what my dad is saying to Janet Ashford."

Grayson followed her sight line to where her dad sat with a dark-haired woman. "Um, no." Whoever Janet was, she was smiling at Doug Strauss. It wasn't the kind of smile one gave about the weather.

It was a you-hung-the-moon kind of smile, and he wasn't going to get in the middle of that.

"Please?"

All it took was one look at those big green eyes. He let out a groan. "Oh, all right." Grayson shuffled his way over, feeling like a cad. "Is this seat taken?" he asked. Doug scooted his chair over. "No, it's yours now."

"Hello, Mr. Strauss—and Janet, is it?"

The woman blushed. "Yes, it is."

Doug's gray hair and robust midline gave him the countenance of a Santa Claus, despite him being sixty years old at most, probably younger.

"Please, you're almost as old as me. Call me Doug." The man winked. "Isn't that how it works? You kids get older and we old folks stay the same?"

"I think Edith Draper once said something like that."

"I wouldn't be surprised." Doug stopped. Opened his mouth. Closed it. Finally— "I heard you got Beth back into the saddle this morning." His voice caught a little. "Thank you." He gave Grayson's hand a hard pat. He glanced at Janet, then back to Grayson. "I haven't seen her so excited about anything in a long time…" He trailed off and his Adam's apple bobbed.

Janet nodded. "It's so nice to be able to get back to something you loved."

"She's a natural," Grayson offered, filling in. And she was. Watching her ride in the early morning hours—having someone to ride with—well, it'd been like unwrapping a gift he hadn't known he'd needed.

Doug nodded, his lips pinched in a wry smile. "She is. So, thank you, again." He stirred the mashed potatoes on his plate. "I lost the heart for the risk and...I don't know. Got scared after her accident. I think we found it easier to lean into each other. I'm sure going to miss having her at the house, though."

"I'll bet. The camp is lucky to have her." The truth was, *he* was lucky to have her. The week ahead was more daunting than a mama bear in a blackberry thicket. And the sight of Beth, grinning as she cantered along the arena rail... He swallowed. An unfamiliar ballooning in his chest lightened his heart. "Well, this job seems to be the best of both worlds, right? She's close by, but also on her own."

"Right," Doug answered, a smile not quite reaching his eyes.

Grayson's phone buzzed in his pocket. He ignored it.

"It's okay—you take that," Doug said. "I think there's a chocolate cream pie calling my name." He slid back his chair.

Grayson hesitated.

Doug gave him a pat on the shoulder and stood up. "I'll grab you a slice too."

"Thank you," Grayson said. He tugged the phone out. Checked the name. Vincent Tucker. For some reason, seeing his name gave Grayson more heartburn than excitement.

MOVING DAY. OH BOY. TODAY, BETH WOULD OFFICIALLY TAKE HER place as the interim assistant camp director.

She wasn't sure if it was nerves or sore muscles that had driven her out of bed three hours before her Monday morning alarm. She could see it now—a wanted poster with her mug on it. The large print underneath would read World's Biggest Impostor.

Not to mention actually driving off with her belongings—at least, many of them—to move into her little camp cabin.

But riding again? That had been far more fun than she'd expected, and thankfully, Vivien had agreed to head to Duluth for a shopping trip.

Beth shoved her last three T-shirts and two pairs of jeans into her suitcase, closed the lid, and snapped the latch. She loaded her laptop into her bag, along with assorted files and reports she'd spent too many hours poring over.

She hadn't expected Noah to hand her three new file folders to go through. Without an assistant, he'd fallen behind. Focused on the highest priority—which apparently was whatever was in front of him. And that hadn't been the horse camp.

She exhaled, long and slow. She could do this. Possibly.

Or she'd grossly overestimated her ability to run the horse camp.

She gave her bedroom a last look before dragging her bags out to the living room. Her suitcase wheels clunked across the floor.

Dad sat at the kitchen peninsula, drinking his coffee. "It's going to be quiet around here."

Aw, Dad.

She walked over and gave him a hug from behind, the smell of Old Spice enveloping her in cozy comfort.

"You'll be able to enjoy your coffee without interruption," she offered, then cringed. That sounded like a rather lame consolation prize. "You can get Eli to come by for a sleepover and take him fishing."

He took a drink. "Yeah. I could do that."

"Or get Dylan to come grill when you're tired of my Crock-Pot freezer meals."

She and Dad had handled Mom's departure differently than Dylan. Her brother had seemed to shake it off—move on, delve into an apprenticeship after high school, and focus on his construction career.

But he hadn't been there in those first hours, when grief tore from her life the dad she'd known. He hadn't heard the soul-deep cries that night when Dad had thought he had the privacy to release his pain.

And here she was. Leaving him. No, not like Mom. But leaving him alone nonetheless. And that stung. Because everything she was and everything she wanted to be amounted to "anything but like Mom." She didn't break her promises.

For the first time, she waffled. Wavered. Wondered.

This might be the best thing for both of you.

"You'll still see me, Dad." She released her hug. "I have the Crock-Pot set up." She checked the heat and timer setting on it. "Tonight at five, you'll have beef stew. And there are mashed potatoes in the refrigerator you can heat to go with it, plus a loaf of Fox Bakery French bread."

"Thanks, sweetie."

The house had never seemed big before, but with the thought of him eating dinner alone in it, night after night?

It seemed...palatial.

Hopefully Janet would come by. Dad could use the company, and Beth hated the thought of him eating alone every night.

Grayson had come back with a big bunch of nothing from his recon at Dad's table. Whatever they'd been talking about, the subject had abruptly changed to her when Grayson arrived.

Yeah, well, she'd seen the expression on Janet's face. She hadn't been talking about Beth. She'd looked to be hanging on Dad's every word. It was well past time Dad entertained a romantic interest.

"Was that Janet talking to you at church yesterday?" Beth measured her words.

Dad stood and scrubbed creamer drops from the counter like they might cause a stain. "Um, Janet? Oh…yeah."

"She seems nice. I haven't had much opportunity to chat with her."

He let out a noncommittal sound.

"You said there's a class reunion trip coming up, though?"

He turned his attention to washing his coffee cup.

Beth raised her voice over the running water. "You should go."

"I'm fine. I don't need a vacation." He rinsed the mug and turned off the faucet.

"But it would be good for you to—"

"I don't need to head out on some European vacation, Beth." He set down his mug on the folded towel. "I've got you and Dylan and Deep Haven, and that's all I need. It's always been enough."

He's afraid.

"I thought you might want a change of scenery. To get out of the house."

"Are you trying to pawn me off on Janet?" he asked, his hand scrubbing over the top of his thinning hair.

"No—of course not." She closed her eyes. Okay, maybe?

"I'm heading to Bible study," her dad said. He pressed a kiss to the top of her head. "Love you, sweetie."

"I love you too."

He stuffed his ballcap onto his head, grabbed his keys, and walked out the door.

Beth eyeballed the entryway. Her bags stood like sentinels, waiting. And she couldn't bring herself to leave.

So, okay, she was afraid too. Afraid of losing Dad.

Maybe even a little afraid Janet could replace her in Dad's life.

She should prep a few more meals for the week. She grabbed

the freezer bags, chicken breasts, carrots, onions, and potatoes. Started chopping.

She lifted her eyes at a knock at the door. It opened and Vivien walked in wearing a yellow empire-waist sundress and wide-brimmed straw hat, a beach tote over her shoulder.

"Ready to head out?" She slipped onto a stool at the peninsula. "We're going to have to hustle if you're getting moved into the cabin today."

Beth sliced into the onion. Blinked. "I want to prep two more meals for Dad. He's upset." And, well, she wasn't ready to drive up Gunflint Trail either. Move into the camp cabin. Sit by herself at breakfast. At lunch. At dinner.

Vivien clasped her hands. "I know this is hard, but he can do this. You can do this."

"Why does it feel so bad?" Beth asked. "I want this job—I want this job like I haven't wanted any other job ever." She sniffed. She could blame the onions, but it wasn't them. "I don't want to hurt him."

Beth went to the sink, washed her hands, a little sob escaping.

Vivien came around the peninsula and wrapped Beth in her arms. "Aw, hon. I'm sorry." She released Beth and leaned against the counter. "Courtney and I found you a little something."

She dug through her tote and pulled out a bookmark with a silver tassel.

Beth dried her hands and took it.

The Lord himself goes before you and will be with you; he will never leave you nor forsake you. Do not be afraid; do not be discouraged. Deuteronomy 31:8

She swallowed. "Thank you."

"Of course." Vivien snuggled her bag back onto her shoulder. "You know, they say in theater, there aren't any small parts— only small people."

Beth slid the cut vegetables into the zip bags. "Is this a joke about my height?"

Vivie laughed. "No." She took the bags from Beth and placed them into the freezer. "You've always been the person everyone else relies on. Often in the background. Sometimes with the thankless tasks." She closed the freezer door. "But whatever you do, you make a difference to everyone around you. We want you to know—no matter what size part you're playing, we're always going to be here for you. God is always here for you. Nothing surprises Him. Not the small parts or the big parts that come your way."

"I wish He'd let me in on His plans."

"He brought Grayson into Deep Haven right when you needed him. Who would have thought?"

Beth carried the cutting board to the sink and turned on the water. "He said he's selling his parents' lot. He's buying a place in Oregon."

Vivien tilted her head. "Interesting. The lot doesn't have a For Sale sign yet."

"I'm sure it isn't easy," Beth said. "But I'm grateful he's here to keep the camp running." She swiped the vegetable cuttings into the disposal. "One of the horses he brought for Noah is this incredible sorrel gelding—and he's beautiful. Coppery-red. That horse has a story." She flipped on the disposal. "He's got a brand, but it's hard to tell exactly what it is. I'm going to see if I can find out any information on him."

"A story? Like, he's famous? Secretariat?"

"He was a thoroughbred—who's buried in Kentucky. No, he looks like a quarter horse. Like Grayson said, not a horse you'd find in a camp string because he's sensitive to subtle cues. Not a horse to have kids flopping around on."

Vivien paced the kitchen. "Hmm…I didn't imagine anyone could get you on a horse again. You were very adamant on Friday. Now you're chasing down horse histories? Riding? He must have been very convincing." Vivie waggled her brows. "If he isn't staying, who knows? Maybe you could head west."

"It isn't like that." Beth scrubbed the cutting board. "The

hardest part was actually getting on. Asking Rex for that first step—and taking it. The mechanics of riding and the feel of it all came back to me."

"That's amazing," Vivien said. "But let's not forget how many times I've suggested it, and you never got on a horse for me."

"I knew you'd say that." Beth rinsed the cutting board and set it on the towel. "I'm kind of sorry I waited so long."

"See? God knew what you needed."

Beth dried her hands. "He could have provided it sooner."

"Maybe," Vivie answered.

Beth's phone buzzed on the kitchen counter. Grayson.

Vivien smirked. "Oh, look who it is."

"You know what? I'm not going to answer that." The last thing Beth needed was Vivie eavesdropping on a conversation with Grayson.

"Why not?"

"Because we're going shopping in Duluth."

seven

. . .

"Do we have to talk about this right now?" Robin opened the bakery oven door and pulled a cake pan from the rack with potholders.

Grayson could almost taste the amaretto. But he wasn't here for sweets, treats, or mouth-watering tarts.

He hadn't wanted to corner her in the bakery after closing Monday night, but he'd come to realize there wasn't going to be a "best time" for their talk. There'd been one thing after another since he'd arrived in town, and he couldn't leave Vincent and Rose waiting for his answer.

Grayson stepped out of Robin's way when she scrambled past him, hot pan in hand. When it came down to it, he didn't want to talk about it right now either. Actually, he didn't want to talk about it at all—but he had an appointment with a real estate agent, and he needed Robin's blessing before he felt right about putting the lot on the market.

If he wasn't going to buy the Tuckers' place, then they had to get it ready for listing. But he'd never find a more suitable location or a better price.

"I don't know how to have this conversation either. Trust me, I didn't know how to bring it up again."

She leaned down, scanning the surface of the sheet cake. "Perfect."

"I get it—it isn't a great time. You don't have to be sarcastic."

"I was referring to the cake." She slid past him and grabbed the second layer from the oven. "I have a lot to do." She set the second pan on the cooling rack. "With the holiday weekend, the schedule's been off, but tomorrow, it's back to business as usual." She tested the spring on the second cake. Somehow her apron was still bright white, despite the cooling racks full of baked goods.

He held out a hand. "Please. Give me five minutes. I can't go to the appointment without talking to you."

She looked up at him, her lips pressed into a thin line. "You're listing it? Today?"

"I'm supposed to sign the paperwork tonight. It'll take a few days for Nathan to get it listed." He looked away from the tight lines that had drawn across her face. The hurt in her eyes. He'd spent hours wrestling it in his own mind.

The bakery's back door opened and Sammy appeared. He set a backpack down on the desk chair and looked from Robin to Grayson.

Back to Robin.

He scrubbed a hand through his blond hair. "Should I come back later?"

Yes.

"No, I'll need your help with a few things," Robin said.

Great. Because if the conversation wasn't already hard enough, now Robin had an ally.

Sammy reached over and gave Robin's hand a squeeze. "I'll, uh…be…right over there." He pointed to the desk, only five feet away.

Yeah, too bad the bakery wasn't a little bigger.

Robin turned back to Grayson. "I've heard your reasons. You want to buy your own place." She grabbed a rag and furiously scrubbed an invisible spot on the countertop. "What about our parents' plans? What about the fact that they bought that land for us to have our family home on?"

He blinked. "It was their dream. It was. And I don't want to let that go any more than you do."

"And yet you are."

Her words slapped him in the face. "Robin—"

"You're going to sell their dreams. Everyone is going to forget them." This time, her tears overflowed, and she hiccupped a little sob.

And Grayson stood there like a clod, unable to move, unable to comfort her, because it was his fault.

Sammy's chair scraped across the floor. He pulled Robin to him.

Grayson looked away. Because this wasn't awkward. Nope. Not awkward at all.

"Hey, you're okay," Sammy said.

Robin sniffed and wiped her eyes.

Grayson slid his wrist onto the countertop to sneak a peek at the time. He had fifteen minutes until his appointment, and he was losing ground.

"It's none of my business," Sammy offered, "but there's got to be a solution in here." He released Robin and she stomped to the storage room.

Grayson followed her.

"There is. Grayson shouldn't sell." Robin hefted a large bag of baking flour onto the shelf. Sammy held out his hand to stop her before she lifted the second one.

"Seriously?" Grayson asked. "You don't think this is hard for me too?"

"It doesn't seem hard enough. You're the one who bailed out of town as soon as you could."

"Does Oliver get a free pass here?"

Robin cut him a look. "He's got his own issues—we both know that."

Clearly. Because their oldest brother had stopped returning

any of Grayson's calls more than a decade ago.

"Is there a way to have both?" Sammy slid another flour bag onto the stack. "The bakery's doing well, isn't it?"

Robin nodded and picked up several large bottles of vanilla extract. "But I don't see what your point is."

Grayson didn't appreciate that her tone with Sammy was far more accommodating than the one she'd taken with him.

Sammy took Robin's hand. "I know what it's like to have to pivot. To let go of who and what I thought I was. To let go of the dreams I had."

Grayson leaned back against the storage room wall and crossed his arms. He knew snippets of Sammy's story. How his legs had been crushed in a terrible log truck accident. How he'd gone from high school athlete to military service to being a man with an uncertain future.

Robin nodded. "I know, but this is different." Her words came out soft, hushed.

"Because it's yours?" Sammy said the words in a whisper, but the impact hit Robin hard.

She nodded, lifted her hand to her mouth, and tears splashed down her face.

Oh, Robin.

Sammy wrapped Robin in a hug.

Grayson ran a hand across his damp eyes. He wanted Vincent's place, but he couldn't break his sister's heart to buy it.

He'd find work at another ranch. Or maybe he could lease a place and pick up some horses to train. He just wished it didn't feel like a gaping wound in his heart to let go of his vision.

"I'll cancel the appointment with the agent." He pulled out his phone.

Sammy said something Grayson couldn't hear, but Robin nodded.

She sniffed again and released him.

Sammy took her hand again and wove his fingers into hers. "What if Grayson buying his ranch and building a youth horse camp could honor your parents more than the vacant lot ever could?"

What? He stopped dialing.

Grayson may have misjudged whose ally Sammy would be.

"I don't know that I can let it go." Robin wiped her eyes. "I didn't even realize what it meant to me until you said you were selling it." She gave Sammy's arm a pat and slipped away from him, pacing the storeroom.

"We're not letting them go," Grayson said. "I'm not letting them go."

"Why does it feel like it?"

Sammy pointed toward the kitchen desk. "I'm going to go check on the delivery schedule."

Robin nodded and Sammy left the two of them alone in the storeroom.

"Trust me, I wrestled with it too. I don't take it lightly. But what if Sammy's right? What if I can make good of this by opening a youth camp in Oregon? Helping kids like me—kids who need a connection. Healing."

Robin looked up at him, her eyes red and watery. "Maybe a family will buy the lot? Build on it?"

He could see it. A cute little cottage facing the lake. A swing set in the backyard. Laughter. He'd be lying if he didn't admit it caused a bittersweet pang in his chest. All he could do was nod.

She felt it too. He could tell when she twisted her lips, then wrinkled her nose. Swiped more tears, then blew out a breath. "It isn't easy. It won't be easy."

"I know." Grayson ran a hand through his hair. "I've crunched the numbers every way I know how, and it's the only way I'm going to be able to move forward in Oregon."

"Okay," Robin said. "I suppose Sammy's right. Embracing new dreams doesn't mean letting go of the memories."

He shifted his feet, wanting so much for that sentiment to soak into his bones.

"I think Mom and Dad would be proud of you."

And those were the words he clung to when he sat down with Nathan Decker five minutes late for his appointment at the Loon Café. Because he'd needed those extra minutes to pull himself together.

He remembered Nathan, whose daughter, Colleen, had been a volleyball star in school.

The man's brown hair looked lighter now, with silver strands throughout.

"Sorry I'm late."

"Ready to get things started?" Nathan spun a stack of paperwork across the table and slid it into place facing Grayson.

"Sure." The word came out a little tight. Pinched.

"I did some preliminary work, based on our phone call."

Grayson nodded and stamped down the emotions swirling inside. He could only hope Mom and Dad would be proud of him like Robin had said. That he wasn't being blinded by selfishness.

Again.

🐾 🐾 🐾

Beth sat down at her desk Tuesday afternoon, her office redolent with sweet hay mixed with aged wood, animals, dust, and leather.

It would have calmed her except the to-do list from Noah stared up at her. She needed to dig into family camp and all that it entailed.

Instead of shopping with Vivien, she should have been at the camp—volunteering hours during her off time.

Sure, Vivien had helped her pick out a few pairs of boot-cut jeans for riding and a pair of turquoise-and-tan Ariat boots that made her smile. She would have called it quits there, but then she'd fallen in love with a jade-green-and-peacock-blue paisley blouse.

She snagged a pen from the desk drawer and enumerated the items on the to-do list. Update the camp registrations, check hay supply and contact sellers, check fencing, review vaccine schedules, update the website, make a list of tack that needed repair, order any necessary trail maintenance, review camp grants, and return all grant renewals.

Oh, and review the family camp activity schedule. She skimmed the rest of the list. Deposit checks at the bank, complete sponsor applications, and have the manure pile turned.

Wow. Was that all?

It was becoming evident that she'd glamorized the job a little. Thought it was all purpose, playtime, and praise.

What had she been thinking? She needed to learn how to say no, because the to-do list was far too long.

She heard Tally moving in her stall.

Add to the list—keep Tally from dying or being permanently lame.

Beth walked to her office doorway. "What do you think, Tally? Am I totally messing this job up?" She lifted the lid on the large metal can in the barn aisle and pulled out a handful of horse treats from the bag inside. "Which one of you wants to help me with these grants?"

The two horses let out deep nickers. Remington's neck stretched over his Dutch door too.

"You're going to get me into trouble, being so loud." She went to Remy first and held out a treat for him. He grabbed it with his lips. Crunched.

Tally let out another soft nicker and took a tentative limp forward.

"Are you volunteering, sweetie?" She fed Tally a treat, the lips tickling her palm. "We're besties now, right?" She leaned to get a look at the bandage, which still held in place since the last wrap change.

Beth gave Tally another treat, then slid a chair into place outside the stall's Dutch door. She grabbed her laptop, journal, water bottle, and grant files from the desk and plopped them on the chair. Tally stepped back, just out of reach.

But she didn't back away completely.

"It's okay. I'm just going to work on organizing this mess of a schedule." Beth slid a hay bale into place as her table and set up her workstation on top of it.

"You can give me some tips."

Tally's ears followed Beth, and she stepped forward and gave Beth a nuzzle for another treat.

Beth rewarded Tally's request and rubbed her soft muzzle. "You're not so bad, are you? You're just afraid of getting hurt." She sat down. "We can keep each other company, right? I need to organize these grant requests and write up some proposals, which, quite frankly, I've only ever done twice. For the library. So this could get interesting."

She'd had no idea there'd be so much paperwork to keep track of.

Beth opened her laptop and clicked on the grant files along with the financial and participation reports Noah had sent her.

Oh boy.

File after file—she couldn't make sense of any of it. It all melded into one jumbled mess of information.

She dug a granola bar from her pocket.

She'd missed breakfast with Dad for the first time since...ever.

The bookmark Vivien and Courtney had given her stuck out from her journal.

The Lord himself goes before you and will be with you; he will never leave you nor forsake you. Do not be afraid; do not be discouraged.

Right.

Do not be afraid.

Except, she had been left—forsaken—hadn't she? Rejected and deserted. So, yeah. She was afraid.

Of leaving Dad. Of failing this job.

She closed her laptop and gave Tally another rub on her head. "This isn't going that well." She snagged her water bottle from the hay bale and wandered to the back barn slider.

Grayson rode Maverick in the arena, the morning light enveloping them in a golden haze through the dust that was kicked up.

Beth watched from the shadows of the barn doorway. The horse's coat gleamed bright copper in the sunshine, his breath leaving puffs of condensation in the cool air. They moved across the arena like dance partners, to music only they could hear.

Low tones of Grayson's voice drifted across the expanse between them.

The pair slowed, Maverick let out a soft blowing sound, and they walked laps for several more minutes. Grayson leaned forward, his hand rubbing the horse's neck, and then he dismounted.

He stepped toward the gelding's head. Its eyes were half closed, and it lowered its head, resting its white-blazed face into the crook of Grayson's arm.

He stroked the horse's neck, and the two remained nearly still.

Beth felt like an intruder, staring, seeing the trust, a thin, soft thread between the pair.

She swallowed, her throat suddenly dry, for in those moments, she'd seen a glimpse of the same Grayson that had made her swoon at fifteen and had broken her heart at sixteen.

The water bottle she held thunked to the ground, her grip loosened by the distraction of her memories.

Grayson and the horse turned their heads toward her, the moment between them interrupted.

She walked toward the hitching post. "Oh. Hey. Hi." Beth's words stumbled out. She gave him a little wave before scooping up her water bottle and wiping the dust from it.

"Hi." He walked toward the barn, Maverick beside him. "How's it going?"

"Good." Was she staring? She probably was staring.

He stopped at the hitching post, removed Maverick's bridle, and tied the lead rope.

She turned her attention to the gelding. "He's got beautiful movement."

"I wish he could talk. He must have an interesting backstory." Grayson rubbed the red horse's sleek neck. "He gave me some nice rollbacks and lead changes."

"Do you think he was a show horse?"

"Maybe. Maybe a ranch horse. Someone put time and money into him."

He pointed to the horse's left hip. "The brand looks like it was bobbled or doctored or something."

"Doctored—as in corrected, or altered?" She looked at the spot—instead of white freeze-branding, the narrow lines were void of hair, making them hard to distinguish on his hide.

"It happens."

Beth ran her hands over the spot. "So curious." She studied Maverick. Heavy muscling across his chest and hindquarters spoke of the ranch-bred quarter horses she'd seen pictures of.

"How's work going?" Grayson slid out the latigo and dropped the cinch.

Beth blew out a breath. So much to do. "Not that great."

She knew Grayson could help with many of the tasks—if he had time—but she didn't want to get used to relying on him.

He'd be leaving, and she needed to remember that. Not let any amount of cards or horses stomp out that reality.

"I'm wondering if I should have stuck with kayak lessons and library circle time."

"Kayak lessons, huh?"

"For Wild Harbor." She grappled for words, the English language somehow lost to the depths of his green eyes and the tan of his biceps. "I am—I was the children's instructor. Let me tell you, that lake never gets any warmer." Good grief, she was rambling.

His Adam's apple bobbed.

She sucked in a breath. "Oh, I'm sorry. I wasn't thinking." Because, of course, Grayson was all too familiar with the lake. He'd been on it with his parents the day they drowned.

He shook her words away. "No, don't be. I mean, Lake Superior's front and center to Deep Haven. No getting away from it."

Realization settled over her. "Unless you're living in Oregon." She looked up at him. "Is that...why you left?"

He slid the saddle off Maverick and set it in the grass.

"Not intentionally." He picked up a curry from the grooming bucket and ran it along Mav's barrel where the sweat had dried. "Partly, though. Yeah." He gently scrubbed at a spot on the horse's coat. "I put my parents' lot up for sale. Signed the paperwork last night."

Oh. "It's never easy, huh?" She tucked a loose lock of hair behind her ear. "But you have the opportunity in Oregon. A ranch. A camp?"

He nodded and dropped the curry, then picked up a body brush.

"You said only partly the reason?" She picked up another brush and set to work on the other side of Maverick, alternating between brushing and using her palm against his soft coat.

Grayson stayed quiet so long she didn't think he'd answer. Then—

"It was my fault." He dropped the brush into the bucket. "The day after they died, I heard my grandparents talking. Grieving. Grandpa kept saying, 'I don't know why they were out there.'" He stopped. Swallowed. "It was all my fault," he repeated.

Beth looked over at him. Waited.

"We were on the lake because I'd begged Dad to take us. I

wheedled and bugged him and manipulated him. I was jealous of the attention I thought Robin and Oliver got."

"You were just a kid. Kids do that kind of thing all the time."

He shook his head and smoothed his hand over Maverick's coat. "When that storm blew in and I knew they'd gone overboard, I pleaded with God to rescue them." He shook his head again. "He didn't."

She had nothing.

He untied the lead rope. "That was the first time I realized I couldn't trust God."

The first?

"I ended up at the camp. I actually didn't even want to come that first day, but you know—there's something about the horses." He lifted a shoulder. "It became easier to dive into work. Keep people at a distance."

Because what better way to protect his heart than to never get close?

He led Maverick down to the paddock and released him. She watched while the gelding shook out the dust and trotted away to graze.

Grayson grabbed the saddle from the ground and walked past her into the barn. "Want to help flush a wound?"

He'd closed the door on their conversation.

"Sure."

He stowed the saddle and she followed him into the emergency stall. Tally nickered to her, soft and deep.

"She likes you."

"We talk a lot. Mostly, she listens to me lament about how ridiculous this plan was."

"Which plan is that?" He put Tally's halter on and handed the lead rope to Beth.

"The camp. Being the assistant director." She palmed her face. "I was serious—I really should have stuck with kayak lessons and library sessions."

Grayson unwound the self-adhesive bandage wrap. "You're

doing fine—more than fine." He carefully lifted the Telfa pad from the wound. "It's good for you to chase after your dreams."

"There's so much to do—more than I ever imagined."

"But you wanted it for a reason, right?" He cleaned Tally's wound and reapplied ointment.

Beth tore open a fresh bandage and handed it to him. "Sure. I always wanted to work in outdoor recreation somehow. I love being outdoors."

"I can kind of see that. You always had a book in your hand, but you'd drag it right up into the tree with you."

She laughed and held out the bandage wrap to him. "I think you and Dylan intentionally sought out bigger and bigger trees, thinking I couldn't—or wouldn't—climb them." As she found the spot on Tally's withers that she loved to have scratched, Beth could imagine Grayson and Dylan scurrying up the tree from her.

"Seems like you do a lot to help out—not only here, as a job, but the theater. The church. The library and the youth center. I don't know how there's enough of you to go around."

I pleaded with God to rescue them.

Maybe he'd understand more than anyone else.

"I guess I was a little afraid of why my mom left us. Worried it had something to do with me—something I hadn't done."

"You can't look at it that way."

"It's hard not to. When someone says they love you, then leaves?"

"Like Lyle?"

"Exactly." She felt herself blush. "He chose a job over me. Just like my mom chose living her 'best life.' Which didn't include kids or a husband."

"They don't deserve you," he said, giving her a crooked smile. "Look at all you're doing here, though." He picked up the old bandages and wrappers.

"Like what?" She removed Tally's halter and led the way out of the stall.

He tossed the used bandages into a trash can. "You've got camp set up, ready to go, right?"

"Weeks one and two. We have full sessions, fees paid, waivers on file. I still need to figure out some family camp activities."

She scooped up her laptop, journal, and paperwork from the hay bale and carried them into her office.

Grayson followed. "See? That's happening because of you." He slid into the chair opposite her desk.

"I don't know that it took any special talent."

"You do have talent. I'm completely confident in your abilities."

His words made her smile. "Thanks."

"Where's the to-do list with my name on it?" He peered across her desk.

"Oh, it's here." She lifted the scroll-length note from Noah. "Anything with horse, tack, or manure on it—it's yours." She grinned. "Think you can handle that, cowboy?"

"Yeah. I've got this." He laughed and checked the list. "Uh, hey—my grandparents are throwing some kind of something on Friday. You should come." He clenched his teeth. "Save me from the social butterflies—they tend to always have a lot of food, laughs, people, and dancing."

"I figured you'd enjoy a hoppin' party. You must've broken more hearts than a country song." She'd meant it as a clever jest. A little poke to find out exactly what his dating history entailed.

Nope.

His jaw tightened and he shook his head. "I'm not that guy anymore."

"I'm sorry—I didn't mean—I was—" She was what? Jealous? Because she'd scraped away the scab on something much bigger than a shard of regret.

She was such an idiot.

"Hey—" Beth started.

He set down the to-do list. "I should get going." His chair scraped the floor.

That was the first time I realized I couldn't trust God.

"No, please." Beth swallowed. "I didn't mean that."

He studied her, as if sorting out something in his mind, then leaned forward in the chair. Rubbed his hands over his face. "It's true—just like I said, I didn't need or want people close to me."

"There must have been someone."

He looked away. Nodded. "Yeah. A woman from Redmond named Harper Pennington."

Beth wanted to know but didn't want to know. She waited, uncertain if he'd continue.

Finally, he rubbed his hands on his jeans, opened his mouth. Closed it.

"We dated for a little while. It was the first relationship that had lasted more than a few dances and games of pool. I liked her—I mean, really liked her—but how does a guy like me give a girl anything to rely on?"

"You seem pretty reliable."

"I mean, um, personal stuff. But I wasn't ready to step into that and she was. I broke things off with her." Grayson's jaw flexed. "She was upset. Wrecked her car a few miles out after tearing out of the ranch driveway."

"Oh no."

He looked up at her, devastation on his face. "She...died." His Adam's apple bobbed. "Six years have passed and I still..."

Six years. She did the math. That's when he'd stopped coming to Deep Haven.

"I'm sorry. That wasn't your fault, though."

He let out a wry laugh. "I felt differently. So did her family. She was on the phone with her mom when she wrecked. She was in a coma for a few days. Man, I paced those hallways, praying." He shook his head.

I realized I couldn't trust God.

Beth fumbled for some brilliant words of support. Anything that might possibly dull the sting.

"But you started going to church again?"

"Yeah. I knew there wasn't any future in the path I was on in my relationships, but I guess you'd say my faith is still a little like Tally's. I'm skittish. Prone to running, bucking, fleeing." His half-hearted smile told her there was more truth than jest in his words.

"She's coming around. Maybe there's hope for you."

"I should get going." He stood and rubbed his bicep with his opposite hand. "All this deep talk is gonna give me hives."

She tried to smile. "I have Benadryl in my first aid kit." She pointed to the oversized white tackle box on her bowed shelf. A red cross had been added to the top and sides, and it looked like it might be a two-person carry.

"I bet. Thanks." He laughed, something genuine and full that broke the weight in the air. "Looks like you have the fix for all that ails."

After he left, she listened as Grayson's apartment door closed, then buried her face in her hands.

eight

· · ·

THE LAST THING HE NEEDED WAS TO BE ENTANGLED IN THE TOWN'S social schedule.

Apparently, no one in Deep Haven had received that memo.

"Grayson, dude! We heard you were in town!"

Grayson tried to place the face of his new best friend at Grandpa's deck party, the one who'd handed him a plate of barbecued ribs and slaw, but...

Too many people.

Everything in Grayson told him he should have hidden out at camp. Hung out with Tally and given some of the camp horses a bit of attention.

He should have listened.

He still couldn't believe how he'd babbled on and on to Beth. About his parents. About Harper.

He hadn't told anyone about Harper. Beth was like truth serum personified.

"Hey, how's it going?" Another new face gave him a nod when he walked by.

If last Sunday's potluck had taught him anything, it was to expect a Friday-night crowd and to fight to lie low. That's apparently how things rolled in Deep Haven.

But...

Laughter and conversation buzzed across his grandparents' back deck, and the smell of fresh-mowed lawn mingled with smoky barbecue.

This time, it was a full-on party.

He actually recognized most of the faces gathered around—people sitting in the white plastic chairs or standing in the shade. He shook hands as he made his way through the crowd. Vivien Calhoun—now Buckam—had introduced her husband, Boone, and explained he headed up the Crisis Response Team.

Add in Dylan, Marie, Eli, Doug, and Beth, and the crowd had spilled off the deck and onto the grass where Noah and his wife, Anne, sat with two teenage boys. Lena stood nearby nursing an ice tea, and Beth's friend Courtney sat with Sammy Johnson and Robin. Even his old high-school coach, Caleb Knight, had stopped in with his wife, Issy.

He remembered Issy. She was the former coach's daughter. Had been in the car with him when they'd had a terrible accident that had ended coach's career.

Megan and her husband Cole—last name Barrett—also involved in the Crisis Response Team.

Nope. It was one thing to spend time with his family, but only one week back in town and they were practically painting him into the town mural.

He adjusted his position in a plastic chair, gulped down his tea, and waved away the barbecue smoke that funneled under the backyard umbrella.

Country music filled the space, just loud enough to make Grayson want to climb inside the song and settle into a sunset horseback ride. Alone.

He should be working. Taking care of Tally, repairing broken rope halters, or picking manure out the paddocks.

He scanned the yard for Beth. They'd had a good week working together, despite him spilling his guts on Tuesday.

You must've broken more hearts than a country song.

The statement had rattled him. All he'd seen was Harper's face. Heard the sound of her car tearing out of the drive. Saw her mom's face.

Beth had left the barn that night by the time he'd ventured out of his apartment to feed the horses, and neither one had brought it up since.

He knew he hadn't owed her an explanation, but still. Something had compelled him to share it, and maybe there was a little relief in not carrying the burden himself. He wanted her to understand. Harper's death had turned him inside out. Changed him. And even if he hadn't quite found solid ground with God, he wanted to be a better man.

Far better than the one he'd been.

And he wanted to believe Beth was right—that maybe, just like Tally, there was hope for him too.

"How's life at the camp?" Dylan slid into the seat next to him.

"I'm wishing I was still there." Grayson pushed his plate aside. The mounds of food were mostly untouched. "It's quiet."

"You're a part of this, whether you like it or not." He lifted his glass toward the chatter and laughter.

Grayson took a drink and watched Marie and Eli take turns on the croquet course that had been set up on the back lawn. "That's a great kid you've got."

"He's amazing. He worries about Marie—too much."

"I'll bet."

"We'll be okay. Marie's fighting hard and we caught it early." He hoisted an oversized brownie and took a bite.

"Dad, come on!" Eli called. "I'm playing you next."

"Duty calls," Dylan said. He took another bite of brownie. "Wish me luck." He headed down to the lawn and took the croquet mallet offered by Marie.

Laughter erupted from Vivien's conversation circle, where Robin was making moony eyes at Sammy.

Beth stood up from one of the card tables set up on the lawn.

Her hair was swept into a messy bun, and her big green eyes met his, creased with a smile.

He stifled the twist it caused in his gut.

She disappeared into the house with an empty tea pitcher to refill and returned moments later. Wove her way to a spot where Vivien, her husband Boone, Courtney, Robin, Sammy, and several others sat.

Grandma picked up a casserole dish from the table. "We're going to start cleaning up. You all take your time."

"We'll need to get going soon too." Megan Barrett stood and folded her chair, as well as the ones the Knights had vacated. They worked to clear out the remaining seats.

Someone turned up the music, and everyone remaining congregated near the dessert table in clusters of conversation.

"Having a good time?" Vivien Buckam nudged Grayson with an elbow.

"Vivie," Grayson said. Vivien had always been a beautiful woman, but he'd be lying if he didn't say she looked radiant now.

"Good to see you." She smoothed her hand down the arm of her husband.

"I want to hear more about what you've been up to." Vivien's blue eyes pummeled him with an expectant glaze, penetrating and unrelenting.

"Working at a ranch." Grayson shifted. At this point, everyone knew his sole income was the camp.

She pulled back the wrapper on a cupcake. "Besides work, silly." She took a bite, using the tip of her finger to wipe the smudge of frosting from her lips. "How's camp?"

He had the distinct impression Vivie was fishing.

"You know how it is. Church on Sunday. Work all week. Spend Saturday playing catch-up."

Dylan lifted his tea glass to point at Grayson. Laughed. "He doesn't have a life." He handed the glass off to Marie and took his next croquet shot.

"Funny." He tossed his balled-up napkin at Dylan, who didn't have a free hand to catch it.

"Sensitive, are we?" Dylan waited for Eli to take his shot.

Okay, maybe it was a little, partly, half true.

Vivien set down her cupcake. "Oh, come on—Mr. Bachelor. You have to have some free time."

Robin cleared her throat. "Grandma says you're quite the two-stepper." She'd fallen for Vivie's bait.

Oh, thank you, sister. He cut her the hardest look he could muster.

"It's true. She said you told her you'd won a dance contest at some radio station's event at a fair."

Oh brother. He should have known better than to tell Grandma that. But she'd badgered him for news. An update. Something about his life. He'd caved and told her about the contest he'd only entered to win concert tickets for Tim McGraw.

"I'd like to see him prove it," Dylan said, a smirk twisting his lips. "This guy's always had two left feet. But you did tell me about those places in Oregon—Cross-Eyed Cricket and Rowdy's?"

Oh, he had to mention that.

"You're denying it?" Robin challenged. "You can't be a cowboy and not two-step."

"That's in the rules, isn't it?" Vivien asked. She crossed her arms. "Let's see some of that action. If it's contest worthy, I'm sure you can teach us North Shore inhabitants a thing or two."

"He can probably only line dance," Dylan goaded him. "Or only knows the electric slide." Dylan, Eli, and Marie had joined the group, their game of croquet over.

Robin grinned from her seat at the end of the table. "I will say, he did have some fancy footwork in high school. Could he have lost his touch, though?"

He wasn't biting. "No way. This is *not* a dance party." He held out his arms. "Not a contest."

"We can make it one." Vivien called to Beth, who was wrapping up leftovers at the buffet table. "Beth—come here."

Beth turned from her work. "What's up?" She walked over, holding a brownie in one hand and cup of punch in the other.

"Aren't you supposed to be cleaning up?" Vivie asked.

"This was the last one left on that tray." Beth turned the brownie in front of Vivien. "I had to help out."

"Well," Vivien said, "Grayson here's going to show us his two-step. He needs a partner."

"Uh…" Beth backed away. "My hands are full." She shoved half her brownie into her mouth and covered her chewing with her cup. "And I'm eating." The words came out muffled.

"Come on—it'll be fun!" Vivien pried the food items from Beth's grip and set them on the table. "They'll be here when you get back." She shoved Beth forward and snagged Boone's hand. "Let's dance, hon. Before I'm so pregnant I can't move."

Robin reached for Sammy's hand and pulled him from the sidelines. "Come on, show us!"

Beth finished chewing and stood facing him in the middle of the impromptu dance floor. Everyone else was dancing around them.

Awkward.

And he just couldn't help it. He laughed. Something from within, so open and expansive it brought tears to his eyes. "You know there's no saying no to Vivie, right?"

She closed her eyes. Nodded. "I know. Oh, I know. It doesn't stop me from trying, though."

He'd missed this. The twist of memories that locked him in. Rooted him. Maybe he just hadn't tried hard enough in Oregon. Always played it low-key. Detached. The cowboy in the bar that was good for a night of dancing and darts.

And a front-door goodbye.

No strings. No attachments.

Because a man like him couldn't risk connecting with others. No matter how tempting.

Especially after Harper.

Yet here he was, in the middle of all the layers of history. Of family. Of community. And he was starting to like it despite every attempt he'd made to stay in Oregon.

Beth began to slip away.

"Whoa," he said and held out his hand to her. Maybe he could give in. Try a little harder. Dig a little deeper. Take a risk. Because somehow, it didn't seem as risky or wrong when it came to Beth.

She stared at his hand for a moment.

"Come on!" Vivien said, her husband giving her a slow twirl.

Beth said something he couldn't hear. He leaned in.

"I don't know how to dance." Her breath tickled his ear, shot rays of electricity down his back and arms and tingled every nerve in his body.

"Just trust me." As soon as the words left his lips, he wanted to exit the area. Who was he to ask for her to trust him?

She teased her lower lip between her teeth.

"If you can relax, all you need to do is let me lead." He waited for her to look up at him. "I really did win that dance contest. Now my reputation's on the line."

She nodded and slid her right hand into his left. He placed her left hand on his shoulder. Let his right hand find the sweet spot on her back.

Instead of a two-step, a strong country swing was playing. He drew her toward him.

He caught Doug Strauss's eyes on him. A little wary. Very watchful.

Grayson looked away and tried to turn Beth. For such a petite woman, it was like trying to move a one-ton round bale. "You're fighting me."

"I'm not."

"Relax."

"I'm trying."

"Don't try—it's like riding. Feel."

What she needed was an old-fashioned distraction. Something to make her quit thinking about her feet and just move with him. "I'm sorry for the way I left the other night," Grayson said.

She turned her head, releasing a citrusy smell from her hair. "I—I shouldn't have said what I said. I'm sorry." She gave him a crooked smile. "I've wanted to apologize for three days, but I was afraid to bring it up again."

"Yeah. I know that feeling."

Her tiny sandal landed on his boot. "Oops. Sorry."

"You'd have to stomp those little feet awfully hard for me to suffer injury."

She laughed, something sweet and light. "Noted." She looked up at him. "Friends?"

He swallowed. "Yes. Friends."

He was in trouble. There was something so soft and sweet in Beth—she made Deep Haven feel a little like…home.

The song ended and rolled into a slow ballad. No one else left the makeshift dance floor. Even Doug had made his way to the dance floor with Janet, though Grayson wasn't sure Beth had noticed.

She relaxed. Let him draw her close.

As fast and as far as Grayson had run from Deep Haven, the buzz of the evening made him wonder if everything he'd been missing had been right here all along.

The only things waiting for him in Oregon were long, hard hours and quiet, lonely nights. And a lot of work getting his would-be ranch and camp up and running. Which, really, was just fine with him. Wasn't it?

It used to be. Right up until Bookworm Bethy stumbled back into his life.

He lost track of how many songs they'd danced to, until Grandma announced that they were going to head inside. And Grayson felt the strangest reluctance in letting Beth go.

She pulled away, smiled, and scooped up a stack of unused

cups to carry inside.

Dylan was watching him from the doorway, his face unreadable.

Wow—two for two with the men in Beth's life.

Dylan walked up to Grayson and glanced over his shoulder to make sure the door had closed.

"Hey," he said, "I see all that." He nodded toward the back door Beth had disappeared through. "Don't hurt her. She's had enough people bail on her."

"We're just friends."

Dylan let out a sound. Cleared his throat. "You just keep telling yourself that."

BETH NEEDED TO STEER CLEAR OF ALL THINGS GRAYSON FOX BEFORE she got caught up in his cowboy ways.

Which was exactly why she'd hopped out of bed early to drive into town and have breakfast with Dad. Why she stood over the stove cooking sausage links and pouring batter.

Her skin prickled at the memory of dancing with Grayson the night before. He'd smelled of aftershave and the outdoors when he'd drawn her into his arms. The tenor of his voice had vibrated against her, and his laughter had lifted in the evening air, so unexpected. Surprising.

Yes. Friends.

And it made some little piece of her wonder what life might be like in Oregon.

Yep. She needed to put some miles between herself and Grayson.

Beth watched bubbles form on the pancakes and rolled the sausages sizzling in the second pan. Waited. Flipped the pancakes. Yep, she needed to ground herself in reality today.

She inhaled the savory smells mingling with the sweet maple syrup.

Breakfast with Dad. Check his freezer-meal supply. Make sure he rescheduled his eye appointment. Then pick up more sausage, eggs, and orange juice.

You might be doing just a little too much for him.

Courtney's words prodded at Beth. Okay, likely there was some truth in that.

The Rhine River cruise pamphlet still sat on the corner of the kitchen counter. Huh.

She plated the pancakes and sausages.

"That smells good." Her Dad padded across the living room in his slippers, stopping at the kitchen doorway. "I've missed this—I'm feeling spoiled now." He pressed a kiss to the side of her head and slipped into a seat at the peninsula. "I didn't realize how much you do around here until you were gone this past week." He took a bite of sausage. "This beats the cold cereal I've been eating all week."

Beth pointed her spatula toward the cruise brochure. "Did you think any more about that Rhine cruise?" She dropped two more pancakes onto her own plate and set aside the plate of extras.

He waved her off with a forkful of pancake dripping with syrup. "It's fine. I don't need to go on a cruise." He took a bite of pancake. Chewed. "I wish I'd known you were coming by, though."

See? Nothing had changed. She was on her own but could still have Saturday mornings with Dad.

He checked his watch. "I'm meeting a friend in about fifteen minutes."

Wait, what? "You're leaving?"

"Yeah, I'm sorry. It's a little late to cancel—I mean, I can, though." He tipped back his orange juice.

The pancakes turned to paste in Beth's mouth. "No, Dad. It's okay. I can do a few loads of laundry and then head out."

130 · Rachel D. Russell

"Sure?"

"Of course."

Beth reminded herself of all the reasons this was good for both of them, though she hadn't planned on sitting around Dad's house by herself.

"Looked like you had a memorable time last night."

Beth stared at her plate, the heat of a flush warming her skin. She cut another bite with her fork. "We always enjoy time with Elaine and Jim Fox."

"Need to be careful or Grayson might just steal you away."

Beth coughed and took a drink of juice. "Don't be ridiculous, Dad. We work together—that's it."

Dad raised a brow. "I remember the last guy who came to town and left again."

"It's fine. I'm fine," Beth said. "We danced. Lots of people were dancing." The morning breeze blew through the open kitchen window and she shivered.

He was still watching her. "I'm just asking you to be careful," he repeated. He reached over and placed a hand over hers. "I'm glad you're enjoying work at the camp and riding again—but he's not staying in Deep Haven."

Beth fidgeted in her seat. "I'm a big girl. I know he isn't staying." She just wished it didn't sting quite so much to admit it. To know Dad was right.

He pulled his hand away to take another bite. "You'll have to give me a call later. I want to hear about how things are going." He downed the last of his juice.

"Of course." She stirred a piece of sausage in maple syrup. She'd lost her appetite.

At least she wasn't in the barn with Grayson. He was all kinds of trouble that snagged her heart and stole it while she wasn't looking.

No way. She'd promised herself she wouldn't be lured by dancing or riding or hours working in the barn together. Nope.

Grayson might not be a player anymore, but he wasn't sticking around.

Just like Dad said.

And she wasn't the kind of girl for a fling. Or a summer romance.

Especially not with their past, let alone the fact that he and Dylan were friends again.

Not that Grayson even liked her like that. Nope. Dancing was something he did with lots of ladies in his life. She'd just been thrust into the position and that's all it was. All it would ever be. That was just fine with her, thank you very much.

"Excuse me," she said. She set her plate on the kitchen counter, went to her bedroom, and tugged on her ratty University of Minnesota sweatshirt. No matter how many holes it developed, it was still her favorite. Aged to soft perfection.

She hoisted her laundry bag and carried it to the washing machine, then returned to the kitchen.

Dad stirred his last bite of pancake in syrup and chewed it.

"I'm sorry to run out on you." Dad stood and put his plate and silverware into the dishwasher. "That was delicious. Thank you." He gave her a squeeze, tugged on his shoes, and opened the door.

And there stood Grayson on the doorstep, holding a box, looking wickedly handsome in a way that seemed wholly unfair. He wore jeans and boots and a snug, tucked-in T-shirt that made him look like a superhero.

He's not staying in Deep Haven.

Dad turned. Shot a look at Beth. "Grayson," he said, his tone flat. "What a surprise."

"Good morning," Grayson said. The rich tenor of his greeting practically made her toes curl.

Dad tugged on his ball cap, stepped past the threshold, and turned back to her. "Please, Beth, remember what we talked about." With that final plea, he turned and left.

So much for steering clear of Grayson.

"Those don't look like cinnamon rolls," she said, pointing to the box. She stepped aside so he could enter.

"I brought you something." He walked to the coffee table and set down the box, opened it, and pulled out a straw Stetson cowboy hat. "You mentioned you didn't have any of your old stuff. I know you and Vivien went shopping, but I thought you might want this too."

"You got me a Stetson?" It had a blue-and-green band on it, and when he placed it on her head, the hat slid into place.

"Something to shade your eyes and face. You've been working in the sun all week."

She stepped in front of the mirror by the front entry. "How did you get me the right-sized hat?"

"Vivie—she was very helpful." He put the lid back on the box.

Beth shook her head. "I'll bet she was." She'd have to have a few words with Vivie—hopefully she didn't try to give him her ring size too.

"You'd mentioned theater." He lifted a shoulder. "I took a guess she'd have your measurements from costumes and stuff."

"How did you know I was here?"

"I didn't. I stopped by to see my parents' lot." He nodded toward the view of the vacant lot out the kitchen window. "Saw your car."

"I thought I was having breakfast with Dad. I just assumed he'd be sitting around the house today." She moved back into the living room. "Turns out he has other plans."

"Isn't that a good thing?"

She scrunched up her face. "I think so?" She shrugged. "I mean, yes. Did you already walk the lot?"

He shook his head and his Adam's apple bobbed. "How come you never went to college?" He gestured toward her sweatshirt. "I always thought you'd go to college. You were such an outstanding student, despite your complete inability to catch me in tag."

"Hilarious. I had planned to go."

"But you didn't."

"No. I mean—yes, I left for college. I didn't even last eight seconds."

"Whoa."

"Okay, probably it was closer to three hours."

"What happened?"

"I was accepted. Went for a tour with Dad." She plucked a stray thread from her sweatshirt. "It probably sounds silly to you, but I didn't know anyone there. I didn't like the girl who was going to be my roommate. I didn't even like the carpet in my dorm room."

Grayson paused. Looked down at her, a little mischief in his eyes. "You chickened out."

"Ouch. But I guess, pretty much. It was easier to come back home. To continue life as usual." She walked back into the kitchen. Grayson followed.

"You didn't want to leave your dad?"

"Bingo." She picked up a washcloth and wiped down the kitchen counter. "You know, it isn't that weird. Seventy-two percent of people live in or near their hometown."

"That's a strangely specific statistic."

"I may have looked it up once." She placed the rag over the sink. "Dylan thought I should have stayed in school."

"He looks out for you." Grayson's eyes stayed on her, a little pensive and tender, even.

Was he thinking of high school—or something else?

She played with the torn cuff of her sleeve.

One thing was for sure. Working with Grayson Fox was going to test every last promise she'd made to herself and Dad. And she couldn't fall for the guy who was definitely leaving town. Because she wasn't, right? She wouldn't. Couldn't. Right?

Probably.

Oh boy, she was in trouble.

nine

. . .

GRAYSON MUST HAVE BEEN KICKED IN THE HEAD AT SOME POINT. That's the only reason he could muster as to why he'd agreed to lead the horse camp.

Could he just go back to riding with Beth? Because a guy could really enjoy getting paid to keep that kind of company.

He'd even ordered twenty tons of hay and made sure the horses were on the farrier's schedule before hopping on the tractor and turning the manure, checking all the camp saddles for maintenance, and repairing the fence Tally had dismantled.

Two days since he'd stopped by her dad's. Since she'd admitted that she'd given up college to stay with him.

Did Doug even know? Was he okay with that?

Grayson shook off the distraction.

He stared down the Monday morning lineup of kids, all eyes on him. He'd rather have a wild Mustang to gentle—was he even cut out to run his own camp? Dreaming it had been one thing. Being faced by children, looking at him with every expectation of an equestrian excursion?

Oh, boy.

But Beth needed him. And Eli needed him. And every one of

the kids in the lineup needed him, so time to pull it together. Fast.

There wouldn't be any ambulances or angry parents this time.

Eli smiled up at him from the group, and Grayson tried to focus on him—he was easy to talk to.

Didn't work.

Beth stood against the hitching post, her brand-new straw Stetson shielding her eyes from the sun. In her Wranglers, Ariats, and hat, she looked like Miss Rodeo USA.

And that suited her, if he were the kind of guy to notice those details about Dylan's sister. Which he wasn't. So he didn't.

He hadn't noticed how she'd smelled like summer—coconut and orange blossoms—when he'd given her that awkward sideways hug last week. Or how much he enjoyed giving her a leg up into the saddle. Or how much fun he had sharing hours at the barn with her—like the way she smiled when Tally came near, brave enough now to accept a scratch on the withers. Or even how Beth looked at him like sometimes she drew a little of her courage from him.

Or how he looked for her car every time he was in town.

Nope. Didn't notice any of that.

Not that she'd care, anyway. She'd be the official camp AD, and he'd be leaving town.

Unless he hadn't imagined the little bit of spark in her eyes when he'd danced with her at his grandparents' party. Or in Tally's stall when they fed the mare applesauce spiked with antibiotics and re-wrapped her bandage.

Maverick nudged Grayson's arm. He checked out the lineup again. "Yeah, Mav. I know."

The campers all still stood, staring at him. Waiting.

And he thought he'd be able to run his own camp?

His throat constricted, tight, as if a horse had landed on him, squeezing out the breath. Not permitting his lungs to fill.

This was a mistake.

It shouldn't be that hard. Beth had helped him tack up the horses, who all stood patiently, tied at different spots around the arena. She'd worked with deft but gentle hands prepping each horse.

Speaking to each quietly as she worked. Calling the horses by name.

They'd already fit the kids with helmets. He rubbed his slick hands against his jeans and took a swig from his water bottle in hopes of getting rid of the cottony dryness, then shoved it back into his saddlebag.

No amount of staring at Maverick could inflate his lungs.

The kids stood, several toeing the dirt. A few wiggling side to side. Out of nine, only six pairs of eyes were on him.

Two of the campers started to tussle, bumping into Eli. Grayson stepped forward. "Hey—we're not going to have any of that."

"We're just playing," one answered.

This day had *train wreck* written all over it.

And he had no idea where to start. Everything he'd rehearsed, gone like front-row tickets to the country music festival.

They stared.

He stared.

Crickets.

This was a lot harder than he'd imagined it in his head.

"Ahem." Beth walked up. Yep—she looked like a pro in her blue camp staff T-shirt she'd tucked into her Wranglers.

"I'm Miss Beth and this...cowboy here is Mr. Grayson." Her voice rose, surprisingly clear and resolute in the barnyard, and the youths leaned in to hear her. "Who's here for a trail ride?"

All their hands shot into the air with a chorus of "Me!"

She glanced over at him, the sparkle in her eyes mischievous.

For all her quiet, demure appearance, Grayson was starting to believe something untamed lived just beneath the surface. Something saucy and sassy and smart.

That maybe all Beth had needed was the same thing he'd needed—the same thing these kids needed. Someone to stand by her and give her a little nudge. Believe in her. Tell her to go for it.

"We need to review over a few safety rules." She held up her finger. "First, listen and obey all the instructions we give you." She held up a second finger. "Second, move slowly around the horses and use a calm, quiet voice." She scanned the lineup for eyes. "Third, do not stand where you could be kicked—namely, behind the horse." She used her arms to gesture toward the nearest horse's hind end like a game-show assistant.

Her audience giggled.

She continued reciting the rules while Grayson pulled himself together and grabbed their radios from the charger in the barn.

He'd spent some time riding each of the horses over the past three days while Beth rode Rex. He could plop a kid on top of these horses and trust it to willingly follow the one in front of it. They'd decided he'd ride Maverick in the front and Beth would bring up the rear.

"Any questions?" Beth had finished her lengthy rule discussion. The kids all shook their heads. "Okay then, we're going to get things ready, then we'll pair each of you with your horse you'll be riding this week, then we'll get you into the saddle."

"Here, take this." Grayson helped her clip her radio onto her belt. "I'm Wrangler-one."

"Yes…Mr. Grayson." She said his name with a teasing lilt, a softness and familiarity that caused him to pause. "I guess that makes me Wrangler-two?"

She was messing with his head. Watching her rediscover a love for horses caused a lightness in his chest. He'd be lying if he didn't admit that she made the very ordinary, easy trail ride something of an adventure. He couldn't help but lean into her laughter and listen for the quiet jokes meant only for his ears.

She had the kids line up, and he matched each youth to a

horse. Lucky for him, these were the horse-crazy kids who were too eager, if anything.

Beth stopped to adjust the stirrups on one of the saddles, and he saw Eli heading for the barn.

Huh.

He hustled over. "Where you heading? Today's our first big ride."

The boy cut toward the gate.

"Whoa there." Grayson caught up, circled in front, and blocked the path.

He caught a glimpse of Beth across the arena. She motioned for him to lower himself. Yeah, he probably looked like a giant. He squatted in the arena dirt. "What's up, Eli?"

"I don't think I want to go."

"But you were looking forward to it—begging me to let you ride last week."

The boy shook his head and crossed his arms.

"What's changed?"

Eli crumpled a little, blinked. Ran his forearm across his eyes. "My mom has an appointment today. A scan. I don't feel like going on the ride."

"Oh, buddy." Grayson reached for the arena rail. Fisted his hand around it. "I'm sorry to hear that."

Eli nodded. "That's what everyone says."

Grayson let out a half laugh. "You know, you're right." He placed a hand on Eli's shoulder. "It's because people care and it's hard to have the words to express all the sorrow they feel for what you're going through." He stood upright.

Eli tipped his face toward Grayson. It was splotchy and his blue-green eyes were rimmed red. "Does everyone think she's going to die?"

"No, no. Not at all. But it is hard to go through these things. People care about you, your mom, your dad."

Eli nodded again.

"I'm going to let you in on a little secret. I actually didn't want to be here my first day when I was a kid either."

"Really?"

"Really. I think you'll find the same thing I did, though. Horses are lots of fun."

Eli looked over his shoulder at the group. Beth had made the kids laugh again. They were laughing almost as hard as she was.

"You know, you can invite your mom to watch you ride at the end of the week."

"I could do that?"

"Sure. But you'll have to be a rider in order to do that." Grayson leaned back against the arena rail. "You know, I need a helper with me on today's ride. I could really use your help."

"Me?"

"Yeah. I need someone I can trust." He pointed a thumb toward the arena. "I'm not sure I can count on that cowgirl over there."

Eli looked over and scratched his head. "Aunt Beth?"

"Yeah."

A giggle. "I'm going to tell her you said that."

Grayson ruffled the boy's hair. "Thanks a lot."

Eli lifted his shoulders, still grinning.

"Okay, I still need your help, though. I'll show you what to do." He paused. Let his words soak in a bit. "Would you be willing to do that?" He pointed toward a little roan mare. She was a pocket pony if he'd ever met one. She might just be part Labrador. All sweet gentleness. Like Mr. Pickles. "You'll also get to ride Lexi, one of the best horses in the herd."

Eli stared at Lexi. "I don't know."

"Would you at least come meet her?"

He wanted to take the boy's hand, but Eli didn't need that—especially not in front of the all the other kids who were watching. What he needed was Lexi.

"Come on." Grayson walked toward the horses. Beth had mounted up most of the kids already.

Footsteps pounded the dirt. Eli appeared beside Grayson. "I like her color. She's red and silvery."

"I do too."

They walked up to Lexi, and the horse stretched out her neck and lowered her head so Eli could rub her forehead. He skimmed his fingers across the silky nose, like he'd done with Remy on his last camp visit.

Lexi blew out a soft breath. Eli looked up at Grayson and smiled. A smile so big and wide that it almost made a grown man cry. This. *This* was why he needed to open a camp in Oregon.

"Ready to hop on?"

He nodded.

Grayson grabbed the nearby mounting block, untied Lexi's lead, and set the block in place. Eli stepped up and Grayson helped him onto the horse, tied off the lead to the saddle strings, and slipped the reins into the boy's hands.

He scanned the arena. Beth helped the last kid on and then led Rex to a mounting block for herself. She swung her leg over and rode up the line. Passed him.

"Good job, cowboy." She leaned in, whispered the words for only him. Her eyes landed on Eli and Lexi, then flitted back to him.

His heart skittered.

"Okay, everyone, stay in line and keep your horses on the trail, single file." He turned Maverick back and rode to the front of the line. He paused next to Lexi. "Okay, Eli, follow me. Your job is to stay about one-horse length behind me. You're the leader for all the rest of the group."

Eli nodded and held his reins against the horn.

He gave the kids instructions on how to guide the horses with direct reining—though for the most part, the trail and the horse in front of them would keep them on track. He led the group in a loop around the entire arena twice, giving him a chance to see how each of the riders was doing, and then stopped at the gate to unlatch it and side-pass Maverick to swing it wide open.

They headed out on the five-mile loop trail, twisting through the spruce and pine trees and catching glimpses of Mink Lake shimmering through the stand.

Every time he turned back and saw Eli smile, it nearly split his heart in two. He couldn't give Marie the miracle she hoped for, but he was here, in Deep Haven, keeping the camp running. And because of that, Eli might experience some of the same healing power of horses that Grayson had.

That wasn't so bad.

They snaked through a hairpin turn on the trail, which let him see the other riders behind him. At the end of the line, Beth was pointing out something to the nearby riders. She looked over at him. Smiled.

And having a partner wasn't so bad either.

🐾🐾🐾

A GIRL COULD GET USED TO HAVING HER OWN LITTLE OASIS IN THE woods. Beth carried the plate of grapes, cheese, smoked sausage, and crackers to the outdoor table and set it down next to the tea glasses on her small back patio where Vivien sat in a lounge chair. Beth's cabin had a forest view, and she loved relaxing to the cacophony of bird song.

Beth's heart had nearly exploded into a million pieces when Grayson had gone after Eli on Monday, and no, she hadn't been the least bit surprised when Eli begged to stay late and help with the horses.

And again the two afternoons since.

Because she knew his mom had been at appointments each day.

And when he'd announced with conspiratorial glee that

Grayson had said she was untrustworthy, all she could do was smile when Grayson winked at her.

She looked forward to the rides—a reprieve from the stacks of paperwork and computer files she'd been working on.

Even treating Tally's wound had become an ordinary part of her day, and Lena had been pleased with the healing when she'd stopped by.

Three days into camp and she wasn't sure whose life it was changing more. One of the kids', hers, or Grayson's.

If she could just gain some ground on the grant proposals and paperwork.

Vivien snagged a slice of cheese and took a bite.

"You should have seen them, Vivie," Beth said. She grabbed her ice tea. Sipped. "It was...I don't even have words for it. This camp makes a difference."

"Mm-hmm." Vivie adjusted in her chair, her blue eyes on Beth. "Guess you're done being my emergency stand-in at the theater. Sounds like you're finding plenty of real life to keep you busy."

"Kind of nice for a change." Beth took another drink of her tea. "It is a lot of work, though. I was up late finishing a grant application, and this morning, I had to delegate a few things to Grayson. He's going to chase down farrier appointments and a load of hay."

"It also sounds like you are a little smitten with the cowboy."

A warm summer breeze blew across the patio, carrying with it the sweet lilac from the bushes planted along the side of the cabin. Beth set her hat on the table.

Summer on the North Shore was what made winter tolerable.

"It's not that. But it is satisfying to be riding again. And he's very helpful." He was leaving. Or not—because the man owned a lot with a premium view of the lake. A lot he was a little reluctant to sell, even though she'd seen Nathan posting the For Sale sign at the corner.

"Right." Vivien rolled her eyes and checked her watch. "You

haven't been going on and on about Grayson this and Grayson that for the past twenty-seven minutes."

"You asked how things have been going. We've had a lot of time together."

"Right," Vivien repeated.

"Seriously. Working. We work together." Beth adjusted in her seat. "My office and his apartment are both in the barn."

"The camp. His grandparents' place. The bakery." She popped a grape into her mouth. "It just seems like everywhere you go, Grayson is."

"It can't happen, Vivien. He's leaving." Beth pulled several grapes from the bunch. "Besides, what about when things fall apart? When we break up? He's one of Dylan's oldest friends. They've just patched things up."

"You're a twenty-eight-year-old woman. They're grown men. They'll figure it out."

"I'm enjoying the horses." Beth tried to shift the direction of the conversation. She wasn't going to start another relationship that would break her heart.

"Are you going to run some barrels again?"

"Oh, racing?" Beth laughed. "No. My frontal lobe finished developing several years back." She crunched a cracker.

Vivien scooped up several crackers and cheese, topped them with sausage on her plate. "You had one accident. It doesn't mean you'll have another one."

"It doesn't mean I won't." Beth wrinkled her nose. "But trail riding? That's fun. Seeing the kids' faces? Amazing."

Vivien chewed her food and chased it with a swig of tea. "They have trails in Oregon."

Beth shook her head, afraid to admit the daydreams she'd had. "I'm not leaving Deep Haven."

"Why can't you?"

"This is all I've ever known. My dad is here, Dylan is here—plus Marie and Eli." She raised her hands toward the cabin and forest. "This is here—all this. You know how long

I've wanted this job, and I'm this close." She pinched her fingers together.

Vivien nodded. "I get it—I do. I left and came back. Sounds to me like you're trying to sell yourself on all the reasons you think you have to stay."

Beth rubbed her palms on her thighs and met Vivien's expectant gaze. "Okay, fine. Yes, I've thought about it. Wondered what it could be like."

Vivien's eyes rounded. "I knew it. Good for you."

"But leaving Deep Haven would be leaving my heart. This is where my life is." Beth looked down and brushed a crumb from her shirt. "Besides, you know I can't leave my dad."

"Speaking of where life is at and your dad"—Vivien stirred her tea—"how's Operation River Cruise going? Did you buy his ticket?"

Beth laughed. "I'm not just going to pack him up on a plane."

"You should—fear holds both of you back. I mean, I'm not a psychologist, but I have played one on stage." She arched a brow.

"You are hardly qualified."

"Humor me. You and your dad both suffered loss. And that makes change scary. But you're here, at camp—living outside your childhood house for the first time ever." Vivien tapped her nails against the tea glass. "And you're both still doing okay."

"I'm only twenty minutes away."

"Still, that's a start."

"I miss seeing him every morning." Saturday's breakfast flashed through her mind. Without her around, Dad had made other plans. Which was great.

And maybe also bothered her.

"I'm sure you do. When my mom moved to Arizona, I was a little crushed. But I could have gone with her."

"Why didn't you?"

"Because that wasn't where I belonged. Sometimes the easy thing to do isn't the right thing to do."

"I made him a promise, Vivie, after Mom left. I promised him I'd never leave him."

"That was a promise made by a young child."

"Now you sound like Grayson." Beth shrugged a shoulder. "I meant it, though. I'm not going to be like her—and I don't need to be. I have this." She gestured again to her cabin. "This job is perfect for me, perfect for my life. My dad needs me."

Vivien held up her hand. "I understand caring for him. You love him." She pulled another grape from the cluster. "I just want you to think about if, perhaps, you need him to need you."

"That doesn't make any sense." Beth piled a cracker with cheese and sausage and took a bite.

"Sometimes it can give us an excuse to avoid hard things."

Like leaving home for college. Leaving with Lyle.

She finished chewing. "That's not it. Lyle could have stayed—he chose not to." And the fact that he hadn't loved her enough to stay, well, that was a heartache she'd spent months recovering from.

"I did see your dad at lunch with Janet the other day."

Oh. Dad hadn't mentioned that. Huh.

Vivien grabbed a cracker, then took another drink. "Since you are planted in Deep Haven, tell me more about your job. Have you still been looking for an assistant wrangler? Someone to take the spot you're filling?"

Heat crept up Beth's neck. She hadn't even thought to continue searching or calling around. Because she liked being Grayson's partner at the camp.

"Ah-ha!" Vivien set down her plate. "You don't want anyone else."

"It's working out for now. I can't think too far ahead." Beth took another drink of tea and then snagged her laptop from her backpack and set it on the table. Flipped it open. "Okay, enough chitchat. I need your help on a few of these grant proposals." She clicked on the digital files. "You said you've done some for the community theater?"

"I did—though I'm not sure I'll be that helpful." Vivie lifted several folders from her tote. "I was awarded one and lost out on one."

"I've only done those two for the library—mostly using Joyce's templates." Beth dug through her backpack and hefted her own stack of files onto the table. "Maybe between the two of us, I can get at least one or two new grants, plus the renewals." She handed Vivien a hard copy. "I think this one is ready to go. Can you take a look at the packet?"

Vivien flipped page by page while Beth proofread another grant proposal.

"You'll want to update these budget numbers. It looks like the ones Noah has in here are several years old." Vivien slid the folder back across the table.

"Excellent point." Beth rubbed her palms against her eyelids. She'd rather be riding than crunching numbers on her computer.

"Nice hat, by the way." Vivien winked.

Beth's face warmed. "I hear I have you to thank for it."

"Not at all—only that it fits. It's pretty handy that I could assist."

"It didn't arrive with the best timing. Dad had just lectured me on being careful with my heart."

"Oh." Vivien held out a hand. "So he sees it too?"

"There's nothing to see." Beth bit into a cracker. Chewed. "Nothing."

Vivie flipped through several pages. "Nothing at all?"

Beth slumped. "Then Grayson showed up and that was the end of it. Dad bailed out of the house."

Vivie raised a brow. "Grayson again."

"Stop." Beth crossed her arms.

"He just seems to be around a lot. And by a lot, I mean you spend more time with him than you do with me." She popped another grape into her mouth. "I'm kind of getting jealous."

"I'm not going to be someone's summer fling."

"He does like you." Vivien pointed at Beth with a slice of smoked gouda. "I knew it."

Beth put her head in her hands. "Vivien."

"I'm sorry. Who doesn't love a love story? I want that for you. The fireworks. The romance. The grand gesture." She threw her arms wide. "You're the kindest, gentlest person I know. You are generous and devoted and loyal."

"Thanks. I think those pregnancy hormones are making you a softy."

"I've always been a romantic."

Vehicle tires crunched on the gravel, followed by the slam of car doors. Moments later, Dylan rounded the corner of the cabin followed by Grayson.

Out of the corner of her eye, Beth saw Vivien's head snap from Grayson back to Beth.

Beth ignored her and focused on Dylan. "Hey. What's up?"

The men jogged up the steps of the deck.

"Thought I'd check out the digs." Dylan scooped up crackers and cheese and handed several to Grayson. "I took Grayson to one of our current home sites."

"Help yourself," Beth said.

"Thanks." Dylan munched on his crackers and scrutinized the cabin and deck. "This is a cute place."

Beth pulled several grapes from the plate. "Right? I like being surrounded by nature. I'm sure it's much smaller than the ones Seth's building."

"Yeah, your cabin is about the size of the kitchen," Grayson said.

"Where's it at?" Vivien asked. "We love the place you guys built for Boone."

Dylan finished chewing. "It's about two miles farther out."

"Nice."

Grayson's phone buzzed and he tugged it from his pocket. "Speaking of homes—it's my real estate agent. I need to grab this."

"Sure," Beth said.

Dylan gave him a nod, and Grayson answered his phone and wandered around the side of the cabin.

Yep. She resisted the urge to lean over and catch any of the conversation.

Grayson would clear out of town and head back to Oregon.

Which had been his plan all along—just like Dad said.

She just wished it didn't bother her so much.

ten

. . .

GRAYSON RUBBED HIS HANDS TOGETHER. THEIR LAST DAY OF CAMP for the week and he'd found himself leaning into the work, the kids. They'd made it through one whole week.

He slid the grooming bucket back onto the tack room shelf.

If only today's schedule didn't include a water crossing.

Sure, it wasn't a raging river or a lake. Just a creek. Barely over the horses' knees. He just needed to get it over with and put it behind them.

He tried to swallow, but his mouth had gone pasty and his throat dry.

"All the horses are saddled and ready to go." Beth stood in the doorway of the tack room. "Is everything okay?"

Tally's head popped over her stall door at the sound of Beth's voice. That horse's heart was being won over by Beth at a rapid pace. He'd caught Beth sitting with her on more than one occasion, her computer, her journal, or her files in her lap. She'd started with a chair and hay bale set outside the stall, but after several days of that, her chair had migrated inside the stall despite his reservations and warnings.

She'd sit in there and work. Carry on conversations with Tally. He'd come to expect the sound of her voice in the barn.

Just like he'd come to expect her easy smile across the arena when they got the kids ready for each ride.

And he'd rely on that easy smile to get him through the day.

"We're on the shoreline loop today. It's the only trail they haven't been on yet that's been checked for winter damage."

"That's right—the other trails need to be checked." Beth closed the tack room door and snagged her water bottle from the table. "Will you be able to knock that out before next week?"

"I'll add that to my to-do list." He followed her out the back barn slider and slipped through the arena gate behind her. If only he'd known to check the trails sooner.

Still, for the first time since he didn't even know when, he'd found himself bouncing out of bed, looking forward to the day ahead. Even with his long to-do list. Even though he was supposed to have gone into town over the past two days to meet up with Nathan and sign updated paperwork.

I promised him I'd never leave him.

Grayson rubbed his fingers against his temple. Why did Beth have to live in Deep Haven? And wasn't that just the stupidest thing he'd ever wondered?

Because Beth was the kind of girl who played for keeps. He needed to make sure she stayed squarely in the friend zone. No matter what that crazy coconut, summery smell did to him or how much her smile lit him on fire.

Whoa.

He shook away the thoughts and turned back to the lineup of horses. "Eli may sign up to join us for the rest of the summer."

She rubbed her hand down Lexi's roan shoulder. "I kinda don't blame him." She wore her camp T-shirt and had her hair down around her shoulders. The sunshine had splashed more freckles across her nose. "What's not to love?"

Man, she was pretty. The kind of beauty that was so natural it radiated from the inside out. Not just the green of her eyes but the way they lit up with excitement. Not just the ashy light-brown of her hair but the effortless way she wore it.

She never even looked like she had makeup on. He liked her exactly like that. Her lips were the perfect shade of rosy pink...

"Grayson?"

He blinked and shifted his glance. Okay, he'd been staring at her. So much for friend zone. All she had to do was show up and he practically lost his mind.

The arena gate closest to the main drive rattled. Saved by the kids.

The crew piled into the arena, their chatter not even fazing the horses, most of which still stood with a hind foot cocked and their ears drooped.

"We went on the ropes course this morning." The announcement was made by Sarah, a curly-haired blonde who he'd learned loved to draw horses.

"Jackson was afraid," Chloe announced.

"Was not," the dark-haired boy protested.

Grayson held up his hands. "Nothing's ever wrong with a little healthy fear. Are we ready to ride today?"

Beth stepped up beside him. "Everyone, walk to your assigned horse and wait to be cleared to mount."

The kids nodded and dispersed. Eli was already standing next to Lexi. Sarah, Chloe, Jackson, Ava, Mason, Ruby, and Aiden all found their horses.

He and Beth worked in tandem, giving the kids a leg up or leading them to the mounting block, as needed.

They rode out through the pine, spruce, and maples. He could hear Beth pointing out the wildflowers. The sunlight sparkled off Mink Lake, and he let the rhythmic sound of hooves against the packed trail soothe his soul.

A bald eagle soared above the lake. "Look at that!" He pointed.

Eli rode behind him. "Oh, cool!"

The response made Grayson laugh. Maybe he already had the best job in the world.

The trail turned away from the lake, and they rode deeper

into the woods, the air fragrant with pine and earth mixed with leather and horse sweat.

His radio clicked, and he moved Maverick to the side of the trail, turned in the saddle. He could see Beth at the back of the line, several of the kids out of position.

"Wait here," he said to Eli.

The trail was too narrow right there for him to ride through.

"She's got a loose cinch," Beth called. She nodded toward Chloe's saddle.

"Serves her right. I hope she falls off." Jackson pinched his lips into a deep frown. Poor kid. It was never fun to be the one being poked at.

Grayson dropped to the ground and led Mav back toward Eli. He wasn't positive the horse would ground tie, but he also didn't think the horse would go far.

He hoped.

"If I fall, my daddy will never let me ride again," Chloe cried.

"You're not going to fall, sweetie," Beth answered. She had enough room to ride up next to Chloe and hopped to the ground.

"Keep an eye on him, would you?" Grayson asked Eli.

"Sure."

By the time he wove his way past the horses and shrubs along the trail, Beth had helped Chloe to the ground and was working to reset the saddle. Beth, Chloe, and Jackson were about thirty feet behind Mason's horse.

"Looks like you've got everything under control."

She nodded toward Jackson. "Not exactly."

Grayson moved up the trail to where Jackson sat on his horse. "It's not easy to be teased. I get that."

Jackson didn't respond.

"Sometimes, kindness works. Not always, but sometimes."

"Her dad is marrying my mom."

Grayson had nothing.

Jackson reached down to his horse's mane and ran his fingers through a tangle of it. "I was the last to know."

"That sounds tough."

Jackson nodded. "They thought we could bond together at camp this week."

"Not working out, huh?"

"She hates me. Like it's my fault."

"It's possible you're both hurting."

Jackson glanced back. Chloe was back on her horse, tears in her eyes. He looked away, his eyes resting on his horse's ears.

Beth still stood next to Chloe and patted the girl's leg.

Chloe sniffed. "I'm sorry," she whispered. "I don't...hate you."

Jackson looked down.

"You stayed with her." Grayson nodded toward Chloe. Jackson should have been up with the other riders, but despite their button-pressing, his actions had shown his true nature.

He cared about his future stepsister.

Beth rubbed her hands together. "We're not counselors, but we can talk to your parents about working with you. Maybe finding someone."

Doubt creased Jackson's face.

"Think about it, okay?" Grayson said. "I've been in some hard places. It can help to talk it through."

Chloe and Jackson nodded.

"Truce?" Beth asked.

They both gave reluctant agreement.

"Let's get moving or we won't make it back in time," Grayson said.

Beth collected her reins and looked at him, her green eyes bright. "Can I...uh...get a leg up?"

Oh boy. "Sure."

Beth was going to be the end of him.

He stepped up beside her, and she bent her left leg up. He

cupped her knee in one hand, his other hand on her ankle, and tried to ignore the heat that lit his body at their touch.

Beth gave a bounce off her right leg, and he lifted her up by the bent left while she swung her right leg over and settled into place.

Yeah. This was the hard part. A guy could get used to having Beth around.

But that meant someone to worry about.

Nope. He preferred to keep everyone at a safe distance.

He walked back to Maverick and rubbed his velvety muzzle.

"Thanks for waiting, guys. Is everyone ready?" He swung up onto his horse and took his place at the front of the line. Beth gave him a nod, and he turned around and took them farther down the trail.

Ten minutes later, they reached the creek. It wasn't as high as he'd feared it might be.

He'd ridden through water on the ranch. That part didn't bother him. Mostly. It was the idea of taking the kids through.

The trail widened at the creek, and he rode out to the side. The other riders all rode up and joined in a group.

He checked his watch. "Well, we could head back now." He nodded toward the creek. "Or we can ride a bit farther past the creek."

"We can ride across the creek?" Sarah asked.

"Yes!" Ruby's eyes rounded.

"I'm okay either way," Mason said.

Aiden shrugged.

"I want to go."

Beth held up her hand. "We can take a vote. If there's anyone who doesn't want to go, though, we'll all be respectful and honor that wish, is that clear?"

Could he raise his own hand to decline?

A murmuring of affirmation responded.

"And that means no teasing—now or later." She gave the briefest pause when her glance bounced past Jackson and Chloe.

Okay, time to cowboy up. "Who wants to go?" he asked.

Every single hand rose.

Well, okay.

Beth wrinkled her nose and gave him a tentative smile.

"Single file again," he said.

He led Maverick through, the splash of hooves against rock sending droplets flying, cooling his warm skin.

Laughter caught his attention.

He turned and saw Mason's bay horse stopped, pawing in the water.

Oh no. "Ride him forward, Mason."

He imagined the horse going down for a roll. Trapping Mason beneath the water.

Mason laughed. "What's he doing?"

"Ride him forward! He's going to roll."

Beth was closer but blocked by four other horses.

The horse turned, pawed some more, and started to drop his hind end.

Grayson saw realization strike Mason at the same time. Panic gripped his features and he yelled, "No!" and nudged his horse just as Grayson splashed toward him on Maverick.

The bay startled and reorganized his legs, then launched out of the water like it was a Three-Day Event course obstacle.

Mason clung to the horn. "Whoa. Whoa!" The bay came to an abrupt stop on the near side of the creek and settled.

Just past them, Grayson could see Eli grinning. He'd blocked the trail on his little roan.

Beth brought up the last half of the crew and took in the scene. Blinked.

Grayson scrubbed his hands over his face. He was pretty sure if they needed an ambulance and a vet call, he and Beth might both be out of jobs.

"That was awesome!" Aiden shouted, loud enough that Grayson was certain it echoed across the lake.

Grayson shook his head. "Okay, we've had a lot of

excitement today. We need to get back to the barn—so, just a reminder: don't let your horse stop in the creek."

Mason gave him a shrug and a smile. "I stayed on."

While not the only goal in horseback riding, it was at the top of the list. "Good job."

Their afternoon crew had a much less eventful ride. Four hours later, after feeding the horses dinner and making sure all of them were settled, he hauled the hay cart back into the barn.

He stopped at the open door to Beth's office, where she sat at her desk, leaning over a stack of paperwork.

"What's up?"

"It's okay—you're busy."

"No, it's fine. I'm about done here. I'm trying to finalize one of the grant submissions, and I could use a break before my brain explodes."

"Want to help me rebandage Tally?"

"Sure." She followed him into the stall. "You did good today. I wasn't expecting all that drama."

Tally nuzzled Beth, her favorite human. All their handling was paying off. Tally wasn't tense anymore when they worked with her.

He nodded. "Thanks. I really felt for those kids. That's a tough family situation."

"I meant at the creek." She handed him a clean bandage. "The water. Actually, yeah—all of it."

He wanted to lean into her words. He was drawn to her just like the kids were. Just like Tally. That peaceful presence.

She embodied a safe harbor—her heart for others, whether human or animal. Always being the one who stood in the gap. The helper.

He finished the wrap, collected up the trash, and followed her out of the stall.

She scooped up her journal and backpack.

"Are those your plans for world domination?" he asked.

A pink blush crept up her cheeks. "No. Just notes I write.

Things I think of." She shrugged. "And my bucket list. Things I might someday do."

"Isn't a bucket list supposed to be the things you set out to do?"

She smiled. "It can be whatever I want it to be." She held it open. "Look at this."

Get back on a horse

Written in her precise and feminine script.

"Yeah—see that?" She pointed to the bold check mark next to it.

"I do see that." He scanned the unmarked items on her list.

See the ocean.
Fly somewhere beautiful.
Buy my own place.
Visit Yellowstone.

"I did that. I got back on a horse."

How many hours had he spent working alone? Thinking it was his preference.

His phone buzzed and he read Robin's message.

ROBIN

Cinnamon rolls need boxing for special order dinner party. No one else available. Made extra. Help?

He punched back a response.

GRAYSON

I'll be there in about sixty.

"Robin says she's got a few extra cinnamon rolls if she gets help boxing an order up for delivery." He wiped his hands off on a shop rag. "You game?"

She ran her fingers down the length of her ponytail, twisting the tips of it. "Umm...I haven't even eaten dinner."

He wanted her to say yes. Not that it should matter—because they were just friends. "Oh, come on. We can grab dinner on the way. They should be just coming out of the oven. Think about that." He should stop himself. Just let her go her own way home. Part ways. But with all the craziness of camp, he was longing for time together. Just the two of them. Like it had been last week.

He craved the time with her more than the cinnamon rolls.

She scrunched up her face. "She's packing up an order this late?"

He waved his phone. "Special order for a dinner party—but she said she'd baked extras."

"It's pretty hard to turn down her fresh cinnamon rolls."

And he couldn't help himself. "With sugar glaze and double-recipe gooey filling," he added, like he was hawking them at a Fish Pic booth.

"Okay, I'm convinced."

And oh, he just couldn't stop himself. "That trail check for winter damage—do you want to ride it with me tomorrow afternoon? See more of the lake and trails?"

Friends didn't ask friends' sisters on dates.

But this wasn't a date. Except, somehow it felt like it was when she smiled up at him and answered.

"Sure. That sounds like a lot of fun."

🐺🐺🐺

BETH HAD NO BUSINESS SITTING DOWN AT THE BAKERY WITH Grayson after hours. She teased open her cinnamon roll and tore off a bite. The sweet filling melted on her tongue. Okay, it wasn't a terrible idea. Not at all. "This was an excellent idea." She looked across the bakery's café table at Grayson. They'd both scarfed down their sandwiches on the drive over, but there was always room for dessert.

"I think so too," he answered, giving her a smile from across the table, something she couldn't read on his face. "We earned this." He took another bite.

Two weeks ago, Grayson and horseback riding hadn't been remotely on her radar.

Now? They'd become an integral part of her daily life. She'd do well to remember this was a temporary life.

Then she'd go back to her simple life. The camp would be lonely once he moved out. "I don't know how I stayed away from riding all these years." Apparently, all it took was for one capable, handsome cowboy to believe in her, give her a challenge, and encourage her to boost her confidence.

"Having a wreck can shake the confidence. You were young. Sometimes that makes it easier to bounce—when you have the right support."

She nodded. She'd fallen into the gap after her mom left. Now it was hard to imagine a day without Rex, Maverick, Remington, Lexi, and every other horse at that camp.

Or Tally. Maybe especially Tally.

"You're really good with the horses and the kids." His eyes held hers. "I wouldn't have made it through camp this week without you."

The compliment landed in her core, a glowing ball of light, filling her with the kinds of hopes and dreams she'd ignored since childhood. The ones that had included finding out she was more than just Dylan's little sister. More than Bookworm Bethy.

"I don't think you need me nearly as much as you thought." She took another bite of cinnamon roll and let the glaze pour over her taste buds.

"I do need you."

She stopped midbite. Met his eyes across the table.

She'd expected something mischievous, but instead, they held a vulnerability. This wasn't garden-variety, playful flirting. In the moment, he was unguarded and tender.

A girl could ride off into the sunset in that look.

"Are you two about done?" Robin called from the counter. "I've got to go pick up the delivery van from the garage. If you can start boxing all the rolls on the rack, I'd appreciate it."

Grayson nodded, his eyes pulling away from Beth's, the cord finally snapped between them. "Yeah. Sure," he said.

"Thanks. I've already locked the front door and turned the sign."

She had? Beth hadn't even noticed.

She ate her last bite, hoping Grayson couldn't see her hand shaking.

"I've been doing some brand searches for Maverick."

He tilted his head. "You have?"

She nodded. She hadn't had much time to put into it, but she'd saved several websites she'd been gleaning through. "I haven't found anything yet, but I'm going to keep looking."

"It's pretty curious, isn't it?" He shook his head. "Someone put a lot of time into that horse. It just doesn't make sense that he was at that camp, sold for hardly anything."

"Maybe his owner passed away?"

"Could be. Maybe the family didn't know what he's worth or know anything about horses." He stood and piled up their trash, threw it into the nearby can. "Would you ever race again?"

"Barrels?"

"Stock cars." His eyes creased with a smile. "Of course barrels."

"No." She waved him off. "Everyone keeps asking me that." She tapped her forehead with a fingertip. "I've got too much sense now."

"I don't know about that." He grinned, not an ounce of insult on his face. Was he *flirting* with her?

"Right, cowboy. We know how skilled you are with a horse."

She was caught between exploring the moment and knowing she needed to walk away from it. Protect her heart. Play it safe. "Let's see how you are with the family business." She stood, followed him into the kitchen, and they washed their hands.

She grabbed a pair of gloves while Grayson pulled a large baking sheet off the rack. Several pastry boxes had already been folded and set on the worktable.

He handed her an apron and slipped one over his own head.

She put her apron on and tied it. "Eli really likes you." She snagged a box. "I think Lexi's going to want to keep him. She follows him around like a puppy."

"That's because I always give him a treat to give her." The shy smile he gave her made her feel like a teenager again.

"That's your secret. You're a horse briber, not a horse whisperer."

He held out his hands. "I made no claim."

"Once you warmed up with the kids, though, you took over like John Wayne in *The Cowboys.*"

"You have not seen that."

"Vivien likes to torture me with classic movie nights."

"Of course."

"I do think Eli's finding camp a refuge from Marie's cancer." She grabbed one of the boxes and set it on the table in front of them. "Did you see his face after he blocked Mason's horse?"

"I didn't know if I should've yelled at him or high-fived him. Not the safest thing to do." Grayson plucked a rectangular cut of cinnamon rolls from the pan and placed them into the box Beth held open. "I do hope he finds healing."

She looked over at him. *I hope you find healing.*

And the sadness of it all poured over her like winter storm waves against the breakwater, the spray of memories and regrets soaking through her.

Grayson was made for the open range and the squeak of leather in a place where snow-capped mountains punctuated the horizon with grandeur and mystery.

"I know the camp meant a lot to you," Beth said. She picked up another box and held it open. "But why do you really want to open your own camp?"

He dropped a set of rolls inside the box. "I was one of the first horse-campers Trinity had."

She kept working, waiting on him, not sure if he'd say more.

Then— "It was after my parents died."

She knew about the boating accident, but mostly what she'd heard as she'd grown older. That, along with snippets of conversation between her dad and Dylan. She hadn't been allowed to attend the service, but she remembered seeing Grayson several days afterward. Right before he was sent away, along with his siblings, to live with an aunt.

She'd thought she might never see him again. And she'd cried. Grieved his loss. Grieved her own loss.

Then he was back to finish school. They were all back, living with their grandparents in the house a few miles out of town. And over time, some of the lightness that had always been Grayson returned. Some.

Not all. He had distanced himself more often. Then that kiss at the pit party.

He stared at the pan of rolls. "I've never been back out on the lake." His words were quiet and woven with regret. "I couldn't."

"I don't blame you."

He released a long breath. "But horses? The camp? That became my other home. Walter was the wrangler there, and I was his shadow. I couldn't get enough of the horses."

"I can see that." Beth grabbed several flattened boxes and began folding each one into form. Setting them aside.

"I want to give other kids that same kind of place to grieve, to cope, to belong and connect."

They worked in silence for several minutes. Her folding boxes, him filling. Her closing the lids.

She set a stack of full boxes onto a cart. "Horses set you off on a westward adventure."

Grayson plopped another block of rolls into a box. "Don't knock it until you've tried it."

She cut him a look. "I like it here."

He picked up a damp towel and wiped icing off the fingertips of his gloves. "I'm just saying—you could do it. Head out on your adventure. Tackle that bucket list."

"I can't leave my dad."

"You could always come back to visit—or even have this as home base."

She shook her head. "It's just not in the cards for me." If it had been, maybe she'd have left with Lyle. Gone on a trek to Texas.

But she wouldn't choose between her dad and her future. Couldn't.

No. She was meant for Deep Haven.

She loaded another stack of pastry boxes onto the cart. "Everything I ever need is here." She waved her hand, gesturing to the room in general.

He set the last baking pan onto the table. "Do you really believe that? There's nothing beyond Deep Haven for you?"

She couldn't answer him. Oh, she'd thought it to be true. Told herself that. Repeatedly, each time a dream began to well up in her, she'd tell herself that she wasn't like Mom. That Deep Haven was all she ever needed. And her kayak had been happily tethered to that dock.

Until Grayson had rolled back into town and started trampling her plans. Invited her on rides and to hang out in the bakery. Danced beneath the twinkly stars.

He's leaving.

Wasn't he? Or was he? Because as he stood there, wearing a Fox Bakery apron and a smile, he seemed right at home.

And that lit just a little hope in her heart that he could stay.

"Looks like that's all of them." He tucked the lid and added the last box to the stacks on the cart.

He stood close—impossibly close—and she could smell his woodsy aftershave. How could a man smell so good?

She dared to look up at him, met his green eyes. A little mix of fire and mischief sparked in them.

Her focus dropped to his lips. She'd first dreamed of kissing those lips twelve years ago.

Grayson reached out and tucked a lock of loose hair behind her ear. His eyes went to her lips.

Kiss me.

The back door flew open and Grayson jumped away like he'd been torched by a vat of hot glaze.

Robin jogged in. "Hey, are you two done? Sammy's going to help with—" She stopped, glanced from one to the other.

"Yep. All done."

Robin looked at Beth, a quirk in her brow.

"Oh yeah. All done here."

"Thank you, both," Robin said. She scooped up a stack of boxes and turned toward Grayson. "I know this was a stretch to fit into your busy schedules." The sarcasm was thicker than the glaze on her cinnamon rolls.

"Do you need help loading up?"

"No. You two can head out." She waved them off. "We've got this."

Grayson grabbed his keys and turned to Beth. "I can walk you out."

"Sure," she answered.

"Don't forget to put that trail ride on your calendar for tomorrow afternoon."

Like she could turn down the opportunity to saddle up, sans campers, and ride the unknown, uncharted trails with Grayson?

She nodded. "Of course."

Okay, so they weren't exactly unknown or uncharted, because he did have a map of them—but no one else had been on them in a year. That kind of made them unknown and uncharted in her book.

Kind of like whatever this was with Grayson.

She should run, fast, in the opposite direction.

His eyes stayed on her, soft, focused as he listened and, shoot. It made her feel a little unstoppable. Made her crave the raw edge of adventure.

And when his eyes paused on her lips for a moment, then met her own upward glance, it made her want to draw him into a kiss far more now than when she'd had a teenage crush.

But she played it safe. And kissing Grayson was anything but safe for her heart.

eleven

. . .

ONLY ONE WEEK IN AND THE RHYTHM OF CAMP COULD SETTLE INTO Grayson's bones, lulling him. Luring him. Making him forget that he had a life and a plan far beyond the spruce forests and lakeshore lookouts of Trinity Horse Camp. And of Deep Haven.

It felt a little indulgent to spend his Saturday alone with Beth at the camp, riding the trails. It was work, though.

Yep. Work. They had trails to check.

He could ride with Beth every day, even if it meant plopping green kids on the backs of babysitters.

Or the ordinary activity of eating cinnamon rolls with Beth and working in the bakery. Sharing glimpses of who they were behind the images the rest of the world saw of them.

And he'd almost kissed her.

I can't leave my dad.

He'd known that, right? It hadn't been a surprise. And yet it had left him with this vast expanse of sadness that had dogged him the rest of the evening.

The passing thought of his vacant lot gave him pause. No, that was crazy. He was in the middle of buying his own ranch in Oregon.

But he had missed several of Nathan's calls and hadn't had it in him to return any of them.

He urged Maverick into a lope down the arena panels, the wind lifting his spirits, letting his soul soar. They rounded the short end and galloped down the far side. The horse's body reached full extension with each stride, the power propelling them forward as one.

Every day, they'd had their two crews of kids, eager for their two-hour ride through the forests in the morning and afternoon. And between him and Beth, all of them had managed to go home safely at the end of the day.

Maybe just barely the day before, but they'd done it.

He slowed Maverick when he saw Beth leading Rex from the hitching post. He hadn't expected her to say yes when he'd invited her to check the trails, but then, maybe he hadn't misread that look on her face in the bakery. When he'd been nearly certain she'd wanted him to kiss her.

She wore a blue T-shirt with her jeans and had her hair hanging loose under her hat.

Like she belonged there. Like it was still natural for her to be leading a horse.

He relaxed in the saddle, drawing in Maverick's pace to a stop near the gate. He let the horse stretch his neck out, long and low. Mav blew out a contented breath. "Ready?"

Beth tilted her head. "It's funny—I love it. I don't know why, but it still gives me butterflies."

She gave him butterflies. Or something. Whatever that unfamiliar rush of adrenaline was called that swirled in his chest.

He leaned down and swung the gate open before side-passing Mav and closing the gate. "And yet you can't help yourself."

She looked up at him and grinned. "It seems so." She rubbed Rex's neck. "This feels really good." She led her horse to a mounting block that sat outside the arena panels and hopped on. All by herself. Like she'd never been away from it.

Okay, he was maybe a little proud at the confidence she'd been building.

"I brought you this." She held out a canteen to him. "I made us sweet tea."

He took the offered drink and snugged it into his saddlebag. "Thank you."

She rode ahead of him on Rex, her hair down her back and her body relaxed. It had been a little selfish of him to invite her along to explore several trails they hadn't yet used. But if students like Eli were going to come again and again, he needed more options to keep things interesting.

Sure, he could have checked the trails by himself, but he'd done enough solo riding in his lifetime.

And it didn't cross the line into anything that might be called a date. Nope. This was work. Didn't raise anyone's radar.

He hoped.

Because he craved her company after she left camp each day—her laughter, the lightness her presence enveloped him in.

Like at his grandparents' party. In the bakery. Had she felt that moment between them? The one that'd arced until Robin had interrupted.

Sunlight cast dapples of light and dark through the forest canopy, and he found himself a little mesmerized at the way golden strands wove through Beth's hair, her locks variegated with sunny highlights.

The trail widened and Maverick and Rex fell into step next to each other, their hooves landing with heavy thuds on the thick duff of the trail.

"I took a picture of Mav's brand," Beth said. "I'm so curious where he came from."

"Did you find anything?"

"No, not yet." She grinned. "I had to put that project aside. Too many other things I'm trying to stay on top of." She pointed to native wildflowers growing along the forest floor and listed names as they passed. Forget-me-nots, butterwort, trillium. Even something called Dutchman's-breeches, which did look like pairs of miniature pants. He'd caught glimpses of her doing this all week with the kids.

"How did you get to know so much about them?" he asked when she pointed out a barely visible starflower.

He would have ridden right past it without a glance.

She shrugged. "Reading. Kayak camp—we take the kids across the lake, then hike around for a couple hours. Explore and identify the flora and fauna. I guess it all stuck." She gave him a bashful smile. "There are a ton of trails around this lake—even a few cabins on the far side."

She pulled her canteen from his saddlebag and took a drink, prompting him to do the same.

He hadn't had sweet tea in a long time. "That's good stuff."

"Maybe I'll share my secret recipe sometime." She wiped her arm across her damp lips and stowed the canteen.

The trail narrowed and he let Rex take the lead to keep long-strided Mav's pace in check. Possibly for Beth's benefit. Probably to prolong the afternoon.

Rex shook his head. Tossed it up and down. Sidestepped into the brush along the trail. Beth flapped her arms at something, swatting with her right hand.

Then Grayson saw them. Wasps or hornets. Dark bodies swarming. "Ride out of them!"

Beth was too busy flailing at the insects to hear him. And by the looks of Rex's prancing feet, swishing tail, and head tossing, he was taking the brunt of the attack.

"Ride forward!" Maverick stomped, his body coiling. "Easy, Mav."

Rex kicked out behind before lunging forward.

Beth yelped, her body jerked forward and sideways with the sudden movement. She grabbed the horn. But instead of moving forward, out of the swarm, she was clutching the reins, holding Rex back. He tossed his head back and forth, then crow-hopped, his back arched and his whole body bouncing with stiff-legged jumps.

Beth slid farther to the side.

"Ride out of them!" Grayson ordered again.

Rex was a camp horse through and through, but even he had his limits. He let out a grunt, a squeal, and finally bolted through the swarm. Beth's scream cut through the trees.

It sent a cold chill through his bones.

"Beth!" The wind ripped her name from his lips.

He'd run down loose livestock plenty of times, but it was different having Beth on Rex's back. Knowing she might come off in front of them. Be trampled.

He urged Mav in pursuit. They flew through the buzzing cloud, too much adrenaline pumping for Grayson to notice if he'd been stung.

Beth's boot had come out of her left stirrup, and her body was hunched forward and to the right. Her knuckles were white, her left hand gripped tight around the horn. But she was sliding.

Grayson moved Maverick to the left side, the scrape of branches slapping his face.

Beth was trying to pull herself upright, back into the saddle, but couldn't do more than hang on.

Beth would not die on his watch. He'd get her off that horse and send her home.

No more rides. No more camp.

Done.

He wouldn't be responsible for someone else getting hurt.

Before the next curve in the trail, Rex dropped to a hard trot. Grayson leaned down, grabbed the loose rein. "Whoa, buddy." Rex slowed to a jog. "Whoa," Grayson repeated. The horse's feet slowed again, this time to a walk, then stopped.

Grayson slid from Maverick and ran to Beth's side. He tried to pry her from Rex, where she clung, half in, half out of the saddle. "I've got you. You can let go now." She was small enough—he plucked her off the horse and carried her to a nearby patch of moss along the trail. She could probably hear his heart racing, and he wasn't entirely sure he trusted his voice. He set her down, holding on so she wouldn't lose her footing.

One look at her and his decision was made.

A white pallor blanched her face, and she wicked several tears away with her sleeve.

"Hey, it's okay." He held her face in his hands. "You're okay."

He had one week of camp behind him, and he could handle the rest of the weeks by himself. They'd stick to the regular trail and he'd ride ahead—like he should have done this time so he could have warned Beth. Could have taken the brunt of it with Maverick.

Protected her.

"Were you stung? Are you allergic?" He inspected each area of bare skin on her face, neck, arms, hands.

"A few stings. I'm not allergic." She rubbed her arm.

He spotted two welts, the stingers still pulsing. He flicked each one out.

"Just in pain. I think I hit the saddle horn too." She touched her hand to her abdomen.

Probably not okay for him to take a look at that. "It might hurt more tomorrow. Can you breathe fine?"

She nodded, blinking back unshed tears.

And it nearly unraveled him.

He drew her to himself, letting the physical presence of her body, safe against his own, calm his own nerves. She wrapped her arms around him, and they stood there, soaking in the relief.

She looked up at him, her eyes bright and green and liquid. Facing each other, like when they'd danced under the canopy of stars last weekend. Like when they'd stood in the bakery.

Heat flamed inside. Oh, how he wanted to kiss her—even more than yesterday.

Maybe it was because his emotions were running high, but he succumbed to the desire. Dipped his face, paused.

Waited for her to lean into it, and then he kissed her—urgent and afraid and relieved, all at once. She tasted of the sweet tea, and he couldn't drink in enough. Her body molded into his when he drew her close, a little sound escaping her throat.

Then he remembered who he was. Who she was.

And Dylan's words of warning etched in his brain for all time.

He loosened his hold. "I—I—" He couldn't form a coherent word. He resisted the urge to push her away.

And then you rejected me.

He wouldn't hurt her like that again. He was a grown man, not an impulsive high schooler—though, maybe he'd been a little impulsive with this kiss too. He swallowed. Everything in him wanted to draw her close. Feel that she was safe.

Rex shoved his head in between them as if to remind them he required attention too. He pressed his big old head against Beth and gave her a little shove against her armpit, causing her to step sideways to catch her balance.

Grayson reached out to steady her, and Rex gave another nudge.

Beth laughed. "Stop—that tickles—oh, ouch, that kind of hurts."

Grayson reached for Rex.

"Okay, wild man." He skimmed his eyes and hands along Rex's body, looking for welts and stingers.

"I don't like saddle horns anymore. They're a very, very bad idea." Beth rubbed her abdomen. "Is he okay?"

"He's got a few on his flanks and belly. Poor guy." He pulled his notebook from the saddlebag and used the firm cover flap to flick the remaining stingers out. Grayson ran his hands down the horse's legs. "Yeah." He rubbed Rex's forehead. "You're a good boy."

The horse stretched his neck down and snatched up a mouthful of grass, the ordeal behind him.

"Well, he's all better now," Beth said, like she was trying to infuse her voice with cheer she didn't feel. She tentatively touched her scalp near the base of her braid. "Ah!" She flinched. "I think there's one more."

"Stinger?"

She let out a groan. "Yeah, maybe."

"Let me see."

She turned around and dipped her chin. "Right in here." Her fingers hovered over a spot.

It didn't take much searching. "Hold still." He lifted the notebook and flicked the stinger out.

"Ahh!"

"Sorry." He checked over her scalp, neck, and arms again. "It looks like that's it."

She wrapped her hand around to her upper back. "My lats are going to be so sore tomorrow."

And he couldn't help it. He drew her back to himself, held on. Because every time he closed his eyes, he could see her coming loose off Rex. Could imagine a terrible fall. Her head hitting a tree or the ground.

It was like watching the storm rip his mom from the boat. Knowing the waves were sweeping her away. Out of sight.

And his dad too. That helpless feeling, being sent below deck. Knowing something awful was happening. Being helpless to stop it.

🐺🐺🐺

BETH'S LEGS MIGHT HAVE TURNED TO JELL-O IF GRAYSON HADN'T lifted her from Rex and pulled her to himself. Carried her and set her down on the ground, his fingers, both work-worn and tender, skimming across her skin. The strength of his arms almost distracted her from her adrenaline-flooded nervous system.

Almost.

She'd maybe stick to feeding, grooming, and saddling the horses. Shoveling manure. Grants, schedules, and greetings.

Anything but get on a horse again.

Because her life had just flashed before her eyes, the very real, clear acknowledgment when the tree stumps and thundering hooves blasted by her head.

This is how I'm going to die.

So nope. She'd just stay in the cocoon of Grayson's laundry soap layered with the warm scent of his body.

A girl could almost forget she'd nearly died. Forget the way he'd called out her name.

How his heartbeat had skittered against her ear, the air swept from his own lungs.

But what she couldn't forget?

Oh, that kiss—like every detail of the last ten minutes had ruptured between them in a flood of emotion.

And if she hadn't had Jell-O-y legs before, she sure had them now.

The kiss had been passionate and intense, foreign and familiar. The touch of his lips on hers had sent her brain and heart on another wild gallop, this one, exhilarating and exciting. Grayson Fox, the man who'd rejected her, had pulled her in and kissed her like she was the very breath of his body.

If only he'd finished what he'd been going to say before Rex interrupted and stole the moment away.

"My head is going to swell up to the size of a watermelon," she said. She flicked her fingertips over the spot where he'd removed the stinger.

"I thought you said you weren't allergic."

"That was before my head started throbbing." She grunted. "I'm kidding. Mostly. Does my face look weird?"

He stared at her. "No. You look..." He ran his fingers through her hair, straightening a tangle. But it sent shivers up and down her body.

Beth had greatly underestimated the power of Grayson's

touch. The tenderness of his calloused hands and the husky intimacy of his voice.

How much she wanted to feel his lips on hers again.

*You look...*what? Awful, terrible? Okay? Fine?... Amazing? *Finish the sentence.*

His eyes met hers, held them. Caused her breath to catch because for a moment, she thought he might kiss her again, and she was totally and completely more than okay with that.

Then he blinked, looked away. Paced as if he were wrestling some inner demon, then cleared his throat. Seemed to collect himself.

He rubbed his cheek. A red welt, probably from the slap of a branch, arced across it. "Do I have a tattoo now?"

"It makes you look tough." She tried to give him a smile and pretend they weren't dancing around the fact that they'd just kissed and neither one of them seemed to know what to do about it.

"Oh, good. I was going for that." His eyes stayed on her, a longing in them, maybe uncertainty. "Here." He handed her Mav's reins and ran his hand down Rex's neck, then checked his legs again. "He's good." He loosened Rex's cinch, straightened the saddle back to center, and restrung the latigo knot.

He led him forward, walked him back, then drew up the reins. With one sweep of his leg, he hopped up on Rex, then nudged the horse forward. He rode him up the trail to the next bend, turned around, and rode back, speaking to him in some sort of cowboy coo the entire time.

Which was kind of adorable to her frazzled brain.

He hopped to the ground and pulled out the map from his back pocket. "We can connect to the other trail loop up ahead so we don't have to go past the ground hive again." He grabbed a pen from his saddlebag, placed the map against the saddle, then scribbled a note with an X marking the hive location and slid the map and pen into the saddlebag.

She rubbed her abdomen again where the horn had

practically impaled her. "How long do you think it will take for us to walk back?"

"Beth…" A tight set locked Grayson's jaw. He pulled off his hat and scrubbed his hand back and forth over his hair, then rubbed Rex's neck and looked at her, a little reluctant and lot wrecked. "You should do it."

The full force of it hit her. He'd watched her near wreck unfold in front of his eyes. She'd felt the wild beating of his heart. She'd felt the need in his kiss.

He'd been shaken and he felt responsible.

Get back on a horse.

Her stomach hardened and her heart rate accelerated. "I can't."

Get back on a horse.

"You can. I know it's hard." His eyes were bright with unshed tears. "But you didn't do it the last time." He gave her hand a little squeeze. "I'll be with you. Right next to you."

She shook her head. Nope. No way.

"You have to." He rubbed her fingers with his thumb.

"Do I?"

He closed his eyes, nodded, and then refocused on her. "And not for anyone else. Not for the job. Not for Eli. Not…for me. You need to get back on that horse for you." He looked down at her, his eyes deep, pure green. "I don't want you to go another twenty years, or whatever ridiculous amount it's been, not riding."

He was right. She knew he was right. Why, oh why did it have to be so stinking hard?

Do not be afraid.

She squeezed his hand and then released it so she could pet Rex. A thought bobbed in the back of her mind.

Ask.

She let out a breath. "If I get back on, will you do something for me?"

"I'm not going to steal cinnamon rolls from the bakery for

you." He winked and ran Maverick's reins through his fingers.

"You want me to face this fear." She shook out the nerves. "Let me take you kayaking this afternoon. On Lake Superior."

His hands stilled and he swallowed. "Not what I was expecting."

No. No, no, and no. The weight of her request pummeled her. What was she thinking?

She held up a hand. "I'm sorry. You don't have to do that. I shouldn't have asked that."

He seemed to process her request for a few moments, his green eyes on hers. His Adam's apple bobbed. "I want to." He reached out again and took her hand. "Yes."

She swallowed. "You don't have to do that. I'll get on Rex anyway."

Man, he was handsome. He stood there, strong and vulnerable all at the same time. "If there's one person I trust to take me out on that lake, it's you."

Oh.

It wasn't an *I love you* or a commitment to stay in Deep Haven, but, wow. Okay.

Now she felt sick. Because not only did she have to get on the horse; she'd committed to taking him out on the lake—which was no big deal to her. But to him?

It would be confronting the worst day of his life.

She looked at Rex. She didn't really want to get back on. But if he was willing to face the lake, she could get on Rex.

"You ride beside me."

She didn't miss the gloss in his eyes. The way he drew his arm across his face as if to wipe sweat off his brow. Except it was his eyes he brushed across.

Buckle up, Buttercup. You asked for it.

Yeah. She'd get on the horse. She'd prove to Grayson that she was, in fact, perfectly and completely fine and he had nothing to blame himself for.

Despite her being not at all fine.

Grayson placed a flat palm on Rex's neck. Bowed his head, making the slightest movement of his lips.

Was he praying too?

Please, Lord.

Surely, between the two of them, God would hear their prayers.

She imagined the inner actress Vivien had instructed her to be. Get on the horse. Ride back to the barn. Smile. Just like any other day.

Don't think about dying. Or hanging off the side of a horse. Or how much her bruised abdomen throbbed with every breath.

"Ready?" Grayson bent down, held out his hand for her knee.

Oh dear.

I can do this.

Grayson had prayed for her. Well, maybe.

Was that presumptuous? Just the thought of it gave her a little boost of courage.

With God all things are possible.

She nodded, held her breath, and bent her leg so he could cup her knee. Let him lift her while she swung her other leg over the cantle.

She settled in, slipped her boots into the stirrups, then drew up the reins.

They caught on Grayson's hands before she could make contact with the bit. He was holding Rex and rubbed the horse's neck again before releasing the reins.

"Right by me," he instructed again before remounting Maverick.

She wanted to tease him with a "yes, sir," but she couldn't. Not when he tried to cover the wrecked expression on his face and nudged Mav forward, alongside Rex.

And the impact of those little details barreled through her. Nothing would be the same between them—and she wasn't sure if that was a good thing or bad.

twelve

· · ·

GRAYSON HAD MADE A GROSS TACTICAL ERROR. SAYING YES TO Beth's request to go out on Lake Superior just to get her back on Rex had made sense at the time. Trading one hard thing for another.

What had he been thinking? He hadn't been. After that kiss he'd have said anything. He'd completely lost his mind.

He waited on the shore near Wild Harbor. The Saturday afternoon weighed heavy on him, yet the lake reflected a clear, cloudless sky.

If he did this—if he conquered the lake—then what? He couldn't actually stay in Deep Haven, could he?

He was buying his own place in Oregon. Starting a camp, by himself. Because he wouldn't have a partner in Oregon.

Okay, he was overthinking. He could hire someone.

Of course he could.

But he wouldn't have Beth.

He blew out a breath. He was getting in far too deep, and that scared him more than the lake he faced.

"Look at you, dressed like a civilian." Beth walked up wearing shorts and a dark-green T-shirt. The cut of both highlighted her athletic figure.

His heart skittered at the memory of kissing her. The way she'd responded.

If only Rex hadn't interrupted them, because, well—what did they say now?

She pointed to his athletic shorts and shoes, and her fingers played with the end of her braid. "I'm so impressed. I didn't know you still owned anything that wasn't straight out of *Western Horseman*." She kept her words light, but he'd been around her enough to know nerves made her twirl her braid.

"I think I already stick out enough in Deep Haven—I don't need to be dubbed the kayaking cowboy."

She laughed. "Good point. Welcome to my world." She fanned her hands out at the kayaks as if revealing a prize up for grabs.

"Great," he said. It came out pinched and lackluster.

She stopped, wrung her hands in the hem of her T-shirt. "You don't have to do this."

"It's fine." He mustered the words, giving her his best rodeo game face. "I need to do this."

Beth reached out and gave his hand a squeeze, then nodded.

For every part of him that thought he needed to do this, there was some serious internal opposition. Still, he couldn't turn back. After all, Beth had gotten back on Rex.

He followed her to the beach, to the two kayaks waiting. Every step closer to the water caused a constriction in his throat like a dallied lariat on the saddle horn.

Nope. This would not be good for either one of them.

His breath hitched, his stomach sinking like his life had in the lake.

She shook out her hands and grabbed paddles that were leaning nearby.

He stopped at the water's edge. He'd ridden horses through water crossings. He'd even drifted on languid stretches of the Deschutes River in Oregon. But this? No, not this. Because this was Lake Superior. This was the unforgiving, icy grave that had stolen his parents from him.

He ran his hand across the constriction in his throat.

"You sure you're okay?"

"Sure." Even though his pulse thrummed in his ears.

She dropped the paddles. "You're a terrible liar." Her green eyes studied him.

Fine. "It's harder than I expected…" With her, he knew he didn't have to finish.

"I'm sorry." She placed her hand on his arm. Her soft fingertips electrified every cell in his body. "We don't have to go," she finished, her voice gentle, a sweet caress filled with care.

The power in her tiny frame emboldened him. This was the girl who had overcome her own fear. Who'd gotten back on when she'd nearly had another catastrophic fall.

The look in her eyes caused a raw kind of courage to take root in him. She had true courage. The kind that was afraid—but did it anyway.

"Yeah. I think we do." He glanced out over the lake. A clear blue sky. The waters flat and blue. "Today's the day."

She handed him a life jacket. "If you change your mind, there's no shame in that."

"Do you tell all your students that?" He buckled the life jacket, wiped away the sweat of his hands on his shorts.

"Seriously—it wasn't fair to ask this of you."

"Oh, so you want an out for yourself as much as me." He tried to jest. Tried to put from his mind the depth of the water. "You afraid I'll be more than you can handle?"

"Possibly? Probably." She grimaced. "I wasn't thinking when I asked you to do this—I was just so caught up in overcoming my fear I guess…I just wanted that for you too."

Shoot. He didn't want her to feel bad. And seriously, how bad could it be after all these years?

He'd said it in the forest, and he still knew it was true. He trusted her. If he was ever going to get out on the lake, it'd be with her.

He took her hand and gave it a squeeze. "Let's go."

"It's pretty smooth today, but if it gets choppy at all, follow my lead. Turn perpendicular to the waves so you won't tip. And balancing is a bit like riding a bike." She winked. "It comes back to you."

They pulled the kayaks out into the water. Even in summer, the water hit with a sharp, brisk sting. He hopped in, grateful to feel the heat of the sun on his skin.

He could do this. He focused on Beth's form, let his paddle dig into the water. Found the rhythm of the stroke. Water flicked off the paddles, catching the sunlight.

He focused on the driving paddle. On the dampness of his seat. On the sun warming his skin.

She paddled out into an arc, turning back toward shore before slowing, waiting for him to catch up.

"You're a natural," she said. "I should have signed us up for one of the races."

He wasn't prepared to see the shoreline quite so far away. Cold prickles rose across his body.

He could practically feel the rain slamming their family boat. Lost. Alone. Waiting for a rescue.

"Grayson?"

"I'll be...okay." He hoped.

Maybe not.

Beth's kayak clunked against his own. She set her paddle across her lap and ran her hand down his arm. Found his fingers. Squeezed.

"We'll head back in." Her other hand adjusted her paddle.

He drew in a breath and held up a hand for her to wait. Just let the warmth of her small hand soak into him, soothing the turbulent vortex within. "They argued over whether we should or shouldn't go." He lifted his eyes to the horizon.

The kayaks bobbed.

Beth's hand held firm.

He shook his head. "I don't know why it was so important to me that day." He let out a sharp laugh that held no humor. "Why? Why did I have to beg them to go?"

He turned to her and she blinked away the glassiness in her eyes.

"You were a kid," she said. "You wanted to have time with your family. That's a good thing."

He lifted his shoulder. "It had started out just fine—cruising, fishing, laughing. But that storm blew in." He stopped.

Even without a cloud in sight, the panic of that day lodged in his throat.

And they bobbed there, rocking. Silent except for the laps of water against the plastic hulls.

And maybe here, on the water, above the depths that had taken the lives of the two people he'd held most dear, maybe this was the place to finally let it all go.

He drew in a shaky breath.

"I told you how I blamed myself for my parents' deaths."

She nodded.

"There's more to it." He paused, trying to compose himself. To finish the story. To tell her the worst of it. "I blamed God." He faced her, all the grief swelling around him. "Deep down, I still do." He swallowed. "When it came down to it, God didn't answer my prayer. He didn't protect those I loved."

He blinked against the unshed tears. "I was left alone with my own shame."

He could still hear the wind raging against the boat. See the lightning. The rain. He shivered, despite the sunshine on his bare arms.

"You've been carrying this burden too long." Beth drew her thumb across his hand.

He nodded and shook away the grief that swept over him. "It was my fault. All my fault."

"You couldn't have known."

"I pressured them."

"I see parents and kids all the time," Beth offered. "Yes, kids of all ages throw tantrums. It happens. Totally normal as they process their own desires and wants, explore independence." She squeezed his hand again. "Here's the thing, though—parents are parents. They are the adults, and they make choices all the time about how they will handle each situation that arises."

She tapped her other hand on the paddle. "If your parents chose to take you on the lake that day, it was one hundred percent their choice. As persuasive as you might think your tantrum was—and trust me, I've seen some very persuasive tantrums in all my work with kids—the adults made the decision. You aren't to blame."

He wanted to believe her. Yeah, okay, if he was being objective, he'd seen that with kids.

Still, the regret clung to him. A little lighter, though. A little less intrusive.

Because every time he'd walked into the bakery, stood by the lake, or celebrated a holiday in Deep Haven, the vacancy of his parents had been too near. "It became too hard to have close relationships."

"And then...Harper."

He dropped his head. Stared at the paddle. "Exactly."

"Vivien and Courtney keep telling me God goes before me—it's from Deuteronomy. That God will not leave me or forsake me."

"Some friends they are—throwing Scripture at you like that." He gave a wry smile.

"Right? How dare they?" She worked her fingers against her other palm, as if kneading her thoughts. "Deep in my heart, I believe it. But out here"—she gestured to the world around them—"it's scary."

He nodded. "I want to be a better man. I want to be the man who believes God didn't—and won't—leave me. But He didn't save them." He dipped his fingers into the icy water. Watched the sunlight sparkle on it. "It's hard to reconcile that with a loving God."

"Hard to trust being close to people…that you won't lose them. That they won't leave."

He nodded. Yeah, she got it. And knowing that made his world feel a little less lonely. "I didn't know all this came with the lesson." He tried to make light of it and flicked the water drops from his fingertips.

"You're getting the extended version." She rubbed her fingers on her paddle. "So, what are your great plans for being a better man?" she asked.

"Ah. Well, I'd like to be a man who is sacrificial. Unselfish. Who puts others first. Who trusts God, even when it's hard."

"Good goals. I think we have to choose who we are every day, with every decision we make. That's what makes you who you are. Each next decision."

"Says the girl who struggles with chasing her own dreams."

"Hey now," she said, but she had a smile in her eyes. "I give great advice. I don't necessarily follow it." She winked, lifted his hand in her own, and wrapped it with her other hand. She drew it to her heart. "I don't know why your parents died that day, but it wasn't your fault. Or God's." Her words drifted out over the water.

Hope. An irresistible, undeniable hope swirled in his soul, spilling over. Rising above the grief. Above the darkness that had fed his childhood nightmares.

He squeezed her hand. "Thank you."

"Of course." A soft smile swept across her face. "Ready to head back?"

"Yeah." He hadn't made friends with the lake, but the dark water had released him from its stranglehold.

By the time they pulled the kayaks onto the shore, the sun was sinking in the western sky.

He turned to Beth after stowing the paddles. "Thanks again."

"You're welcome." She threw her arms around him in a triumphant squeeze, then released him just as quickly. Her eyes were bright, and joy curved the corners of her lips.

Those lips... He stared at them, a spark igniting in his core. He didn't know how much longer he could avoid his feelings.

He wanted to kiss her again. Wanted to take her in his arms and loosen her braid. Run his fingers through her soft hair, let his touch skim across her neck, and kiss her without interruption.

It turned his entire body molten.

She smiled, the kind of gentle, sweet smile that stirred his soul like the first rays of sunlight breaking through storm clouds. The kind that lifted his spirit. Made him feel whole again.

"There's a staff campfire tonight." She scooped up her towel. "I can help you at the barn first."

In that moment, he wanted to be anywhere she'd be. "I'll pick you up."

He caught sight of Dylan exiting Wild Harbor and walking toward them. Grayson took a step back.

Don't hurt her. She's had enough people bail on her.

He couldn't turn back the invitation.

Not that he wanted to. But he should. Should pack up and tell Beth she'd have to find someone else to be her head wrangler. Because he was the guy leaving town.

Right? Buying Vincent and Rose's place. Horses. Kids. Camp.

Except, Deep Haven already had a horse camp in operation— and he'd have a few years before he'd be up and running. He'd have to build a reliable string of horses. That wasn't going to happen overnight.

He rubbed his hand across his face.

"Sure. I'll see you tonight," she said. And the way the breeze lifted her hair and the excitement of their adventure lit her eyes, he couldn't help but imagine the crazy possibility of staying in Deep Haven.

BETH STARED INTO THE FLAMES OF THE CAMP'S FIREPIT, SHIVERED, and shook away the sense that Grayson had bailed on her.

"Do you want another marshmallow?" Noah held out the bag to her.

Beth shook her head. "Not yet, thanks."

"I'll take another chocolate bar," someone to Beth's left said.

One of the camp counselors pulled one from the supply box and it was passed around.

Still no Grayson.

No, she hadn't needed him to pick her up. But when he'd called to say he'd have to meet her later—at the campfire instead of picking her up—she hadn't realized he meant much later.

She yawned.

The fire popped and the embers lifted into the dark night, then faded.

She'd been certain when they came in from the lake that he'd kiss her again. She'd been so excited for him—the way he'd pushed through his fears and shared the moment with her. She'd practically thrown herself into his arms. He'd been wearing the face of a man who'd just ridden out of the storm.

And she hadn't missed the way his glance had skipped to her lips.

Then Dylan had shown up, prompting yet another brush-off.

Yep. She was falling for Grayson. Leaning into his laughter, the resonance of his voice, and the warmth of his body. And the fact that he'd confided in her and entrusted her with the pain he carried… She didn't have words.

She looked at her watch and yawned. Everyone—including herself—would be calling it a night soon. She tried not to sink into the swirl of disappointment.

She knew he'd have a good reason. He just hadn't shared it when he'd given her a brief call and told her to go without him.

"How are the plans for family camp going, Beth?" Anne, Noah's wife, sat on the wood bench across the firepit, in the crook of her husband's arm.

"Good, um, yeah. Good. We've got four or five families signed up for the first week—which falls over the Fourth of July."

"Excellent." Noah nodded. "That's really good news."

Several of the camp volunteers and counselors from Wilderness Challenge filled the spaces around the fire. Beth recognized most of them, even if she didn't know all their names.

Anne looked down the trail. "I thought Grayson would be done with the real estate agent by now."

The words slammed Beth like she'd been dumped from Rex. He was with Nathan?

Noah leaned forward and took the stick from Anne. "Kind of late for that, isn't it?"

"Not for here—for Oregon. Pacific time zone. He said it was a call about that ranch he's buying."

Right. Because he was leaving.

Beth swallowed and took a marshmallow offered by the blonde next to her.

"Thanks."

"Is it nosy to ask what's going on with your dad and Janet?" Anne asked.

Dad and Janet? Had she missed something? "I don't know— what do you know?"

Noah waved them off. "Anne's just playing matchmaker. Don't worry about it."

"That seems to be a common theme around town," Beth answered. She'd only moved out to camp a week and a half ago.

"I've just seen them together a few times. At church and around town."

Oh. Interesting. "They are old friends." Maybe Dad wasn't as lonely as she'd imagined.

Anne smiled, nodded, a little glimmer of knowing in her eyes.

Huh. Beth wanted to feel excited for Dad. She should be happy—it'd been her idea that he go on the Rhine cruise. So what was this little sting she was feeling?

Why hadn't he told her?

The girl who'd offered her the marshmallow stood and wiped her hands on her jeans. "Okay, that's enough sugar for me."

Several others added their agreement and proceeded to collect the extra marshmallow sticks into a stack, setting them into the empty coffee can Noah kept near the far bench.

She turned away from the conversation and laughter that rose with the smoke into the darkness of the inky black sky swathed with the sparkly bands of the Milky Way.

"We were wondering if you'd make it," Noah said to someone. "We were all starting to wrap things up."

Beth's head snapped around. Grayson stood across the firepit, his face unreadable.

He'd changed back into jeans and wore a dark-blue flannel over his T-shirt. The man was impossibly handsome, like straight out of an epic romance.

"Sorry, I had a call," he said. He looked straight at her. "Am I too late?"

"It's getting late for us," Anne said. She passed the bag of marshmallows, chocolate bars, and grahams to Beth. "But you're welcome to stay."

"What about you guys?" Noah stood and passed his marshmallow stick to Grayson.

"I need some sleep." A dark-haired woman stood.

"Me too." Another Wilderness Challenge counselor grabbed her sweatshirt from the bench.

The fire crackled as the group finished collecting their belongings.

Beth did a quick count—everyone but her and Grayson was leaving.

And she wasn't sure what to say to the man who might be taking her heart. Or maybe breaking her heart. What was that call to Oregon about?

"We'll put out the fire," Grayson said. He'd apparently made the same assessment. And wasn't ready to leave. He sat down on the bench next to her.

"Good night," Noah said. "There's a bucket of water over by the shrubs."

A chorus of *good night*s followed, and the group disappeared to cars and cabins.

The quiet settled over them, a heavy blanket of her own uncertainty.

"You really know how to clear a party." Beth tried to squelch the questions brewing in her mind.

Did she ask him and risk their entire evening?

She added a marshmallow to her stick.

Grayson laughed and speared several of his own marshmallows. Set them above the flames next to hers.

He smelled soapy and masculine, and it made Beth's nerves buzz.

The longer Beth listened, the more she heard. Crickets. An owl. A few thousand frogs.

She watched the telltale flickers bouncing around the tall grass near the tree line. Pointed. "Fireflies."

"They always remind me of childhood," Grayson said.

"All those dusk games of tag and hide-and-seek?"

"Yeah."

"Me too. There's just something so…whimsical about them."

"Whimsical? About a bug whose butt lights up?"

She laughed. "Don't make fun."

"I'm just teasing." He rotated his marshmallows. "You love Deep Haven."

"Of course I do," she said.

"Sometimes it seems like you have all these dreams, but you keep them to yourself."

"They're just that—dreams."

"But the camp? Is it one of your dreams?"

"I love the camp—more than I ever dreamed I would." The thought lifted her soul. She let her gaze sweep across his features, the firelight accentuating his strong jawline. "I like the horses too. It is one of my dreams."

"The horses are hard not to like." He used his free hand to snap apart his graham cracker and set it on a paper plate. "What stops you from living out the rest of those dreams?" He added a square of chocolate.

He'd called her on it while they were on the lake. Asked her why she didn't take her own advice. Focus on each next decision.

"You want this one?" He offered her the s'more.

She waved him off. "Oh, I've almost got this marshmallow toasted to perfection."

He laughed. "You seem like someone who thrives when you take on new things, but it also seems like you don't pursue everything you might want to." He took a bite of his s'more, and they sat in silence. "I know you do a lot for your dad. It just feels like it's at the expense of…you."

"Says the man who wants to be sacrificial." She paused, testing the marshmallow on the end of her stick before pushing it back into the fire.

"Okay, true." He chewed another bite. "There's a balance somewhere, isn't there?"

"Maybe. I'll let you know if I find it."

He sandwiched another toasted marshmallow between graham crackers and chocolate and took a bite.

Beth's marshmallow caught fire, and she pulled it from the fire and blew out the flame.

They sat in the easy comfort of the campfire.

"You don't have this in Oregon," Beth said, chafed that Grayson had kept the truth from her.

"We do have marshmallows, chocolate bars, and grahams," He said as he set down his plate.

She swallowed, her mouth sticky and dry. "I meant this—the whole greater experience."

He studied her in the firelight. "No." He smiled, something soft and warm that just might break her heart. "I don't have this in Oregon."

"Anne said you had a call with a real estate agent." She closed her eyes. "I thought you were finalizing plans."

He slipped his hand around hers, weaving their fingers together. "It wasn't the agent." His thumb rubbed across the back of her hand. "I...uh...I've been avoiding Vincent's calls."

"The owner of the ranch you want? Why?"

He shook his head. "I came here for the summer. I didn't really want to come, but Noah needed me and I needed the money—and then...you. You in that silly costume." He squeezed her hand. "You on Rex. You with the kids. The lake today." A deep husk thickened his voice. "It's kind of thrown my plans into chaos."

She tried not to dive straight into his words like the last cinnamon roll at Fox Bakery. "Have your plans changed? What did you tell him?"

"I told him the truth. That I don't yet have the money for the down payment to secure the loan. I can't sign for the loan or purchase contract yet." His fingers traced the line of her jaw. "That I've got things here to take care of." He lifted his shoulder. "I mean, I don't even have horses to run a camp. It's a bit of a long haul to get things running."

Beth shivered in the breeze. He hadn't committed to Oregon.

He leaned back to shrug out of his flannel, then wrapped it around her.

"Won't you be cold?"

"I'm okay."

They sat in quiet, the chorus of crickets interrupted only by the occasional owl hoot from the nearby forest.

He drew her close.

The heat of his body warmed her against the cool night, and she leaned into it. Leaned into the smell of soap and flannel. The tenderness of his touch. The safety of his broad shoulders.

She dared to look up at him.

He released her hand, cupped her face in his palms, and she waited. Wanting.

Instead of kissing her, he leaned his cheek against hers, grazed her cheek with his lips. Held her against himself and let out a long exhale. As if resisting. Doing the right thing.

Which was smart. Safe.

But she was tired of playing it safe. Instead, she turned her head, let her lips meet his.

Take a risk.

She kissed him, pouring into it every wave of longing and hope.

He accepted her kiss and returned his own with an urgency that melted every last bit of good sense in her brain. His arms wound around her body, holding her against the heat of his own.

The smell of campfire smoke clung to him, and he tasted like chocolate and marshmallows and sultry summer nights.

Then, a creak and sway beneath her. A tug that nearly pulled her from his arms, leaving her a little dizzy.

He tightened his hold and she opened her eyes. Gasped.

A snap and then his body dropped beneath her, taking her with him.

Falling.

Falling straight through the wooden bench.

Beth's clipped scream turned to laughter. With dust billowing around them, she landed on top of Grayson, his arms wrapped tight.

"We broke the bench!" she said into the fabric of his shirt.

Nuts. Add that to her to-do list. She was going to have to order a bench repair.

"You must be okay." The timbre of Grayson's voice vibrated against her. She could lean into that voice and hold on. "That's too much laughter for pain."

She sighed. "I'm okay. You?" She lifted herself up enough to look him in the eyes. He'd lost his hat, and his eyes held a bright clarity.

"Never better." He plucked grass from her shoulder, let out a little breath, and ran a hand through her hair. "Beth?"

Yes.

She didn't answer out loud. Instead, she lowered her lips to his again, delighting in the feel of him. Leaning into the moment she'd been thinking about since the trail ride. Maybe even since that regretful blunder in high school.

Tender and sweet and ardent. It was starlit nights and laughter and oh, so much of everything. Everything she'd boxed up inside. Every dream, every hope.

He ran his hands through her hair, and when they parted, he traced her lips with his fingers.

She swallowed.

"My back may have been impaled by a broken plank." He shifted and shoved a chunk of wood out of the way.

"Oh no!" She drew her hand down his chest and realized she was still lying haphazardly on top of him. Oops.

She sat up and scrambled to her feet. "Do you need me to take a look at it?"

He got a silly grin and looked up at her. "My back?"

Oh dear.

He reached out, caught her hand, pulled her back down, and wrapped her in the cocoon of his arms. "Don't think you're not going to help me clean this mess up."

She laughed and he brushed his fingertips across her cheek, captured her face in his hands. Even in the moonlight, their eyes met. His sparked with something like...delight. "What are you doing to me, Beth?" he whispered, then drew her closer.

He'd conquered the lake. He'd admitted he'd missed things about Deep Haven. And this?

That wasn't the kiss of a man who was leaving town.

Yeah. Maybe Grayson Fox was truly coming back to stay.

He'd kissed her right here, on purpose, beneath the velvet sky that sparkled with a million diamonds. Sweet and tender and oh so perfect.

thirteen

. . .

THE LIGHT OF SUNDAY MORNING SHOULD HAVE CAST REGRET OVER the kisses Grayson had shared with Beth. Instead, it left him feeling like what Robin would call a giddy idiot.

Don't ever look at my sister like that again.

He rolled from the bed and stood on the cold floor. Groaned and got dressed.

Dylan was going to kill him. Because no matter how hard Grayson had tried, he was falling hard for Beth, and that was bad. Very bad, because his life wasn't in Deep Haven. A reminder that had arrived via text from Nathan Decker.

Because his lot was still very much for sale, and now several offers were in the works.

He was losing as sure as he was winning. Getting himself all muddled up in his head.

And no, he didn't want to hurt Beth. It was the last thing he wanted to do. But the girl kept a bucket list—and maybe he was building his hope on that bucket list.

She'd made him completely doubt everything he'd believed about the safety in living life unfettered from all the responsibility of grown-up relationships.

He was leaving, wasn't he?

He could still see Beth talking about the bucket list she kept.

Get back on a horse.

She'd shown off the bold check mark next to it.

See the ocean.
Fly somewhere beautiful.
Buy my own place.
Visit Yellowstone.

Each one written in her perfect penmanship, enumerated by curly designs and tiny sketches.

Oh, Beth.

She had all these dreams tucked away. He couldn't help but wonder if she just might be willing to go on an adventure…with him.

Once the offers on the lot came through, he wouldn't be able to put them off for long. And then he'd owe Vincent an answer.

When had his life gotten so impossibly complicated?

He grabbed his day-old coffee. Took a swig of the cold, bitter brew, then opened the small refrigerator, snagged a carrot, and headed out of the apartment.

First stop, Tally.

He looked over the stall door. Her bandage had slid down her leg, leaving the wound bare and soiled. "Aww, girl." He ran his hand through his hair and checked his watch. "You know I'm going to need to fix that before I head to church."

The mare shook her head. Stomped the foot. It was probably getting itchy as it healed.

"I don't know what I'm going to do." He spoke to her while he grabbed the bucket of first-aid supplies. "I feel like I'm making a mess of things." He stepped into the stall, and the buckskin backed away. "I know, you care about her too."

Tally set a wary eye on him and pinned her ears. "Easy, girl." He pulled the carrot from his back pocket. Offered half of it.

She took the carrot, chewed. Lingered. Didn't back away quite so fast.

"You're okay." He rubbed her head. "You gonna let me take a look at that?" The mare stepped sideways, leaving her hoof off the ground, ready to strike. "Okay, maybe we start with your bute." He pulled the tube from his other pocket and set the dosage dial. "I thought I was your new favorite." He held her head and administered the paste into the back of her mouth.

He checked his watch. He wasn't sure he'd still have time to make it to church by the time he rebandaged.

Which might be more personal preference than actual reality. No one was going to care if he ducked in the back door late. He just didn't want to run into Beth.

Well, he did. He did want to see Beth and maybe even spend the day with her.

He didn't want to run into Dylan. Especially not Dylan with Beth.

Grayson heard the telltale hum of Noah's truck.

Moments later, Noah appeared in the stall doorway. "Our camp bench seems to have been decimated last night."

Oh. "Sorry—we were just sitting—" And kissing. He could still feel Beth in his arms. The way she'd kissed him, so sweet and tender and...loving. She'd tasted like promise and possibility.

Yeah, he'd leave out that part. "I'll fix it this afternoon."

Noah nodded. "You need a hand?"

"Thanks." He ran his hand along Tally's shoulder. "There's more going on with this horse than its wounds."

"Always is—whether it's humans or animals."

"I thought I was making progress with her. Beth sure has." He pulled the other half of the carrot from his pocket as Noah entered the stall. "She tore her bandages off last night, and she's really wanting none of it to get that cleaned and rewrapped." Tally took the carrot and crunched it. Eyed Noah.

"She's a wary one, huh?"

"She adores Beth. I think her size is less…" He looked Noah up and down. "Intimidating."

The man laughed. "I get it. I'm not exactly small." He let Tally sniff his hand and then slid his hand down to rub her neck.

Grayson haltered her and handed the lead rope to Noah, then collected the bucket of bandaging supplies.

"Are you almost done in here?" Anne stood in the barn doorway, her Sunday dress billowing in the breeze.

"Getting there," Noah answered.

Anne came to the stall door and watched them work.

"You've both known Beth for a while," Grayson said.

"Sure," Noah said.

Anne nodded her agreement.

"She's pretty tight with her dad." Grayson removed the rest of the soiled bandages and flushed Tally's wound.

"Mm-hmm."

"But she's also got this bucket list of things she wants to do." Grayson looked up at them. "Do you think she'd ever leave Deep Haven?"

Noah let out a laugh, and Tally startled. "Oh, sorry."

"Why is that funny?"

"It isn't. Ignore him." Anne leaned against her arms on the top of the stall door. "Is there something going on between you and Beth?"

"No," Grayson said. Conviction heated his face. "Yes. Probably. I don't know." He added ointment to the Telfa and replaced the pad, then used his teeth to pull up the leading edge of the bandage wrap.

"I knew it," Noah said. He gave his wife a nod. "You know, when Anne and I first worked together at Wilderness Challenge,

I wanted her to join me in Minneapolis—but that was the one place she wouldn't go."

"True story—I was adamant about it."

"What happened?"

Noah turned to Anne, who met him with a tender smile. "You want to tell him?"

"We'd both been touched by tragedies and traumas. For me, I wasn't sure where God was in the darkest moments of life."

Grayson stilled. Yep. He knew that question well. He'd been chewing on the answer ever since the sermon on James.

"A lot of things happened that summer. I learned God is good. His grace is sufficient. If I trust Him, He carries me through any and every hard thing life brings."

Tally stomped a front foot.

Anne's words couldn't placate Grayson. He scooped up the wrappers and old bandages. "I don't know." He hated admitting his disbelief.

Noah passed off the lead rope so Grayson could remove the halter. "She's worked really hard to get this position. It would be asking a lot for her to leave her dad and this job."

"Are you trying to make it worse?" Anne asked.

"I don't mean he shouldn't." Noah opened the stall door while Grayson stepped through, then slid it closed behind him. "I meant that it is exactly the kind of big thing to give over to God. To trust His plan."

Anne nodded. "Ah. Instead of making his own."

"Exactly."

Grayson liked being in control. He shook his head. "I have to leave for Oregon at some point, don't I?" Not that he'd figured out how he was going to extract himself.

"We know. Trust God has a plan," Noah said. He walked toward the door. Stopped. "We're heading to church. "Want to join us?"

Grayson shook his head. "I still have chores to finish before I go. Thanks for the offer."

"Sure."

After morning chores, he needed to round up lumber to repair the bench while he figured out what to do about Madam Librarian and her Amazing Book of Adventures. If he got lucky, it would keep him busy long enough, and he'd be able to dodge Dylan for the day.

Because there was no possible way the man wouldn't know. Grayson was a big brother too. He understood these things—and he definitely understood the code he'd violated.

Fifteen minutes later, Grayson parked the empty hay cart in the barn, grabbed Remington, and led him to the hitching post. "How about some exercise for you?" He rubbed the gelding's face.

He dropped a bucket of grooming supplies next to the hitching post. By the time he returned to the tack room to grab the saddle, all he could think about was Beth in his arms. The way she'd turned to kiss him when he'd stopped himself. How perfect and right it'd felt to share the darkest pieces of himself with her. And her wholehearted acceptance of him.

Not an escape like he'd sought in the past, but a true salve for his soul. The thrill of that realization sparked in his heart, spreading like wildfire through his body.

And the second kiss. Oh boy. An inferno that'd decimated the charred remains of his resolve.

Yeah, Dylan might kill him.

But it might be worth dying for.

A car door slammed, and Beth came running through the barn, her breath clipped in huffs.

"I've made a terrible mistake."

BETH TRIED TO CATCH HER BREATH AND CALM HER ROILING stomach.

"What's going on?" Grayson asked. He put the saddle he was carrying down on the hitching post next to Remington.

Five million different kinds of panic fired in Beth's brain all at once. "I'm going to be fired. What am I going to do?" Remington stepped away from Beth.

Grayson reached out and ran his hands down the horse's neck. "Easy." He turned to Beth, a bit of a flush creeping from his collar upward. "If you're talking about our..." He gave an awkward nod toward the barn door. "If you're talking about that kiss—you aren't actually my boss. You're not going to get fired. Noah signs my check."

Heat flashed through her body. She gasped—she hadn't even thought of that. "Oh no! I'm going to get fired, and I'm a terrible, no good, very bad interim assistant camp director."

"Seriously, Beth, it's okay." He placed his hands on her shoulders and drew her close. Her fingers touched the soft, worn cotton of his button-up shirt, and he smelled rich and masculine, like he'd been working for a while.

When she looked up at him, the earnestness on his face made her want to grab hold of that confidence. Cling to it.

She shook her head. It wasn't the kiss or the fact that she was imagining what life could be like in Deep Haven if Grayson decided to stay. If he built a house on the vacant lot.

Nope. It was her gross negligence as the ACD. Because if she caused the camp to close, well, then he wouldn't have a reason to stay.

Except for her.

Would that ever be enough?

Not to mention Eli and every other kid who counted on the camp would lose out. How selfish could she be? Her first thought hadn't been about the kids—it had been about herself.

What she wanted.

"I messed up the camp funding." She blinked back the stupid

tears. Assistant directors didn't cry. "It was a conditional grant renewal, and I missed the deadline." Except, the harder she tried to hold it in, the tighter her throat felt, until she finally hiccupped a sob.

Grayson held her and cupped her head against his chest.

He smelled good, his musky scent mingling with his aftershave.

She wanted to lean into it, rest in the strength of his arms. His fingers ran through her hair and smoothed a wayward lock. She could hear his heartbeat, and she let the rhythm of it slow her breathing.

He released her but kept his hands on her shoulders. "First, explain to me what's a conditional grant?"

"It's a grant that requires the camp to submit paperwork requesting annual renewal. Each year, for the five-year grant period, I'm supposed to submit a report with the renewal application." She cringed. "I didn't get it done—I missed the deadline."

He rubbed her shoulders. "It's going to be okay." He dropped his hands and paced the barn aisle. "This deadline," he said, "there's got to be a fix to that." He dug in his bucket for a hoof pick and asked Remington to lift a front hoof. "What if you talk to them about this being your first year and send it in now?" He moved to the next hoof. Paused. "This is my fault—you've been helping me above and beyond. I should have said no."

"It's not your fault. I chose how to spend my time." She groaned. "I checked their guidelines. To maintain the integrity of the process, everything is done with strict and firm requirements and deadlines." Beth stepped around the end of the hitching post to scratch Remington's forehead. "No exceptions." She ran her hands over her face. "How could I mess this up?"

"You have a lot going on, and I've asked you to help me with Tally and the trail rides. I'm sorry." As soon as Grayson bent down again, Remy lifted his next hoof.

"I wanted to help."

"What if you pick up some local sponsors?" He finished the last hoof and dropped the hoof pick into the grooming bucket, pulled out a dandy brush, and flicked the remaining dust off the bay's coat.

She mulled the idea in her mind.

She pressed her face into Remington's sun-warmed neck. "It might be my last act as assistant director." She groaned.

"I always thought Vivie was the dramatic one, but you might have her beat." He winked at her.

"Funny."

"Seriously, let's think this through."

She inhaled the sweet smell of horse. "I'm glad Remy and Mav have worked out. When the entire camp herd has to be liquidated because I failed, they'll be more marketable." She ducked under the hitching post and slumped against the barn.

"Come on, you're the indomitable Bookworm Bethy. You always have the answer."

"I really hated that nickname, until I decided to make it into a compliment."

He gave her a crooked smile. "It was—you know, it was my silly little boy way of pressing your buttons and getting your attention. You were so smart and always had the answers to pretty much everything." He set the saddle pad on Remington's back. "And you were one of those annoying people who got straight A's without trying."

The name had flustered her as a kid, but now when he said it, it was with this gentle tease. It sounded far more endearing than she'd ever imagined.

"You're distracting me."

He hoisted the saddle onto Remy and settled it into place.

"How would the assistant camp director think?" Beth asked. She stood back up and paced the barnyard. "How do people raise money? Think... A theater show? But Vivien's booked. Too much work and time involved."

He drew the latigo through the cinch ring and looped it for the hitch knot, then snugged it up. "Bake sale?"

"That would be a lot of éclairs." She swatted at a fly. "Auction? Concert?"

"Those both can require some setup and connections. Do you know any bands?"

"The Blue Monkeys. But they can be heard locally on a regular basis."

"All the bands I know are in Oregon."

"Is that a lot?"

He laughed. "Maybe more than average, but only because the ranch owner has some guest cabins he rents out to a few big-name musicians when they come through on tour. The rural stop is a nice break from their big-city tours."

"Wow. Hoity-toity."

"Actually—what about a wilderness trail ride? Take adult riders out on the trails surrounding Mink Lake. We wouldn't even need to haul the horses anywhere."

"Would that make enough money?"

"It could—commercial businesses charge fifteen-hundred dollars for those multi-day, overnight rides. We've done a few on the ranch for cattle drives."

"There aren't any cattle to drive."

"No, but we could plan a scenic ride. Set up a campsite in advance. Riders arrive there after the first all-day ride, then we do two day-trip rides with the camp as our base. Didn't you say you were trying to come up with additional family camp activities?"

"Family camp?"

"Yeah—we have them sign up and pay for the add-on."

Oh, that was a good idea. In fact, it was a great idea. "That's possibly brilliant. There's an old primitive campground on the other side of the lake." Beth turned the idea around in her mind. "So you're thinking a four-day ride? What about food?"

"Three-day might be better. Two nights. I'll bet I can get my grandparents—well, Robin—to donate some food. Ask a few other businesses too."

"You really think people would pay fifteen-hundred dollars?"

"Not as a camp add-on, but I think four hundred per rider is fair." Grayson adjusted the stirrups on his saddle. "We'll have to look at the costs and crunch the numbers."

"We could give them the option to donate more to the camp." She started running calculations in her head.

"Yeah, that might work. It's for an important cause, so a portion may be tax deductible for them—and they get to do something the camp has never done before."

Beth rubbed her hands together. "How many riders could we take?"

"How big was that grant?"

She groaned. Swallowed. "Ten thousand. And this would have been year four, so it's this year and next year. Plus a pad for the following year, really."

Grayson didn't quite keep a poker face. His mouth dropped open. "Oh, ouch."

"You see, I'm not being dramatic—if I don't fix this, the entire camp will be in jeopardy. Keeping these horses is expensive."

Grayson rubbed his chin. "The camp has, what? Around twenty-seven horses?"

She nodded.

"I'd have to make sure enough of them could pack." He adjusted his hat. "I think we could pull it off. We could take fifteen to twenty riders."

We. That little word blossomed in her chest, filling her with the kind of hope she'd never thought possible. "You'd do that—help me fix this?"

"Of course. I mean, my boss has to approve it." He laughed and gave her another wink.

Boss?

He took off Remington's halter and put the bridle on. "Noah has to approve it."

Beth froze. "I was hoping my catastrophic failure could be fixed without him knowing."

He ran his hands over the bridle, then cinch, making sure all his tack was ready. "You haven't told Noah?" He met her gaze over the top of his horse.

She shrugged. "I was hoping I wouldn't have to."

Grayson picked up his lariat, flipping it with each pull so it coiled perfectly in his hand. "You have to tell him—he has to approve it. Pretty sure he'll notice most of the horses being gone." He looped the lariat around the saddle horn. "Not to mention when the majority of the family camp families disappear. You don't want the Crisis Response Team crashing the ride."

"Well, he'll miss the ten grand too." She covered her face with her hands. "I've got hay coming in to pay for. And the farrier. And vetting." She frowned. "Salary."

He rubbed Remington's nose.

"I'm going to lose my shot at this job. Then what? My future is riding on this."

"You won't lose your job." Remington leaned into Grayson's hand as if to ask for a harder rub. "Let's figure this out—the better we have the details lined up, the more likely it is that Noah will sign off on it."

"We could run it at the end of June with family camp. Head out on Friday." Beth watched him work. "If you'll still be here."

"Sure," he answered. "That's family camp?"

"Yeah, that's right—there's no regular youth horse camp the first week of July." She wanted to revisit the *Sure* part.

"We could do a Sunday morning cowboy church." He pressed a quick kiss to her cheek.

"You gonna preach?"

"Okay, we can skip it. Or we get Noah to come out." He

swung into the saddle. Winked. "We can do this, Beth. I think it's a good plan."

"You're the best."

He tipped his hat, a big grin slapped across his face. "How about you help me replace that wood bench this afternoon?"

Oh. "I can do that." Her heart fluttered a beat.

Because together, they might just pull off saving the camp.

They had to.

fourteen

. . .

"So, you're going to take a bunch of city slickers into the north woods?" Grandpa set his coffee down on the bakery's bistro table Monday afternoon. Twenty-four hours in and the plan was molding into shape.

"Yes." Grayson looked up from the notebook he'd been scratching lists into. Supplies. Food. Gear.

"For three days?" Grandpa folded his arms. "That's quite an undertaking."

Grayson leaned back in the bakery chair and put down his pen. "Beth needs this."

"Seems like you need it too." Grandpa's eyes stayed on him. "I know that camp means a lot to you."

He shrugged. Maybe. Or maybe it was starting to terrify him just a little. "Beth's already reached out to half the families, and all have signed up."

"Isn't that a good thing?"

"It was one thing to plan it as this vague idea, brainstorming in the barnyard. Now it's updating payments, getting new waivers, food arrangements, coordinating all the gear for that many people. Noah and I will pack in the tents the day before and get those set up. There's an access road near the campsite. It's a lot to come together."

"I expect it is. You'll do fine," Grandpa said. "Pray and trust."

Trusting God with outcomes wasn't in Grayson's nature.

"You two about done? I'm ready to put Grayson to work," Robin called from the counter.

"I suppose." Grandpa stood. "I need to get going. I told your grandma I'd be back before dinner." He put a hand on Grayson's shoulder. "Grayson, it will come together exactly as it needs to."

Oh. Okay. Grandpa's words mingled with Anne's.

He carries me through any and every hard thing life brings.

He was still mulling Grandpa's words when he joined Robin in the bakery kitchen. She was rolling out fresh croissant dough, wearing her bakery apron, her hair pulled back in a ponytail.

Grayson set his notebook on the back counter. Now to persuade Robin to help out with the trail ride meals.

Robin grabbed one of her knives and cut the dough. "Can you cut this into triangles?" She demonstrated the first several slices. "Once those are cut, pull away the excess and roll the croissants."

"Sure." He followed her directions, waving off her quality control when she leaned over him and tidied his lines.

"Well, you've got to do it right."

Right. Except his thoughts were elsewhere. Campfire. S'mores. Kiss. Ugh.

"Was that a groan?"

Grayson met Robin's squinty gaze. "Uh…yeah. I guess."

"Is something wrong?"

"Nope." He kept cutting and rolling.

"Do you want to talk about it?"

He placed several croissants onto the baking tray. "About what?"

"Vivien came in yesterday afternoon and mentioned how much Beth is enjoying working at the camp." Robin gave him a look that was filled with all kinds of accusation and assumption. "With you."

Leave it to Vivien. "It's her job. She likes that I'm there to fill in." He swallowed. Hoped Beth hadn't told Vivien about their kiss—because if she had, who knew who else might know by now.

"There was that...thing...I walked in on between you two when you were packing cinnamon rolls. And now you're planning this huge trail ride together."

"Huh."

"Come on. Give me something." Robin picked up the baking tray and slid it into the oven. "What's going on with you?"

"Nothing."

"You're blushing, and you don't blush, which means something is going on with you."

"Did you need me to change anything on the daily specials board?"

"That wasn't even a little smooth. No, the board is already updated for tomorrow. Spill." She plopped another ball of dough onto the work surface and rolled it out.

"It's nothing."

She kept rolling out a large rectangle of dough, shaping and thinning it with each stroke. "Nothing? Will it be nothing if I ask Beth about it later?" She looked up from her work.

Man, the kitchen was warm. "Why do you think it has anything to do with Beth?" He held his hands up, palms out, signaling his innocence.

"Because you turned the color of maraschino cherries when I said her name. She's sweet, kind, loyal. You should ask her out." She stepped aside so he could cut the dough. "You know, besides stuff you can try to classify as work."

Now he could feel the heat flood his face. That kiss had most certainly not been work. He swallowed. Rolled the croissants. Plunked them onto the next tray. "I'm supposed to be leaving at the end of summer."

"It's a date, not a marriage proposal. Besides, no one is forcing you to go back to Oregon."

"Hello? I live there."

"People move all the time." She shrugged. "I left Paris and moved back to Deep Haven—and Paris used to be my dream."

"I'll never have another opportunity like buying Vincent Tucker's place. There isn't a youth camp in the area—and it's a huge need." He cleaned the scraps from the work surface and balled them up with the others, then handed them to her to add to her next batch. "I've met kids through church who needed a camp like Trinity, but there isn't one. And truly, I like it in Oregon—the winters aren't as long and cold as here. We have four full seasons." He did like it there. As much as he'd landed there by chance, it was home.

"Ask her to go with you." Robin slid another tray into the oven.

"You know how well that worked with the last guy." He wasn't ready to trust God like Anne and Noah had. Like Grandpa.

"True. But he wasn't you."

"No. I couldn't do that to her. I could never ask her to leave everything she loves—everyone she loves." He shoved the mixing bowl away.

Robin's timer went off, and she pulled a tray of croissants from the oven.

The buttery smell made his stomach rumble. "Those look and smell delicious."

She held out a hand. "Not yet—they're too hot. And you can't eat all my profits." She pulled off her oven mitts. "You could stay. You haven't closed on the lot."

"Robin—"

"I'm still okay with you selling it—I'm just saying, it's there. It's still an option."

He scrubbed his hands over his face. "I don't know how to

fix this. I can't make sense of what the future could possibly be. The camp in Oregon—I feel *called* to that."

Called. It was the first time the full meaning of the camp connected in his soul. Called to minister to youth, especially the hurting. Called to start something new. In Oregon.

Instead of anchoring him, the realization released him.

"Tragedies like ours—they happen everywhere, including Sisters."

"Of course they do." Robin's voice softened.

"There were two siblings brought into a foster family at church because their parents had died in a house fire. They don't have an aunt or grandparents or anyone else in the world. Sure, they have the foster family—but what if they had a place like Trinity? And, what if some day, I could even bring on counselors?"

"That would be amazing," Robin said. "Have you even asked her, though? Explored the options? Why are you so stubborn?"

"Because for once I want to be unselfish. Look at Beth—she didn't even go to college because of her dad. I could never, ever ask her to leave him." His words tumbled him back into the same tussle. He couldn't solve this.

Robin reached out and put a hand on his. Squeezed. "I'm sorry to press you."

He nodded. Swallowed. He wanted to talk about anything but leaving. "We're working on a fundraiser for the camp—in fact, we could use your help."

Robin wiped her hands on her apron. "Like?"

"This private trail ride will be three days, two nights. But we need meals."

"Oh, intriguing. They're going to survive on cinnamon rolls and croissants?"

"Not exactly, but if you could help—donations would be tax deductible. Maybe ask a few of the restaurants in town if they'd donate?"

"I'm sure I could do something. When is it?"

"The event is at the end of June. Runs into July."

Her eyes rounded. "Short turnaround." She checked her calendar, flipped from June into July. "Yeah, I could help with that."

"There's an access road not far from where we'd be staying. Meals can be prepped offsite and delivered—not the full chuckwagon experience, but on short notice, it's the best we can do." He snagged his notebook and added a checkmark next to her name on the to-do list.

"I don't think anyone spending all day in a saddle is going to complain about a delivery van bringing fresh meals in. It'll be an epic epicurean and equine adventure."

"Um, sure. Exactly."

Robin nodded. "We could make it work. It sounds like fun." She put another tray of croissants into the oven.

The kitchen door opened and Dylan came in. "I've been looking for you." He turned to Robin. "Sorry to crash in here—I did try knocking up front, but I don't think you could hear me."

Uh-oh. "You've been looking for me?" Grayson cut another croissant.

"Yeah. I thought you might want to go fishing, hit our old spot on the shore."

"Oh. Well—" He sought a save from Robin in the form of the long list of bakery tasks she needed him for.

"That sounds like fun—let me pack up a box of pastries for you to take."

That was what sisters were for.

"I heard you guys had a staff campfire Saturday night."

"Um, yeah." Grayson's voice wavered and he tugged at his collar. He knew. He had to know.

Dylan stared at Grayson a moment and opened his mouth—

"How about a fresh croissant?" Grayson interjected. He picked up a roll off the nearby pan.

Burning. Hot. Burning. "Ow!" He dropped it onto a plate.

"What are you doing?" Robin's scolding cut through the bakery. "That just came out of the oven."

"What *are* you doing?" Dylan looked at him.

Grayson shook his head—clearly, he wasn't using it. He grabbed his notebook. "Let's go fishing."

Nope. Definitely not using his head.

Ten minutes later, they'd parked in the same shoreline spot and climbed down to the rocks where they'd spent many an afternoon during high school. Fishing. Talking. Laughing.

Just like old times.

"Beth's been having the time of her life at camp." Dylan cast his line.

Not like old times. Grayson measured his words. Tried to sound casual. Beth's-brother's-friend-like. "Yeah. She's a natural."

The warm air closed in, a little sticky, and a swarm of gnats hovered over the water.

Dylan played his line in the water. "Always has been."

"Teaching comes easy for her, and the kids love her."

He instantly regretted using the word *love* in a sentence about Beth.

Dylan released a little more line. "Is there anything going on between you two?" He kept his eyes on the water.

"Define 'going on.'" Grayson's line snagged and he worked it, trying to free it.

This time Dylan turned his head, his eyes on Grayson and a look of knowing on his face.

"I saw Beth earlier."

Grayson's line snapped and his pole jerked back, nearly toppling him.

He stayed silent. Busied himself with the broken line.

"She told me about the fundraiser—your idea to save her job and the camp."

Oh.

"On and on. About the horses, the kids. You."

Grayson restrung his line.

"For the first time in her adult life, she's finally stepping into her own. When she talks about the camp, she glows."

Grayson smiled. He knew the look Dylan was talking about. The way Beth's eyes sparkled and she wore a smile. How she'd sit and chat with Tally. Watch for signs any of the youth needed a little extra encouragement. How her gentle spirit changed the atmosphere.

Dylan reeled his line back in. Recast. "And when she talks about you, I can't help but wonder how much of this change is because of you."

"I...uh...I'm just the hired help." A lightness filled his chest, and he rubbed his hand across his chin, as if he could stop himself from smiling. "It's all her."

A swallow dipped and dove above the water's surface.

Dylan shook his head. "I know I warned you away from her—and I mean it. I don't want her getting hurt. But if you care about her the way she seems to care about you, then...I don't know. Don't mess this up."

Great. No pressure there.

〜〜〜

BETH COULDN'T EVEN BELIEVE HOW FAST THE FIRST THREE WEEKS with Trinity campers had passed. She soaked in the sunlight on the back deck of her camp cabin, the hum of summer buzzing in her veins. She may have botched the grant renewal, but this trail ride had all the makings of a spectacular adventure.

Courtney sat across the table, her hair piled in a messy bun.

Beth clasped her hands together. "We're one week from departure, and we've filled all the slots with family campers." She punched the numbers from her accounting sheet into her phone's calculator. "Everyone has paid. I have the registration forms. Almost all the waivers."

Courtney leaned forward and poured another glass of ice tea. "Amazing, Beth. That's completely amazing."

And she had Grayson, who made all this work seem not so much like work. They'd fallen into an easy routine. Every morning, she spent two hours in her camp office before helping Grayson saddle the first group of horses. Trail ride, untacking. Another two hours of work with lunch squeezed in. The second group of horses saddled—sometimes by Grayson alone, though Beth tried to get enough work done to jump in and help every time she could.

"Have you talked to Jesse?" Courtney asked.

Beth wanted to ignore the question. Sure, she needed to reach out to Jesse and find out when he'd be returning, but he hadn't reached out to her, so there was that.

"Beth?"

"I don't know—what if he isn't coming back?" she asked.

Courtney scratched her head. "Um, pretty sure he is. Once his leg is healed—Grayson's only here for this summer—or, until Jesse gets back, right? Whichever comes first?"

Beth lifted a shoulder. "I'm just saying, I haven't heard from him. Maybe he won't want to come back."

"He's got a family to support."

"I get that." Beth held up a hand. "But we don't know how his leg is healing or if he'll be able to ride come late summer or fall."

Courtney blew out a breath. "Look, I know you like Grayson, but he isn't staying, is he?" She frowned. "He's leaving."

"I know." Beth's response was a little short. She just couldn't wrap her mind around what the future looked like. Grayson seemed like he wasn't in any hurry to get back to Oregon.

And if he was, where did that leave them? Her?

"So, are you two a couple?" Courtney eyed Beth over her tea glass. "Because every time anyone sees you in town, the two of you are together. And we all know you spend nearly every moment here at the camp with him."

"He isn't here now." She didn't have the answers about the future, but ever since the night they'd kissed, leaving hadn't seemed to be on Grayson's mind.

And yeah. That had bolstered hope. The light, inescapable, joyful hope that obliterated every bit of doubt and fear she'd carried.

"Let me remind you, I had to schedule this visit." Courtney wrinkled her nose. "And as I recall, you said, 'Let me check with Grayson.'"

"I did no such thing—I said I had to connect with Grayson. About some work items." She gestured toward her laptop and the stack of papers. "This trail ride is a big deal."

"Okay, don't answer me. Your non-answer is an answer."

Beth mistyped a number in her calculator. "You're messing me up."

"I just want to say that Vivie and I called it." Courtney jingled the ice in her glass.

"I didn't say we're a couple." Beth stood and poured more tea into both their glasses. The thought of Grayson caused a flip-flop in her belly.

"Again, you didn't have to. It's all over your face."

"That's sunscreen." Beth grinned and went back to her calculator. Punched in the last few numbers and hit the equal sign. "That can't be right." Beth cleared the screen and started over. Ran through the checks and credit card receipts again. She turned her calculator. "Did you see this total? If we run a few of these sessions, we'll cover the lost grant funds and then some."

She had Grayson to thank. She touched her fingers to her lips.

"Who needs grants?"

"We'll have a few other expenses, but not too much. Grayson got a few area outfitters to loan us some rental pack equipment."

Beth made a notation on her spreadsheet. "I'm picking that up this afternoon.

"And you've got food covered?"

"Robin's coordinated snack and meal donations from her bakery, the VFW, Loon Café...I can't even remember where else." Beth took a long drink of her tea. "It's like everyone is rallying behind the camp."

And even behind her.

A gust of wind loosened Courtney's messy bun, and she re-tucked the loose locks. "I'm so excited for you."

Beth flipped open her laptop. "The last of the waivers should be in my inbox." She opened the program.

"Yep." Waiver. Waiver.

She looked through the list of new emails. "Oh, here's someone who wants to schedule it for next year's family camp. We hadn't even planned for future years."

"Wow."

A new email from the Equine Youth Rescue Foundation caught Beth's attention. The subject line didn't start with a congratulations. "Oh no." She clicked on the message and skimmed it. "No!" Her heart sank and she let out a groan.

"What's wrong?"

"We didn't get one of the grants I totally expected we would get." She reread the email. "Says they loved our proposal, that the competition was stiff, and that the funds have been awarded to other camp programs." Her shoulders sagged. "It says to reapply next year."

"Oh." Courtney frowned. "I mean, it's bad news, but it's also good news. You're not going to get every grant you apply for, but they liked what they saw."

"Yeah, I know." She tried to shake it off. To focus on the positives. "Well, you know what? We won't need that money, because we're running a trail ride next weekend."

"That's right." Courtney gave her a fist bump.

"Knock, knock," Grayson called. He rounded the corner of

the cabin and swept up the steps. He wore jeans and a T-shirt, and his lips were drawn in a frown. "Sorry to drop in," he said. "I have some bad news and some really bad news."

"Really? That's all you've got?" Beth gave Courtney a look. "I was just gushing with good news, then I got my own bad news. Then I decided to focus on the positive."

"Way to kill the mood," Courtney said.

"You have bad news too?" He removed his hat and slid into the chair next to Beth.

"Unfortunately."

"You go first," he said.

"We didn't get the Equine Youth Rescue grant."

"Oh." He rubbed his hands on his thighs. "That makes my news really bad news and really, really bad news. Which do you want first?"

Beth let out a squeak and covered her face. "I guess it doesn't matter."

"Okay, the hay prices are up this year, so hay's going to cost an extra hundred per ton." He placed a note page on the table with all his numbers on it. "With the number of horses we have, that's over eleven thousand dollars extra for the year."

She stared at the bottom figure with the dollar sign and a long line of digits following it. Ouch. "Is that the really bad news or the really, really bad news?"

"And the tractor is broken and it'll be around three grand to repair."

Beth blinked back a tear. Opened her mouth. Closed it. Swallowed. "We don't have that kind of money."

"I'm sorry, Beth," Courtney said. "You could raise camp prices."

"We can't do that midseason—besides, we try to keep the camp affordable."

Grayson leaned forward, head in his hands. "If we can irrigate the pasture and put up cross-fencing, we might be able to manage pasture grazing better—that'll save on hay costs. Not by much, but at least a few thousand."

Beth reviewed his calculations. "There has to be a mistake here. Four tons per horse times…nearly thirty horses. One hundred…" Nuts.

"Will the fencing cost as much as the hay?"

Grayson shrugged. "Maybe—but then you'll have it in place for next year."

Beth wanted to whimper. Wanted to just fall apart and surrender. She'd tried not being afraid, and look where that was getting her. "I guess we're all-in on this trail ride now."

Grayson nodded. "It matters more than ever."

Courtney set down her tea. "You guys, it's going to be great."

"I know. You're right. We can do this." She looked to Grayson for validation.

He smiled and put his hand on hers, but his smile didn't reach his eyes. And that left a swirl of doubt in her gut that the touch of his hand couldn't ease.

fifteen

· · ·

WATCHING BETH TRANSFORM INTO A TRAIL BOSS THE MORNING OF the fundraiser ride was like watching a still-wet foal go from her first wobbly steps to galloping across the pasture ten hours later.

Wearing her boots and Wranglers, her hair loose and a clipboard in her hands, she walked into the barn as the edge of dawn spread across camp, a golden lining of sunshine peeling back the darkness.

Dew glinted off the grass, and the day held the promise of adventure and success despite the message from Vincent that might set his camp up ahead of schedule.

Five weeks had passed, and he still hadn't figured out how to find compromise between the life waiting for him in Oregon with his new life in Deep Haven.

Because Beth wouldn't leave, would she?

He'd listened to Vincent's voice mail three times. A Klamath Falls dude ranch was closing after devastating wildfire losses. Their entire horse string was available at a fraction of the full price because the owner didn't want them going to auction. They just couldn't handle any mouths to feed when they'd lost their own house in the fire. The man didn't need the full down payment yet, but he needed a commitment and a portion of the money.

If Grayson didn't act soon, he'd lose any shot of starting a camp in Oregon in the near future.

He needed to keep reminding himself of that. Trinity Horse Camp already had a full-time wrangler. Jesse would be back at the end of summer at the latest—sooner if his doctor gave him the clearance.

And Grayson had been sitting on the offers Nathan had sent him. The clock was ticking on his response.

Tally nickered over her stall door.

He stopped to rub her face.

"Can you believe how well she's doing?" Beth asked. "I saw Lena last night. Told her she'd have to swing through and take a peek."

The wound had closed up. Left a scar at the joint, but Tally was sound, willingly offering a walk, jog, and lope in the outdoor arena. Even a few feel-good bucks and kicks to boot.

No, she wouldn't be a competition header or heeler and wouldn't win any barrel races. But she'd be a fine ranch and trail horse once he finished working with her.

"Pretty amazing," he said.

"You're pretty amazing." She grinned. "Look at all this." She waved the stack of waivers.

At least something could go right. He lifted a shoulder. "This is easy—I know how to do this kind of thing."

"That reminds me—I sent out an inquiry on two horses I found online that could be Maverick."

"Really?" He hadn't put much hope in her search.

"Yeah. One of the brand searches led me to a Facebook page for people searching for horses they used to own." She lifted her shoulder. "I figured it doesn't hurt to ask."

Except, he hoped the camp wouldn't end up losing Maverick in the process. If the horse had been stolen, the camp would lose out.

Still, she looked so excited and hopeful. And they had this ride ahead of them. "Good work, detective."

She grinned. "Okay, I have our roster." She tapped her clipboard. "Most of our group are families from Duluth, the Twin Cities, and surrounding areas, but I do recognize a few names from town. I gave Colleen Decker a half-price ticket so she can act as our trail medic. She's a nurse."

"Smart," Grayson answered. "Nathan's daughter, right?"

"Thank you." She smiled. "And yes, she is." She gestured toward the arena. "This idea, this ride—it's going to save the camp and save my job."

Man, she was cute. She wore her cowboy hat and a Trinity T-shirt and looked far more Sisters, Oregon, than Deep Haven, Minnesota.

They worked in tandem, bringing the horses they'd selected for the ride into the arena to tack up. They were almost finished when Noah's truck rolled up.

"Need any help?" Noah entered the arena and looked at the lineup.

Grayson finished checking a cinch. "We're almost ready."

Beth hefted a saddle onto one of the horses. "We will never, ever turn down help." She nodded toward Grayson. "He likes to think he can do it all, but he hasn't seen how long my to-do list is."

Ouch.

Noah laughed. "You pull this off and we might have to start including it as an option in future years."

Grayson tucked the first aid kit into his saddlebag. He wouldn't be here for next year's event, would he?

He couldn't even think about the follow-up conversation with the bank. In addition to the horses being available, loan papers were heading his way for a digital signature.

Could Beth go? Would she go?

Was it even right to ask her?

He pushed the questions away. For now, he just wanted to be in the moment and enjoy the experience.

"We've already pulled it off," Beth said. She drew the latigo through the cinch ring.

Grayson had already ridden their route four times since they'd planned it. A two-hour ride to their lunch stop. Time to eat and explore for a couple hours, then another two-hour ride to their campsite.

Their first stop would give the horses a breather before the second leg that would take them to their evening destination.

The best part of having horses as his business was that he could be completely confident. He'd put nine-year-old kids on the horses over the past four weeks. If they were trustworthy with children, then every one of the adults could handle the slow-paced, nose-to-tail ride, no matter how many miles they covered.

Ten minutes later, Noah lifted the saddle onto the last horse in the arena, and Beth set to work cinching it.

"Horses tacked—check." Beth finished looping the leather strap and adjusted it, then grabbed the pen off her clipboard and made a notation on her page.

Grayson's phone buzzed and he pulled it from his pocket. "Hello?"

"It's Robin. I've got some bad news."

He apparently had his volume up too high, because Beth stilled and looked up at him, her mouth a little slack.

"There was a problem with the refrigerator the food was in—almost half of it is spoiled, including the rib eye steaks."

Noah looked up from the horse he had stopped to pet.

Grayson headed into the barn with Beth on his heels.

"What are we going to feed them for dinner?" Beth whispered. She paced the aisle.

So much for their gourmet dinner. "You know what? Just go to the store and buy a bunch of hot dogs and chips."

Beth's jaw dropped open. "We can't charge them four

hundred for hot dogs—this was supposed to be an epicurean adventure as well as an equestrian one."

"She's got a point," Robin said. "I'm so sorry." There was shuffling on the other end of the line, then she continued. "Okay, I can do homemade buns and have them ready by dinner time, and Sammy suggested we also have a pot of homemade chili— the award-winning recipe from last year's contest."

"You're thinking chili dogs?" He wasn't sure Beth would qualify it as the epicurean adventure she'd been hoping for.

"Or as a side, and I can make another batch of the strawberry-spinach salad with the champagne vinaigrette."

"With hot dogs?" Even he didn't think they could pull that one off.

"Look, I'm a pastry chef, remember? I don't usually prepare meals. If you want to feed them cheesecake and croissants, I've got you covered."

Beth rubbed her hands together. "Can she do some sort of fruit salad?"

Grayson switched his phone to speaker. "Did you hear Beth on that?"

"Yeah. Okay, I can use the strawberries for a summer fruit salad. Add some kiwi and maybe find a dressing to jazz it up. I can have Grandma and Sammy help."

"What about tomorrow's meals?"

"We've got breakfast and lunch covered, and I'll have time to put something together. I'll reach out to the Loon Café for an assist."

"We'll do what we can—and I do have some cheesecake in the freezer I can thaw. I'll throw that in too."

He looked to Beth, who gave him an uncertain nod.

"All right. Let's do it," he answered.

"Is everything okay?" Noah stood in the doorway.

"Just a few last-minute menu changes," Beth said.

Grayson disconnected his call and led the way back to the arena, Noah and Beth close behind.

"Looks like it's showtime," Noah said. Three cars came down the drive, the swirl of dust not quite settled when several more pulled in. Parked.

He gave Grayson's horse a pat on the neck. "I'm impressed. I wasn't sure this could all come together this fast."

Beth smiled.

Yeah, they'd fill Noah in after they got back.

Beth greeted each rider, directing them to Grayson and Noah, who paired them up and helped them stow their gear into the borrowed saddlebags they'd attached to each saddle.

John and Mary Kane, joined by their daughters Leia and Ginny. The twelve-year-old twins were only possible to tell apart by their different colored tops. Bright blue for Leia and red for Ginny.

Zero riding experience. Grayson matched them up to two sorrels, a bay, and an Appaloosa.

Beth sent the Jaspers family his way. At eight years old, their daughter, Samantha, was the youngest on the trail ride. He put her on Lexi, Eli's favorite red roan.

The girl's wavy golden locks had been tamed by a hair tie. "Will we see lots of wildlife?"

"I hope so," he answered.

Jessica Jaspers put out a hand. "Not bears though, right?"

Um— "Well, it's possible, but probably not." At the furrow on Jessica's face, Grayson added, "We're a big group, and we'll naturally be making enough noise that we won't surprise any dangerous wildlife."

The woman nodded. Her husband, Marvin, gave her hand a tug. "Come on, this'll be fun."

Beth continued checking in the families and sending them his way. The group included a single mom with her thirteen-year-old daughter, grandparents with their two preteen grandchildren, and another couple with two boys.

Grayson directed several to Noah to be matched up, and he took a little time to tell the riders about their assigned horses.

Seventeen guests plus Colleen, who'd waited while all the families checked in and were matched up to their horses.

No problem. They could totally do this.

"Thanks for coming." He paired Colleen Decker with a chestnut mare named Ace.

"To be honest, I jumped at the chance. This is going to be a blast."

He and Noah continued working until all their guests formed a large circle around the arena rail, standing next to their mounts, just like at daily camp.

Beth cleared her throat and took the bullhorn Noah handed her.

"Hi, can you hear me?" Her voice was soft and swallowed by the wind.

Noah stepped up and said something to her, then made an adjustment to the bullhorn.

"Okay, how's that?" Her voice came through clear, with maybe a little wobble of nerves. All heads turned her way. She looked to Grayson with a shy smile, and he gave her a thumbs-up. "Again, welcome to the first—hopefully annual—Trinity Horse Camp Family Camp Trail Excursion."

A buzz of comments and returned greetings rose from the crowd.

She reintroduced herself and Grayson.

"Colleen Decker—raise your hand, if you would," Beth said.

She lifted her arm and waved.

"Colleen's our trail nurse—not that we'll need one, but if you have any concerns along the way, she's our go-to," Beth said. "But please, the most likely issues you'll have are sunburn or bug bites. We have plenty of sunscreen and bug spray if you've forgotten yours."

The riders all nodded.

"We'll ride out two hours, then take an hour-and-a-half to two-hour break for lunch and some lakeside exploring. Then we'll ride another two hours to our evening campout site.

Grayson will be the lead rider, and I'll bring up any of you stragglers. If you have any issue along the trail, please raise your hand so we can hold up the line and address that need."

Noah stepped up beside her and took the bullhorn. "I think most of you met me in the early family camp sessions, but I just wanted to take the opportunity to thank each family for jumping on board for this new offering. I can tell you that you're in very capable hands here. You're going to have a beautiful trip, great food, and make a lot of great memories."

They'd just have to see how the food turned out. Beth shot Grayson a toothy grin.

Several of the participants looked his way and nodded.

He swallowed, the magnitude of the event settling over him. Noah needed this. Beth needed this. The camp needed this.

Noah handed the bullhorn back to Beth. She finished her briefing and then announced a last call for the porta potty that had been staged outside the arena and offered sunscreen and bug repellent to those who'd forgotten theirs.

The entire arena cleared to use the facilities, and a handful of riders snagged a spray of repellent or swipe of sunscreen on the way back through. Beth finished up, clipboard in hand.

"Okay, that's everyone." She met Grayson's eyes across the arena.

Noah took the bullhorn again. "Would you all join me in prayer?"

Grayson bowed his head while birdsong punctuated Noah's words.

"Heavenly Father, we ask for Your blessing over this ride. We pray for safety and opportunities for spiritual growth. Lord, we ask that You would use this ride to encourage these riders, to bless them, and to draw them closer to You. Thank you for what this opportunity brings to Trinity and for the many ways You've provided for us."

Amens rumbled through the group.

"Let's mount up and head out." They set about ensuring the riders were settled on their horses.

Grayson returned to Maverick and led him over to Beth. "Ready for this?"

She nodded. Squeezed his hand. "This is all going to work out, right?"

"Absolutely." The skies were clear, the families were smiling, and Robin was busy scraping together something that he hoped wasn't going to land anyone in gastroenterology.

Beth looked like she was ready to take on the world—heading out on a grand adventure.

"I'll...be at the back," she said. "Lead the way."

He'd have loved to ride alongside Beth, but he supposed if they lost a horse at the rear, it wouldn't be good for the nonprofit.

He gave her a leg up onto Rex and then hopped up on Maverick.

Noah stood at the arena exit with the gate swung wide.

They had three pack horses with the group. Grayson took two and Beth took the other.

He called out to the riders and lifted his finger into the air, looping it to tell the riders to follow. Beth rode past him, ponying her pack horse, a grin plastered on her face, and never, not ever, had he enjoyed riding so much.

It made him wonder if maybe he didn't need that ranch in Oregon after all.

She paused on the other side of the gate to wait for the riders, and they rode out onto the trail.

The first portion of the trail followed one of their daily camp sections before branching off. They wound through the woods, the trail snaking through spruce, pine, and larch. Maverick kept them moving at a steady pace.

Every so often, Beth would key her mic, his cue to stop so she could point out flowers, wildlife, and geographic points of interest.

She could be the trail boss, for sure.

It took closer to two-and-a-half hours to reach their lunch stop. He'd specifically picked this spot for the open grassy knoll where the horses could rest in the shade. It was on a small finger of Mink Lake, and the riders were able to eat and then walk down to the water, cool off, and explore.

The riders chatted with Beth and each other, snippets of conversation lifting on the breeze that had picked up. A computer programmer from Minneapolis, married to a memory care nurse. A horse-crazy daughter. A family from Duluth. First time riders and those who'd ridden horses as kids.

Laughter and smiles all around. This would be the easiest money the camp ever made.

"I hope I'm not kicking up too much trail dust," Beth said, giving him a wink and squeezing his arm.

She was glowing. She was just as good with the adults as she'd been with the kids.

He did a quick headcount as the group made its way back to the horses. "Everyone's here. Are we ready?"

Beth nodded and turned to the group. "All right, everyone, it's about two hours to our destination. Let's mount up—head on out." They made sure everyone was remounted, then Grayson gave her another leg up. Sure, she could have used the tree stump like everyone else.

But it allowed him to linger with her a little bit longer.

"You want to lead?" he asked.

"Me?"

"Why not?"

She smiled, bright and confident. "Sure. Okay."

She rode past him, her hand drawing across his arm in final contact before she took Rex and her ponied pack horse to the front and he took his place at the back of the line with Mav and his own two pack horses.

The afternoon leg of the ride went a little slower, Rex setting a more grandfatherly pace than Maverick had. But other than one loose shoe he had to pull and replace with a temporary hoof boot, their riders entered camp saddle sore and smiling.

He and Noah had set up a tent in advance for each family in a broad arc of the clearing. The tan canvas shelters stood as welcome respites from their ride. All day in the saddle didn't faze him, but he figured their riders were ready for their overnight break.

Grayson pushed Maverick ahead and dismounted next to Beth. They briefed the riders on the order of business—horses first, then humans—and he set about stringing the highline with Marvin Jaspers and John Kane so the horses could be secured and untacked for the night.

Three hours later, they'd had their fill of Robin's gourmet hot dogs on croissant buns, fruit salad, macaroni salad, chili, and flame-cooked Dutch-oven brownies. She'd worked her pastry prowess to bring their hodgepodge meal together with a blend of savory-sweet flavors that tasted intentional and maybe even a little inspired.

The guests mingled in the waning campfire light with conversations about the constellations overhead, the wildlife sightings of the day, and whose horse was the best.

The firelight on Beth's face set her eyes aglow when she turned to Grayson, and he slid his hand over, wrapped her hand in his, and gave it a squeeze.

"This has been an amazing day." She leaned in close, her breath sending fiery blazes down his neck. "Look at all these families—they're having this experience because of us, because of you. This was your brilliant idea."

He couldn't help it. The way she looked at him, her confidence, her pride in him—it stirred an unfamiliar, expansive restfulness inside. Both settling and encouraging.

He was in no hurry for the night to end. Didn't want to think about Vincent's place or the Klamath horses or anything else.

He just wanted to live in this moment.

But when he finally laid his head against his sleeping bag, a roll of thunder rattled through his bones.

🐺🐺🐺

OH BOY, THIS HAD BEEN A BAD IDEA. BETH HAD NEVER BEEN SO cold or wet in her life. She wasn't sure when her tent had started leaking. All she knew was that she'd woken up to a lake inside of it—one that rivaled Mink Lake itself. She'd slid her feet off her air mattress and plunged them right into the icy surprise.

She'd scrambled to dry off and dress—while on her mat, her very own life raft.

Now, rain slicked off her face and down her neck despite every attempt to snug her poncho tighter. Her teeth chattered so hard she thought they might chip.

When she found Grayson saddling the horses, a hard line cut his brow.

"Sorry I'm late," she said. "My tent leaked."

"Yeah, I think they all did." He gestured with his head. Nearly all the families were huddled under the tree line. "I'm wondering if we should turn back."

Her heart sank. "Then my job is over—we won't have funds to keep the camp running. If we push on, we can still make a go of this."

"Push on to what? No one wants to ride in this, and their tents are soaked through." Rain sluiced off his hat, punctuating his point.

Yeah, she was soaked through too. "We can shelter and wait for it to pass. I think our best bet is to proceed with riding up the north fork trail. There's that picnic shelter. We can wait this out under a hard roof." The shelter wasn't well maintained, but it was the best they had. "And I sure hope the rain stops. This wasn't in the forecast."

234 · Rachel D. Russell

"I don't know, Beth."

"We can do this. It'll be fine. The sun's going to shine and dry out all the tents while we're gone." She waved off the wrinkle in his brow and moved Rex forward. "The picnic shelter is closer than trying to ride all the way back. I used it with the camp kayakers last summer."

He nodded. Opened his mouth to say something. Closed it with a grim press.

This was the real, bona fide ranch trail experience. Good thing they'd treated all the saddles at the beginning of the season to protect the leather.

After everyone had stuffed down their runny eggs and watery sausage, Beth and Grayson pulled lunch from the coolers Robin had left behind to pack into the panniers, then had everyone mount up.

An hour into their ride to the shelter and no part of her was dry yet.

"Is everyone good?" Beth shouted over the monsoon downpour. Head nods and weak thumbs-ups were the responses. Not a smile among them, though. Not even a fake one.

She swallowed, her heart sinking.

Grayson rode to the back of the line, where he took the lead line for his pack string from one of the guests.

Beth wasn't sure if she'd picked up the pace or if Rex had done that all on his own, but they'd gone from a languid plod to a slow jog-trot. Not even the driving rain could drown out the sound of mud suctioning off hooves with each stride.

She twisted to look behind Rex when they rounded a curve on the trail. The line was spread out now, each rider hanging back to avoid the thick balls of mud kicking up from each horse in front.

So much for their scenic ride.

As if to punctuate her despair, a ball of hail thunked her hat and bounced to the ground, followed by another. And another.

Until they were being pelted by ice balls the size of asteroids.

The riders behind her looked as tired, worn, and miserable as she was feeling—with grimaces and downcast faces. She tucked her chin and kept riding forward, staying as close to the trees as she could to protect the group. Rex put his head down, pressing onward like a trooper. Her pack horse followed, equally obedient and soaked.

The hailstorm diminished after several minutes, and Beth dared to raise her head and look back. There were still a few frowns, but murmurs of conversation lifted above the squeak of leather and thud of hooves.

She couldn't read anything more than focus and drive on Grayson's face, but if she looked hard enough, sunshine cut the blackened sky along the horizon, offering the hope of a dry afternoon.

If only the slate-gray clouds overhead would yield a little relief for the time being.

Forty minutes later, the trail widened, the forest surrendering the picnic shelter from the spruce and pine. It had a fire break cut around it—enough of a clearing to give them room to easily gather.

It was like they'd finally reached the Promised Land. A land of dry clothes and a warm fire. A chance to redeem the whole day.

Sunshine split the clouds, offering the assurance of a dry spell.

Hallelujah.

She expected the riders were ready to get their saddle-sore backsides off their horses too.

She turned her face to the sun, relishing the golden glory of it.

"Look at that!" Colleen pointed in the opposite direction. It was the first glimmer of excitement she'd seen or heard from their riders since the monsoon had begun.

Beth turned. A vivid rainbow arced across the sky.

Ah. God hadn't forsaken her. Hadn't abandoned her.

She rode Rex to the side of the clearing, giving the other riders room to pass.

Oh boy. She sure hoped dry weather and a warm fire could brighten their spirits.

Grayson brought up the rear with the other pack horses. Hopefully those panniers were waterproof too.

"Okay, everyone, we've had quite an adventure since last night's storm rolled in. We'll dismount, and if you can hold your horses for a few minutes, that'll give Grayson time to set up new highlines where the horses will be tied. They'll be up under those trees"—she pointed to a spot uphill from the shelter—"so they can dry out and take a break too."

She sought confirmation from Grayson, and he gave her an encouraging nod. "He and I will help you untack your horses again."

Her words were met with silence and soggy-headed nods. Only a few halfhearted smiles.

So much for their immersive family camp ride. She had to find a way to salvage this mess.

"Once that's done, we'll head under the shelter and have lunch and dry out by the fire." Beth hopped down from Rex and led her two horses to Grayson.

"You are a rock star." Grayson dismounted. "I thought your idea was a little crazy, but this is a good spot."

"You think so?" Something about the confidence and pride in his eyes made her go a little mushy inside.

The picnic shelter was a broad wood structure. Weathered and worn to gray, but it had a solid north wall with a large brick fireplace built into it, including a brick hearth. The other three sides were open, and the span of it held two broken picnic tables and three mostly solid—if bird poop covered—additional picnic tables.

Hopefully they could find a makeshift tablecloth or two in the panniers.

"I do." He unpacked the highline from his saddle bag, and she took his lead lines for the pack horses and Mav.

Grayson smiled, and that was enough to warm her from the inside out. "Once they can all dry out and eat, everyone will come out of their funk."

"Exactly. We can do this."

He grinned at her, the weight of the storm lifting. "We've survived a flood and hailstorm today. I'm thinking you can do anything you set your mind to." He wrapped her in a hug, and she leaned into his strength.

Together, they were pretty much undefeatable. No storm was going to spoil their fundraiser.

The riders dismounted and stood, waiting in a haphazard line while Grayson set up the highline with the help of several of the men.

Ah, see? Fostering teamwork was a bonus.

"Would you hold these horses?" Beth snagged a couple helpers on their way back from the highline. "I want to get that fire started for us." Several of the younger riders hovered around the picnic shelter's dark, empty brick fireplace.

"Sure." They stepped up to hold the pack horses, Maverick, and Rex.

"How can we help?" Marvin and Jessica Jaspers stepped up. The woman's dark hair was plastered to her skull, and both of them walked a little bowlegged. She wasn't sure if it was from soreness or the cold, wet pant legs.

"You should find downed pieces of dry limbs under that tree line." She pointed past the last horse. "Can you haul several chunks over to the fireplace?"

They nodded and met her back at the brick expanse with wood a short time later.

"Anything I can do?" Colleen stepped up next to Beth, her arms wrapped around her drenched torso.

"Sorry—you've gotten more than you bargained for on this excursion."

Colleen shook her head. "Builds character, right?"

Beth laughed. "Right. That'll be our tagline for the next camp. 'Join Trinity Family Horse Camp. We build character through all nature's elements.'" Beth scraped away the cobwebs and placed the wood into the fireplace like a log-cabin square, then added the kindling to the center. "Can you find me some dry twigs and leaves?" she asked Colleen, who returned a few minutes later with mostly dry tinder. "Perfect."

Beth added them to the center and pulled her weatherproof matchbox out.

Please light.

A flicker—then a breeze snuffed her flame. She lit a second one, this time holding her hand around the delicate light until the tinder smoked and burst into flame.

A whoop startled her. She looked up to see the smiling faces of the riders, who applauded.

Go her. She could start a fire.

Clearly, expectations had been lowered. Well, she'd take it. They hadn't mutinied, or whatever it was called when cowboys raised resistance and rebelled.

For the first time since last night's campfire, conversation buzzed again as the riders each shared their tales of woe from the grand adventure.

See? It built character. And with the dark clouds pushing west, there was something celebratory in the air.

"Nice work. You're a regular Girl Scout," Grayson said. His warm breath tickled her neck. Made her smile.

"I'm sorry I didn't listen to you—we should have turned back."

"I was feeling a little panicked." His gaze flicked away. "Storms and I aren't good friends."

"I should have thought of that."

"It's okay. We got through it and it worked out. You want to snag a couple people to help unpack the lunches? By the time everyone is dry and fed and happy, these will just be funny stories to recount." He smiled. "See that? I'm working on trusting God's plan."

"You must have had a conversation with Noah and Anne."

He nodded.

"Sure, I can do that. I'm looking forward to food, sunshine, and putting this sad, awful, soggy morning behind us too."

"Exactly." He nodded toward the gear stowed under the trees. "I'm going to round up a few hands to water and feed the horses, then help me dry off the saddles."

"Before I grab the food, do you have extra line? I want to string a clothesline for outerwear."

"Excellent idea." He pressed a kiss to her forehead and reached into his back pocket, then handed her a bundle of extra line. Smiled.

She let their hands linger, the touch electric, even through the cold and damp.

He towered over her, all muscles and brawn and wilderness know-how.

Wow, he was handsome.

She forced herself to pull away and looked for a good spot to hang the line. Two trees near the trail, protected by the forest. Perfect. She hiked over and tied off one end of the line, then stepped up to the side of the path, seeking purchase with her boot. Found a chunk of solid ground near the rocks and pressed into it.

Except it gave way, both feet sliding out from under her in an instant.

She screamed as she fell, and her head slammed on the ground.

sixteen

. . .

GRAYSON'S HEAD SNAPPED UP WHEN HE HEARD BETH'S SHRIEK AND saw her halfway through a fall onto jagged rocks. He dropped the water bucket he was carrying and was running before she hit the ground.

He slid up next to her. "Beth—" He caught his balance, then knelt beside her. The cold mud soaked through his jeans. "Beth?" He swept her hair from her face and tucked it behind her ear, careful not to jostle her.

His hands came away bloody.

No. This was not happening. He stripped off his coat and the long sleeve Henley he wore over his T-shirt, then used the shirt to apply pressure to the wound on the back of her head.

She roused. Blinked up at him. She'd landed flat out on her back, her head against the rocks.

"Don't move." He shifted next to her, the goopy mud tugging him down the slope. "Are you okay?"

She scrunched up her face, closed her eyes. Opened them. Looked at him. "What happened?"

She lifted a hand, brown with mud, and smeared it across her face before he could stop her.

"Let me get that," he said. He wiped the mud away with his coat sleeve.

Green eyes searched his face, and then she flopped her body to the side by rotating her hips.

"You shouldn't move."

Someone knelt next to them. Colleen. She had her medical bag slung over her shoulder. "Hey, I saw her fall."

Beth peered up at Colleen, then back to Grayson. "What happened?"

"You slipped," Colleen answered. "Try to stay still for a few minutes. I'm just going to make sure you didn't break anything." She leaned in and pulled back the shirt Grayson held against the wound enough to look at it, then moved his hand back into place. "Keep that there."

He nodded.

Beth stared at them. Blinked. "What happened?"

"This isn't right," Grayson said. His heart sank.

Colleen moved her hands around Beth's body. "Nothing seems broken."

Beth tried to rub her hand over the back of her head where he was applying pressure. "What happened?"

Colleen met Grayson's look, and she gave a little shake of her head.

Yeah, this wasn't good.

He should have turned them back when the storm first rolled in.

"You slipped," Grayson repeated. "Do you remember?"

Beth didn't answer.

A blade of lightning sliced the sky, followed by a heavy roll of thunder.

So much for trusting God's plan. Despite Anne's words, Grayson wasn't feeling it.

"It isn't safe here," Colleen said. "That lightning's close."

"I'm okay," Beth said. She moved to sit up.

"Please, don't move just yet," Grayson said.

Beth turned, looked at him—well, looked his general direction. "Who are you?"

His jaw went slack.

"Ha!" she said. "Just kidding." Her lips turned upward.

Except, she didn't seem like she was actually joking.

Grayson tried his radio. "Wrangler-one to Base?"

Static.

"Wrangler-one to Base?" He'd expected they'd lose contact with Noah at some point, but he didn't expect to have an actual emergency. "Noah?"

More static.

The rest of the group had left the fire and the horses. Circled around them. "Is there anything we can do?" someone asked.

"I need the satellite phone," Grayson said.

Colleen nodded toward the shelter. "It's in my bag. The bright blue one on the picnic table."

"I'll get it," a female voice called from behind Grayson. Moments later, a phone was shoved in front of him.

He turned to Colleen. "Can you sit with her?"

She nodded. It was a stupid question, but, well, he'd pretty much lost his mind.

He punched in the prefix and Noah's cell number, though he was probably the last person Beth would want Grayson calling. He walked out of her earshot.

Noah answered the line.

"It's Grayson—there's been an accident. Beth fell and hit her head. We think she has a concussion. I mean, I know she has a concussion."

Thunder rumbled again, closer now.

Great. Just what they needed.

"Is she okay? I mean, is it mild?"

He didn't even know how to answer that. "Colleen is treating her. She's confused. I mean, Beth's confused, not Colleen." He couldn't even get his thoughts straight. He'd seen enough concussions at the rodeo grounds over the years. "Like, really confused."

"Can she ride out?"

"I'm not sure...she keeps asking what happened, even though we keep telling her...and she said she didn't know my name, then laughed like she was playing it off as a joke." He ran his hand over his face. "It's not good."

Grayson heard Beth announce, "I'm going to be sick." She promptly leaned over and threw up in a cluster of weeds and wildflowers.

"The crisis response team's helicopter's probably going to be grounded due to weather." A shuffling of papers over the phone. "If you can get her to the west end of the lake, I think an ambulance could get to you. There's a camp service road back there."

"Okay, I'll have to ride with her at least that far. We're at the old picnic shelter, not at the main camp."

"I'll get things moving from this end."

Grayson jogged back to Beth and Colleen.

"This cut on the back of her head is a pretty good one. She'll probably need stitches." Colleen had pulled gauze from the medical bag and held it pressed it against Beth's skull. The bright white fabric had turned red. "Head wounds always bleed a lot."

She was probably trying to reassure him. It wasn't helping.

Colleen used a roll of self-sticking bandage, wrapped around Beth's head, to keep the gauze in place.

"I'm fine," Beth said, but she was still looking at them like she couldn't quite make sense of anything.

She sat up, leaned over, and threw up again.

Grayson bent forward, hands on his knees. He might just be sick too.

"You still there?" Noah asked.

"Yeah."

"Okay, I'm going to get ahold of emergency services and the

244 · Rachel D. Russell

CRT. Let's get her out of there, then we'll deal with hauling the horses and riders out from the access road if we have to. Don't worry about that."

Grayson wanted to punch a fist through something. Rail at God. Ask Him where He might possibly be in all this.

"All right," Grayson said. He looked over at Beth.

She was still in her sopping wet clothes, mud now up her backside too, her hair matted to her face.

She demanded to stand and clambered upright. Swayed.

"Have the ambulance meet us at the access road. I'll get her there."

"Hang in there," Noah said. "We're on the way."

Grayson disconnected and handed the phone back, then scooped up Beth and carried her up the rise toward the horses.

"What happened?"

"You slipped and fell."

Colleen followed him.

"They're bringing in an ambulance or the CRT or something. I don't even know. I just need to get her to the access road."

She nodded. "Okay, how can we help?" Marvin Jaspers, John Kane, and several other riders came to help.

"I need to saddle my horse."

John Kane stepped forward, and Grayson passed Beth over to him.

"Is she okay?" Ginny peered out from behind her mom.

"We're going to get her the help she needs," Colleen answered.

Beth was still asking what had happened.

Grayson's hands moved quickly, snugging Maverick's cinch and sliding the bridle back into place. He led the sorrel out from under the trees and swung into the saddle.

Riding double was never the most comfortable thing. He lifted Beth from John's arms and held her petite body tight against himself. "Thank you."

The man nodded.

"Colleen, you've got things here?" Grayson swallowed. Because, yeah. Otherwise, he was leaving an entire crew of campers behind to fend for themselves in the middle of the North Shore woods.

"You take care of her. I've got this here."

"Thanks." Grayson turned Maverick away from the group, who wore heavy lines of worry on their faces.

"I need you to do this for me, Mav," he said. "Slow and steady."

Beth clung to him. So much wet and mud and blood. The bandages that Colleen had wrapped on Beth's head had soaked through.

And the new front of clouds had rolled in, bringing with them enough rain to soak the Sahara. Grayson's hat kept most of it out of his eyes, but he couldn't do much for Beth.

He gave Maverick his head, and the gelding picked his way along the muddy trail. Not even the rolls of thunder shook the horse.

He was solid.

By the time they reached the rendezvous spot, Robin and Sammy were waiting with the fresh meals, parked right next to an ambulance. Noah and Anne's vehicle was parked behind the bakery van.

Robin's hand covered her mouth, and she let out a little gasp. "Oh, Grayson," she whispered.

The medics opened the back of the ambulance and lifted Beth from his arms.

Noah stepped forward. "Go with her," he said.

"The horses? The riders?" Grayson wiped the rain from his face.

"We'll take care of it. I've got Walter coming up with a trailer, and the church is sending up a van.

"Walter's here?"

"He just got back to town. Trust me—we've got this."

Grayson leaned into Maverick's mane. Rivulets of water ran down the horse's sides. "Thank you," he whispered.

He passed the lead line to Noah and climbed into the back of the ambulance before the doors closed.

❧❧❧

BETH OPENED HER EYES. WHITE CEILING. HER BED IN HER BEDROOM in her dad's house. Her bedside lamp was on.

She ran her fingers along the floral quilt, her fingers going up and down over the stitching.

She blinked, hoping that might clear the fog. She couldn't remember getting into bed. Or why her head felt like a steam engine had run it over.

"Hey," Dad said. He sat on the end of Beth's bed. Haggard lines creased his face.

"What's going on?" Beth rubbed her hands over her eyes and scooted into a sitting position. "What time is it?" She touched the wrap on her head. A bandage.

"Go easy." He put a hand on her leg. "You'll be able to take that bandage off tomorrow. You have a couple stitches. It's almost eleven."

Stitches? Eleven? Beth stared at her curtains. Darkness. "What day is it?"

"It's Saturday night."

Beth checked the calendar on her wall—May. That didn't seem right.

Dad stood, lifted the calendar from the wall and turned several pages. "Your calendar is wrong. It's July first."

Memories, vague and fuzzy, spun in Beth's mind. She had no idea what she'd had for breakfast. She tried to make sense of how she'd gotten into bed. She was wearing athletic shorts and a T-shirt, but she couldn't remember putting them on.

She'd been wearing jeans. She thought.

Horses. Right? Yes, horses, riders. Wildflowers. Laughter. Rain. They were snapshots, not full memories. Just disconnected pieces.

She sucked in her breath. "The ride—we were on a ride, right?" She remembered rain slashing across the trail. The storm. "Oh no!" She covered her face in her hands. "The storm ruined the ride?" She scooted upright in the bed. Wobbled. "Where is everyone?"

"Hey, slow down. The riders and horses are fine."

"Was the ride canceled?"

Dad nodded. "Don't you worry about that. Noah and Walter hauled them back to the barn, and the riders were bused back because the weather forecast changed. We're expecting storms the rest of the week. Do you remember the ambulance?"

Beth shook her head. "No—but if the ride is over, we won't have the camp funds. It's not going to be enough." She'd lose everything she'd hoped for. "My job. The horses. We won't even have enough hay." She swiped away the tears from her cheeks.

Dad handed her a tissue. "Let's worry about one thing at a time. You need rest."

She'd be processing refunds for the next two days.

Dad sat down on the bed next to her. "You scared me." He leaned forward and wrapped her in a hug.

"I remember opening my eyes, and I didn't know anything for a few moments. Not even my name." She pulled away. "That was the scariest moment in my life. I couldn't remember my name...but I remember Grayson's face."

Dad seemed to stiffen.

Oh, Grayson. She had a memory of being in his arms. Holding his hand in the ambulance. His face...wrecked.

Then being in a room with large equipment at the hospital. She picked up the stapled discharge paperwork from her nightstand.

Her fingers brushed across the back of her head where a tender spot ached.

"Be careful. You have some stitches."

Eww. Stitches? She read through the hospital's printout. "This says you were supposed to be waking me up every hour."

"We were. You don't remember?"

"No. We?" And yes, she hoped it meant Grayson.

"Courtney's here." He shifted on the bed. "And Janet."

Oh.

Beth blinked. She remembered none of it.

She heard voices down the hall.

Courtney leaned into the room. She wore an oversized sweatshirt and leggings, her hair in a loose ponytail, like she'd dressed to sleep on the couch. "You're awake." She shifted, looked at Dad. "You have company," she said. "Grayson's here."

Dad stood, his jaw tight. "I'll check in on you in a bit." He disappeared out the doorway. Voices, deep and hushed, exchanged words down the hall.

Then Grayson filled the doorway, his face drawn and pale.

It stirred memories… His coat wrapped around her. Rain pelting them.

"Hey." His Adam's apple bobbed.

"Hey."

He stood with his hat in his hands, his fingers rubbing the edge of the it. "You scared me."

"I don't remember much." But yeah, she did remember the look in his eyes. The one that still tore her heart in two. "Only bits and pieces. I'm sorry."

He nodded, his lips pressed. He stepped farther into the room. "They said you might get back some of your memory."

"Most of the day is a blank. I remember it seemed like everything was fine. I don't know."

"It's okay. Give it time."

"I remember being afraid to let on how confused I was. Which doesn't make any sense."

"You kept asking what happened." He stepped closer to the bed. "It didn't matter how many times I told you. You'd ask again. You couldn't remember." He sat down next to her.

He smelled soapy and clean, and she wanted to lean into him. Get her bearings.

"Seeing you on the ground, unconscious—it was—" There was a scrape in his voice, and he paused. Closed his eyes. "It broke a part of me." He tucked a lock of hair behind her ear, his hand lingering on her cheek.

She covered his hand with her own. "I'm sorry."

"It isn't your fault—if anything, it's mine. It was my idea for the trail ride."

"Stop—look, I'm fine." Beth spread open her arms. "I'm fine. God brought us through that and, yeah, I don't know what's going to happen with the camp or my job, but...I want whatever that is to include you." She sounded pitiful. Just like when she'd begged Lyle not to go.

She blinked and bit down on her quivering lip.

Because this wasn't Lyle. It was Grayson. And even with a head injury, she was pretty sure she was falling in love with him.

"I came to Deep Haven thinking I'd work the camp for the summer and head back to Oregon—I thought I could just do that. No strings."

"You have. You're doing a great job." And okay, maybe she was hoping she was the string he seemed to imply getting tangled in.

"I should have never agreed to this. I knew I had to leave for Oregon. But seeing you hurt, watching it all happen like some horrible slow-motion movie..." He ran his hands through his hair. "I'm so far in over my head."

"You're not—it's okay. I'm okay."

"I tried to convince myself it would work itself out—you know, trust God with the plan. Look where that got me." Anguish contorted his features.

"He took care of me. Do you realize how much worse this could have been?"

"I can't lose someone else, Beth."

"I'm here—you can stay. We'll figure it all out. You could stay and run the camp if we can find a way to save it. We'll keep running it together."

"It's Jesse's camp to run." He shook his head. "We knew that all along. He's the head wrangler."

A retch curdled in Beth's stomach. "What are you saying?"

"I think this is where I need to go." He looked away. "I talked to Walter. He said he'll cover until Jesse's back. His doctor thinks he can be back by mid-August."

"The kids need you."

He shook his head. "I'm sorry I made such a mess of this." He took a breath. "I'm needed back in Oregon. The purchase on my new place is finally going through." He shifted. "I have a lot of work to do there."

Beth closed her eyes. No. This wasn't happening. "Now? I need you here." She tried to will the fog in her brain away. "You love being here."

He took her hand. "We always knew this is how it would end, right? We knew it."

She shook her head. No. She'd imagined he'd stay. That he would love her enough to stay. Be a part of her life in Deep Haven.

"You're a great interim assistant camp director." He ran his hand down her arm. "You'll do great in that job."

"I'm not even going to have the job anymore."

"You will. And you have your dad. Dylan. Marie. Eli."

She blinked back the tears. "Stay."

"I can't." He shifted his weight. "I have to go. I'm getting horses for the Oregon camp—I was going to tell you before the ride, but we didn't have time."

"What horses?"

"There's a dude ranch that's closing, and I can get good

horses for a fraction of the time and cost it would normally be."

She wanted so much to be happy for him. So much to just say she'd go too.

But she wasn't the kind of person who just up and left her family.

He leaned forward and placed a kiss on her forehead. Held her. "I have to leave early Monday."

She inhaled him. Clung to him. "Don't go. Don't run away."

He stiffened. "I'm not running away, Beth."

"Aren't you? Because you're afraid you'll lose me, like you lost your parents? Like Harper?" She sat upright, her heart racing and her head pounding. "I may not remember today, but I remember you being the guy who wanted to trust God."

"I'm trying really hard to trust Him, but He isn't making it easy."

"You only trust Him if everything is going your way—you don't really trust Him if His plans are not in alignment with your plans."

"Are you sure that's me you're talking about?"

Oh.

"Because if I'm clinging to fear—and quite possibly I am—then so are you."

She recoiled at his words.

"I've done all kinds of things that scared me," she said. *Like falling for you.*

"But there's one thing you can't do, and I won't ask you for it." He ran his hand through his hair again, leaving it rumpled. He stood. Backed away from her bed. "I don't want to hurt you, Beth. I never, ever wanted to hurt you."

And then he was gone.

Beth waited until she heard the front door open. Close.

She buried her face in her hands. Hiccupped a cry. She knew the sound of the slippers in the hallway. And when the sobs overtook her and racked her body, she leaned into Dad's embrace.

seventeen

. . .

GRAYSON DROVE AROUND DEEP HAVEN TWO DAYS AFTER BETH'S accident, trying to capture the images for the last time. Java Cup. Wild Harbor. He rolled the windows down and inhaled the breeze off Lake Superior.

Joyce, the librarian, waved when he passed her on West Second Avenue. He lifted his hand. Felt like a traitor for leaving town.

He could still see Beth lying in the mud. Rain pelting down.

As much as he wanted to trust Him, Beth was right. He didn't. Couldn't.

It didn't feel like God's grace was sufficient—because he wanted that to look like something more comfortable. Safer. Reliable in a worldly way.

He should have heeded Dylan's warnings and stayed away from Beth.

He kept driving, then pulled his truck into his grandparents' driveway and found them on the back deck.

"We heard what happened," Grandma said. She wore a bright purple top with her white linen pants, like she'd just gotten home from lunch.

"I figured."

"Are you okay?"

He shook off her question.

She gave him a sad smile. "You don't have to go. We've treasured your time here—it's been a blessing."

He wasn't feeling very blessed. "I've got horses to pick up and ranch financing to deal with." No, he hadn't figured out exactly how he'd fund it all, especially once he put his plan in place for the camp.

He was still hoping he could convince Vincent to go into a partnership or maintain ownership while Grayson took over operations and paid rent on the place.

"That seems kinda fast," Grandma said.

Grandpa shifted in his seat. "It wasn't your fault. You couldn't have known that storm was coming in."

"I'm the head wrangler. It was my job to have a contingency plan and to turn back the group."

"I mean the day your parents died."

Grayson's throat went dry.

"I know you'd asked them to go." Grandpa leaned forward in his chair. "It was a horrible accident."

"God could have saved them." Just like Harper Pennington. "And if I can't count on God to save them, it's on me."

Grandpa shook his head. "It's hard to understand how God allows terrible things to happen. But you aren't in control."

"I know that—"

"I know part of you does." Grandpa tapped his temple. "But you don't believe it here." He put his hand over his heart.

No. He probably didn't believe it in his heart. Because how could he accept that?

"You're still blaming yourself. You don't want to open your heart because you don't want to lose your illusion of control."

Noah's words needled Grayson. *Trust God has a plan.*

Grayson shook his head. "You know I've always needed to go back."

Grandpa nodded. "Go for the right reasons, though. And

don't be afraid to take a risk. To ask the question. I think if you look at the past month, you'll see God's been with you all along. He's the One you *can* trust."

The memories of Beth tangled in his mind. He'd been a complete jerk because he wouldn't ask her to do the one thing he'd wanted.

No, he couldn't ask her. Couldn't put her in the same position Lyle had. "I can't make her choose."

"That's right—you can no more make her choose than you made your parents go out on the boat that day. But you can ask. And you'll never know what's possible if you don't."

It was a lose-lose question. If she said no, then he'd be leaving his heart in Deep Haven. If she said yes, he'd be risking his heart to her in Oregon and stealing her from her dad.

Who was he kidding?

He slid into the chair between his grandparents.

Grandma placed her hand over his. "Give it up to prayer, Grayson. We like to pretend we have a lot of control in this life, but the fact is, we have very little. But we have faith."

That was the problem. Grayson wasn't sure he could buy all that. Even if he wanted to.

"This was always the plan, and no, I'm not proud of leaving after this camp disaster, but I've ruined it for Beth. I think it's best I just get out of town and take care of my own business in Oregon. I spoke with Walter Kreder. He's going to fill in at the camp."

Grandpa nodded.

"And I'm going to give the lot to the camp."

Tears pooled in Grandma's blue eyes.

Grayson swallowed. "It's the only way I can make any of this right."

She squeezed her hand over his. "It's okay. I think that's a beautiful gift." The warmth of her hand spread across his. "But what about your place in Oregon?"

"I've got some ideas there. I'll work something out." Blood

flooded his ears, a tidal wave of nature's fury. The right thing wasn't always easy. "I need to stop by the bakery and say goodbye to Robin." He stood and Grandma wrapped him in a hug.

An hour later, he was loading up the last of his gear, still hearing his own voice from his goodbye with Robin.

I do love her. That's exactly why I have to go.

Noah's truck pulled up. "You're sure you want to do this?" Noah asked. "You don't have to leave today."

Great. Him too. "I have to—I've got horses to pick up for the new place. And staying—it's just going to prolong the inevitable. I'm sorry."

"Think about what Anne said. God's grace is sufficient. You can trust Him, even in the darkest hours."

No, he couldn't. And that was the problem.

He shook his head. "I don't see it."

Noah studied him. "You know I came from a rough past in Minneapolis. I'd done a lot of things wrong in my youth."

Grayson stared at the ground. He remembered Noah's testimony from his early days in camp. A past with gangs and violence. The very past that led him to starting Wilderness Challenge.

"God still used me—put me in a place to intervene and save Anne's life. Neither one of us would have ever planned the trials and tragedies we faced—and it hasn't been all roses ever since." Noah let out a breath. "For all that you think has gone wrong, there's been a lot of things that have fallen into place."

Grayson swallowed, a little convicted by Noah's words, but unwilling to yield.

"I just want you to consider if everything that's happened hasn't been to fulfill some bigger purpose."

Grayson let the words ping through his brain and shook Noah's hand. "Thank you." What else could he say? He couldn't be the man Noah thought he was.

He reached into his truck and pulled out the new quit claim

deed. Time he let go of this last piece of the past, though hopefully not his chance to work a deal out with Vincent.

He held it out to Noah. "Here. This is for Trinity. If the camp sells that lot, it'll be more than enough to make up for the shortfall this year." For all the funds they'd refunded the riders. "Nathan's expecting to hear from you. He has several offers on the table."

Noah took the papers and read for a moment. "You don't have to do this."

Grayson held out his hands. "I want to. The camp needs it."

"This is a prime location in Deep Haven." Noah shook his head. "You're sure you want to let it go? This was your parents'…"

Grayson nodded. "I knew I had to sell it at some point. It's time for me to quit holding on. Walter will be here later today." Grayson rubbed his fingertips across the stiff edge of his Stetson. "He can stay until Jesse gets back, and that should give Beth time…" Oh man, he sure hoped Beth still had a job.

Noah's brows rose. "Really? How'd you swing that?"

Grayson had spent all morning tracking down Walter and begging him to come out of retirement just long enough for things to be worked out. For Beth. For the camp.

He'd failed Beth, he'd failed the camp.

He'd even failed God—because he wasn't the man with the faith of a mustard seed.

"He loves the camp too. Wanted to do what he could to keep it open." Grayson nodded toward the barn. "If it's okay with you, I'll buy Tally from you. She's not a camp horse." And he wanted to take Tally because it felt like he was taking a little piece of Beth with him. Every time he looked at her, he could hear Beth's gentle voice. Her chitchat.

Noah tapped the quit claim deed on his hand. "This more than covers her."

"Thank you."

Noah shoved his hands into his pocket. "You really don't have to go—certainly not right now," he repeated.

But he did. Because his life wasn't in Deep Haven. Beth's was. And they'd both known that all along.

"I'd love to have Beth stay here, but you know—if you asked her to go—"

Grayson looked away. Stared at the hay bales where they'd played cards for hours. "I can't do that. Everything she loves is here."

Noah tipped his head and glanced out over the paddocks, turned back to Grayson. "I don't think it's everything."

🐺 🐺 🐺

BETH PULLED INTO TRINITY HORSE CAMP TUESDAY MORNING AND didn't even try to stop the tears. Her windshield wipers squeaked. A large, vacant spot remained where Grayson's trailer had been parked.

Not nearly as big as the hole in her heart.

She walked into the barn and avoided looking at the apartment door. Still, everywhere she turned, she could see Grayson.

Just four days prior, they'd been tacking up for their grand adventure.

She could imagine him hauling saddles out. Leaning against the wall, talking about their day at camp. Out at the hitching post, saddling up Maverick.

She could smell him—his soap and the cottony flannel he wore. The rich, masculine scent of a day's work.

Lyle's leaving hadn't hurt like this.

Did you just expect Lyle would move right into your dad's house with you?

Vivien's question from over a month prior settled over Beth.

Maybe she'd never pondered it because she'd never cared to think that far ahead. Lyle had checked a box, but no—she'd never loved Lyle quite like this.

The realization sank in with teeth. Hurt that much more.

Grayson had been the one to urge her into the adventures she'd longed for. Allowed her to shine.

She walked to Tally's stall.

Her heart sank. It was stripped down. Fresh shavings had been left behind, the water bucket turned upside down.

She walked past Remington's empty stall and stared out at the paddocks. The horses grazed in the drizzling rain. Remington, Rex, and Maverick lifted their heads.

Nickered.

Yeah. She missed him too.

In all the bustle of the trail ride, she'd barely had the chance to tell him what she might have found on Maverick's past.

One person had already responded that Mav wasn't the right horse. But the second? She was still holding out hope. It sure looked like the same horse.

His brand didn't quite match, but it was close. Like maybe it really had been altered.

The markings all matched and, if it was true, someone had been looking for Mav for a long time.

She turned back to the barn and opened the tack room. All the saddles had been cleaned and dried. Every piece of tack hung in its place. Tidy. Organized. Orderly.

Everything she didn't feel.

She'd miss this place. She'd already called Wild Harbor to find out if she could get back on the schedule. There wouldn't be too much available, but it was a start.

She sat down at her desk and grabbed a pen. Started making a list of all the items she'd have to close out before leaving the job. Leaving camp. She had no idea how they'd pay for the hay order—or even how they'd keep the camp open the rest of the summer.

The silence of the barn buzzed in her ears. Wholly and wretchedly alone.

Forsaken.

"Hey."

Beth jumped.

Courtney stood in the office doorway, Vivien beside her.

"You startled me. I didn't hear you pull up." Okay. Not alone. "I'm not in the mood." Beth rubbed her arms. "I told you both he was leaving."

"He's not like your mom, and he's not like Lyle." Vivien's words poked at Beth like a hot iron.

"Really? Do you see him anywhere around here? Did you see his truck in the drive?" She left the office and flung her hand toward the empty stall. "He didn't even have the decency to leave Tally."

Courtney tapped her lips with a finger. "I thought she wasn't suitable for the camp."

"I don't mean for the camp. I meant for me." Her words scraped her throat.

She was losing all the pieces of her life. Just like when Mom left.

Her job. The horses she loved. Her cabin.

"Why did you push me to believe?" The weight of it all pressed in on her.

"This is our fault?" Vivien asked.

Beth held up a hand. "You both should go."

Courtney stepped away.

"No," Vivien said. "We're not leaving." She stepped past Courtney in the barn aisle, dusted hay from a chair, and plopped on it.

Courtney reached for her. "Vivie—"

"Nope. Not leaving." She crossed her arms.

Beth frowned. "Fine."

"Fine."

Courtney turned, searched the barn. Finally settled on a hay bale.

"Does he know how you feel?" Vivien asked.

"I asked him not to go—pretty clear there."

"Have you considered what that did to him—seeing you like that?"

"Have you considered what it did to me? To have him pack up and leave town so fast the trailer door was barely latched?" Not to mention the hole he'd left in her life. Her heart. The camp wasn't the same. Deep Haven wasn't the same.

"He left because he was afraid you'd get hurt."

"Hello—he did hurt me. Far more than this." She pointed to the residual lump on her head where stitches held her flesh together.

"It was probably like watching his parents all over again." Courtney spoke up from the barn aisle.

"Well, watching him go is like waiting for five hours after school for Mom to pick me up, except she never arrived. Then watching my dad fall apart. Completely lose the man he was."

"He said goodbye."

"Oh, goody for him." Beth glared at her.

"He's not like your mom. He didn't abandon you—he had a property to return to." A furrow creased Vivie's brow.

"Coincidentally, when I needed him most."

"I get that it's not the ideal departure. He didn't get it right. But don't think it didn't cost him dearly."

"Whose side are you on?" Beth asked. "And don't tell me 'love's.'" She slid into the other chair. "I don't think I can buy into the whole matchmaker thing again."

Vivien drew her lips together and closed her eyes. "How could he ask you to go with him? He knows how close you and your dad are."

"He could have stayed."

Vivien shook her head. "And done what? Bagged groceries?

Served up coffee at Java Cup? It's not like we have any open range around here. He's a cowboy."

"He had the camp."

"It's Jesse's camp—Grayson was filling in."

Yeah. That's exactly what Grayson had said. Beth leaned forward, her face in her hands, and tried to hold in the sobs. "Please. Let me grieve. I just want to be alone."

Vivien moved her chair over next to Beth's and wrapped her arms around her. "You think he didn't love you enough to stay," she said, her words resolute. "Maybe you need to consider if you love him enough to go."

Vivie's words hung in the air.

She did love him.

"I do love him," Beth whispered. "I do. But I also love my dad. And Deep Haven. And Trinity. What kind of choice is that?" She swallowed.

"You can still love your dad and choose something for yourself. They're not mutually exclusive."

"It feels like it."

A car door slammed. Moments later, Noah came through the barn door. His eyes landed on Courtney, Vivien, then Beth.

"I can come back later."

Beth blew her nose and shoved the tissue into her pocket. Pulled away from Vivie. "I figured I'd get things squared away for the week. Clean out my office."

Noah's brow furrowed. "Why would you do that?"

"We don't have funds to keep the camp open. I'll have to process the refunds from the ride." Beth dropped her hands into her lap. "I'm so sorry, Noah. I thought I could do this job. All I've managed is to shut down the camp entirely. I will take responsibility for feeding the horses until they can be fostered or adopted out or whatever will get done with them."

Noah held out a piece of paper.

Beth stood and took it. "What's this?" She skimmed it.

The deed. He'd deeded the lot to the camp. His parents' lot.

Feels like letting go of their plans. Permanently.

It gutted her.

"Why would he do that?"

"Why do you think?" Noah asked.

Vivien's hand wrapped around Beth's. Squeezed.

Beth swiped tears from her face.

"Walter will be here soon. He's going to run the camp until Jesse's back. Sounds like August sometime."

Courtney stood and wrapped her arm through Beth's other arm. "How did you get Walter to come out of retirement?"

"I didn't." Noah looked toward the vacant trailer spot. "Grayson was more persuasive than I'd been. Walter couldn't tell him no."

Oh.

"So for now, back to business. I spoke with Nathan Decker, and I'm meeting him tomorrow morning to review the offers. It'll close fast and then we'll have the cash we need for the camp—plus a hefty cushion."

Of course they would. That was the sacrifice he'd made.

Noah dug in his pocket. "He asked me to give you this." He held out a small white box wrapped with a deep-green velvet ribbon.

Beth took it.

"I'll...uh...leave you be. I told Walter I'd feed the horses tonight." He grabbed the hay cart and disappeared out the back barn door.

"Oh, Beth," Courtney said.

Beth stared at the box in her hand. Tugged the ribbon.

Let it fall.

Pressed her eyes closed for a moment, then lifted the lid from the box. A necklace with a jade horse. Perfect and unbroken.

And she wept.

eighteen

· · ·

"YOU HAVE TO LET HER GO, DAD," DYLAN SAID. "YOU CAN'T HOLD on to her."

Beth paused in Dad's front doorway. Dylan stood at the kitchen peninsula, both arms outstretched, his hands on the countertop like it was a podium and he was giving a lecture. Dad sat in a chair facing him, his lunch untouched.

"What's going on?" Beth stepped inside. Closed the door. "Let who go?"

Dylan pressed his lips together and his jaw flexed. He stood upright.

Dad blanched and stared at his meal. One she'd prepped for the Crock-Pot.

Neither one spoke. Beth walked to the end of the peninsula. "I'm not a child. What's going on?"

Dylan looked from Dad to her. "That's right. You're not a child. So let's stop treating you like one." He cut a look at Dad.

Dad sucked in a deep breath. Exhaled.

"I'm sorry, sweetie." Dad stood and pressed a kiss to the top of her head.

"I'm fine," she said. "If this is about Grayson, it's not a big deal." It was a huge deal of catastrophic proportions. Not that she was measuring.

"I think it is," he answered, and glanced toward Dylan.

He picked up the Rhine cruise flyer. "You kept asking me about this trip. About Janet. About getting on with life." He set down the flyer. "I turned it down outright because...I've been afraid. I've held on to fear like a shield. As if it could protect me."

"Dad, you don't have to explain or justify anything." She turned on Dylan. "What did you say to him?"

Dylan let out a breath.

Dad held out his hand. "I never wanted to admit that you were holding on to your promise all these years." His blue eyes watered. "I should have. When you came up with reasons not to go to college, I rolled with it because I wanted you here. I guess I've been selfish."

The look on his face destroyed her. "You aren't selfish."

"I have been. I've let you cook, clean, and shop for me." He gestured toward the refrigerator. "When I sat down with Janet and was telling her about my life, I was embarrassed when I realized how much I've leaned on you." He ran a hand over his gray hair. "I don't know, one year turned to another." He lifted his hands. Dropped them. "And here we are." He slumped back into his chair.

Beth sank into the chair next to him. "You've given me a home and support and encouragement. I love my life with you." She looked up at Dylan. "I chose this."

Dad held up his hand to stop her. "I've held you back. Your brother's right." He gripped the edge of the kitchen counter like he dangled over a five-story precipice. "I've held myself back." He glanced over at Dylan, who gave him the slightest nod.

And why, suddenly, did it feel like Dad was rejecting her too?

"Are you saying you don't want me to come by? Don't want Saturday breakfasts together?" Her heart sank.

"Not at all—but it's time for one season to end and another to begin." He tapped the peninsula. "You should visit Oregon. See what you think of it."

Oh. Beth's throat thickened. "Deep Haven is my life."

"It'll still be here. I'll still be here." He waved the flyer. "I mean, when I'm not on this cruise."

"You're going to go on that cruise?"

"Yeah. I think it's time I spend some time exploring the world too."

Maybe you need to consider if you love him enough to go.

Dad scrubbed his hands over his face. "I've lived in fear for so long. I guess I just fell into what was comfortable. Easy."

"We both did," Beth answered.

He nodded.

"Life is too precious to waste." Dylan's words were spoken like a man who knew. Who was watching his wife battle an insidious foe.

Beth reached out and took his hand. Squeezed it.

Dylan leaned back against the far countertop. "I owe you an apology too, Beth. I didn't want things to be weird with me and Grayson. I probably played the big brother card a little too hard." He ran a hand across his beard scruff. "He's a good man—a changed man."

A whole man.

Do not be afraid; do not be discouraged.

Beth sat in the kitchen beside the two men who'd always been there. Thousands of meals shared at that very peninsula. And they were telling her to go?

"Who'll make pancakes on Saturdays or pick up the eggs you always forget?"

"You don't have to take care of me, Beth." Dad gave a wry smile and nodded toward Dylan. "I'll just crash his grill nights if I'm too tired to cook."

"Who'll remind you of your appointments and make your coffee—Dad, your coffee is awful."

"I'm not the first person who's had to learn how to cook for myself. Dylan, Marie, and Eli are here." He flushed. "And Janet."

Wait—what? "Are you two dating?"

Dad lifted his shoulder. "We're getting reacquainted."

"He means yes," Dylan said. "They're both going on that Rhine cruise."

Oh.

"It's time for you both to venture forth." Dylan raised his arms, as if ushering them onward.

"I have the camp responsibilities. I actually still have a job." She turned to Dylan. "Did you know that Grayson gave the camp the deed to the lot?"

Dylan shook his head. "I'm not surprised, though. As for the camp, Noah and Jesse can figure out the assistant camp director position. You said there were a ton of applicants from Minneapolis before Noah agreed to put you in as interim."

Her camp, though? Could she give up her camp?

Beth ran her hands through her hair and leaned forward onto the kitchen counter. She tried to imagine packing her bags. The long drive to the airport. Good grief, she'd never even flown before. Oregon felt like it might be halfway around the world.

"I don't know if I can leave Deep Haven."

Dad placed both hands on her shoulders. "Sweetie, Dylan's right. I don't think you can stay."

No amount of golden Oregon sunrises or miles in the saddle would ease the void in Grayson's heart without Beth. Even after his cross-country drive and more than two weeks in Oregon, he still missed her.

The sweet softness she brought into the day. Her laughter floating on the breeze across the paddocks.

He'd rolled out of bed early to drive to the back end of the property and replace fencing. That was part of the deal he'd made with Vincent. Sweat equity and an owner-carry contract. At least until Grayson could afford to buy the place outright. Without the money from the lot sale, his bank loan had dissolved.

Unfortunately, repairing the fence didn't hold the satisfaction Grayson had hoped for. What was the point if he didn't have anyone to share it with? And not just anyone. Beth.

Nope. Being back in Oregon hadn't dulled the ache in his chest. And Tally? He'd thought she'd ease the pain. Instead, she made it worse. He couldn't look at the horse and not see Beth or hear her voice, chitchatting with the buckskin like they were old friends.

"So, let me get this straight—you had the girl and you just up and left her?" Vincent drew his arm across his forehead and set another fence post. His short gray hair stood up on end, a little wild from the hours of labor.

"Not my best moment," Grayson said.

He'd thought the best thing he could do was put miles between himself and Deep Haven. Focus on his new property.

Because he'd left *for* Beth. He hadn't left Beth.

Not that anyone else would ever get that. Probably she wouldn't, either.

"Uh-huh." Vincent paused. "You know, I was hoping to get out of this property before the fence needed replacing. I'm too old for this." He let out a laugh and rubbed his shoulder.

"I'm sorry." Grayson took a breath. Yeah, it was hard work, and he used to find a lot of pleasure in it. "I'm going to make this contract worth your while."

Vincent nodded. "We'll get it sorted. I'm just glad you were able to get the bulk of the Klamath string."

Grayson couldn't see the horses from his vantage point. They were all being held in the paddocks near the barn on the front half of the acreage. Hopefully they didn't have any fence pushers, because he and Vincent had a long way to go to replace the sketchy old strands of barbed wire with hotwire tape. Maybe someday he'd be able to afford split-rail fencing.

They'd been out working since sunrise and had a long way to go. The hours slogged by. At least yesterday's rain had softened the ground a bit.

Grayson had hoped to keep his mind busy with the ranch. Unfortunately, he couldn't even lose himself in work. Not when Vincent had turned to twenty questions over what was eating at Grayson.

He slid the post driver over the top of the T-post. Slammed it down. Again and again.

Dylan's call on the drive back to Oregon hadn't helped.

I don't want her to get hurt, Grayson had said.

I think it's too late for that, don't you?

Dylan's words had pummeled Grayson.

He'd tried in every way he could to not leave her like her mom or Lyle had—and that was exactly what he'd done.

The conversation had made him want to take the next exit and turn back east, straight back to Deep Haven. How could he possibly align the two separate lives that he and Beth lived?

He could live in Deep Haven, where he'd...do what? Ranching and horses were who he was.

He couldn't ask her to leave her family. To leave the town she loved.

Not for him. Because he had to allow her to do what her heart felt called to do. Be with her dad. Work at the camp. Live in the community she loved.

Oh, how did doing the right thing feel so wrong?

He sank the post down and hefted the driver off the top, set it to the ground, and wiped his brow.

Vincent grabbed another T-post from the truck bed and placed it into position.

Grayson hoisted the driver into place. Began the rhythmic pounding. He slammed the post driver down again and again, feeling the blisters build even under his leather gloves. He'd lost count of how many fence posts he'd replaced on autopilot.

He was lucky he hadn't smashed a post straight into his foot.

Robin hadn't been any help either.

He'd stood in the bakery, telling her he was trying to do the not-selfish thing.

Slam.

How he couldn't ask Beth to come to Oregon.

Slam.

She had her dad there.

Slam.

And Robin had had a quick retort. *You'd rather just walk away. Pretend you don't love her?*

He stepped away from the fence post at the memory. At the words he'd said. *I do love her. That's exactly why I have to go.*

And just like that, he was riding next to Beth, the sunlight weaving those golden threads through her hair, courage and delight lighting her eyes. He was catching her subtle scent of coconut, citrus, and tropical flowers. Listening to her infectious giggles that started as a titter and grew until her whole body shook and tears streamed down her face.

He was being lit on fire by her kisses.

He loved her. He loved every nuance of her. Her sweet nature. Her humor. Her wisdom. Her intuition.

He loved her enough to let her go. Wasn't that what the cliche said?

Was he fooling himself?

He'd made the decision. The sacrifice. He'd expected it to feel a lot better than it did. Nope. He didn't feel noble. Not at all.

"Hey, I'd like to finish this section of fence today," Vincent said. "Do you need me to do that for you?"

Grayson blinked and walked to the truck. He leaned forward against the sidewall of the truck bed.

He'd been an idiot to leave Deep Haven like that. He'd let down Noah. The camp. The kids. Beth.

Noah had been right.

For all that you think has gone wrong, there's been a lot of things that have fallen into place.

Grayson stared out across the meadow, the pines, the blue mountains.

He had so much to be grateful for, just like Beth had said.

He took care of me. Do you realize how much worse this could have been?

God had been with him in the darkness.

He carries me through any and every hard thing life brings.

Anne's words anchored in Grayson's soul, the clarity washing over him for the first time.

God had rescued him from the storm—as well as Robin and Oliver. He'd given Grayson grandparents who'd raised him, loved him. Friends.

Trinity. The horses.

Beth.

Grayson gripped the side of the truck and leaned forward, his head on his hands. "Oh man." He'd only focused on what he'd lost.

"Want to talk about it?"

"I don't know. I don't even know...I'm thinking I've had some things all wrong." Grayson looked up at the older man, whose dark eyes held more than six decades of wisdom.

"How so?"

Grayson waved him off. "I don't know how to explain it." How could he possibly explain the truth that had just settled over him?

"Try me."

"All these years, I thought God left us—literally left my siblings and me in the storm. That I couldn't trust Him when things got hard. I didn't see Him."

Vincent pressed his lips together, the weathered lines of his face creased. "And now?"

"He saved us. Rescued us. I'm realizing all the good things God's brought into my life."

"Amen to that." Vincent wiped his brow. "Every good and perfect gift comes from God." He pointed toward the fence they'd been working on. "This camp you're getting started...it's going to be its own blessing to a new generation of youth. The lost. The hurting. The lonely." Vincent looked back to Grayson. "You're equipped in a special way because of every experience you've had."

A lump formed in Grayson's throat. Was Beth one of those good things too? "I wish I had left Deep Haven the right way."

"Call her." Vincent stood on the other side of the truck bed, facing Grayson.

Grayson shook his head. "I've tried. I dial." He gave a sad laugh.

"Dialing isn't calling."

"I can't hit Send." Grayson leaned forward, his head in his hands. "What would I say?"

"Talk to her."

"I can't..."

God is good. His grace is sufficient.

Beth had been right. He hadn't truly been trusting God. He'd been going through the motions. Trying, he'd say. But not doing. Not actively surrendering, praying, and trusting, despite believing that he'd been called to start this camp. That he could help kids like Eli, Mason, Chloe, and all the rest.

He'd been expecting God's answers to his prayers to look like his own vision for his life.

The horizon, stitched to the sky by the ponderosa pine and mountain peaks, stretched wide and blue. The same horizon that used to bring him peace now left him restless and lost.

Grayson tugged off his leather gloves, grabbed his water bottle from the tailgate, and tipped his head back. Let the cold water scour his throat.

Everything in him knew he needed to be in Oregon.

272 · Rachel D. Russell

"Seriously, I think you should call it a day. Rose would be more help than you. And she has arthritis in her hip."

Ouch. Grayson held up a hand. "I'm good."

"You aren't one for lying." Vincent set his gloves on the edge of the truck bed. "And you're about as good at it as you are at playing poker."

"That's what I hear." He set his water bottle back on the tailgate.

Trust Him.

"Give me a sec—I need to do something."

Vincent laughed and shook his head.

Grayson grabbed his phone. Punched in Beth's number.

She might say no. She could say yes. But he had to tell her what she meant to him. He had to ask.

Hit Send.

His pulse turned to humming static in his ears.

Ring... ring... ring...

Voice mail.

"No answer, huh?" Vincent asked. "That's weird."

"Why would that be weird?" Grayson shook away Vincent's comment. She was probably busy at the camp. Heading out on a ride with Walter and a wild gang of kids eager for some miles on the trails.

He grabbed his gloves, walked back to the fence line, and lifted the post driver.

"We get pretty good reception on this acreage. Surprises me she didn't answer." Vincent shrugged. "Could be she left her phone at home."

"Huh?" Grayson looked up from the post he'd set the driver down on and followed Vincent's line of sight.

Rose's old mare, Daisy—as arthritic as her human—lumbered toward them, and on her back, Beth.

He swiped his hand across his eyes. Looked again. Stared.

It was Beth. Beth, riding right toward him. His heart skittered and he let go of the driver, his feet cemented to the earth.

She wore her straw Stetson and a pale green T-shirt tucked into her Wranglers. The breeze lifted her long hair, tugging locks across her face and neck. She rode right up like she belonged there.

She drew Daisy to a halt.

"I don't understand." He blinked away the blurriness in his eyes.

Vincent let out a deep laugh, smacked Grayson on the back, and walked back to the truck. "I think we're done here. I'll see you back at the barn." He threw the gear into the truck bed. "Why don't we pick back up on this tomorrow." He got in, started up the truck, and drove off.

Grayson took a step toward Beth. What in the world?

Beth sat atop the bay, her face glowing. "Hi." She was wearing the jade necklace he'd given her and, oh, how he wanted to trace his fingers along the delicate notch of her collarbone that it had settled into.

"Hi." The greeting was far too small for the million different thoughts and emotions pinging through his brain. "I'm sorry." Well, that sounded so pitifully lame. "I shouldn't have left like that." He swiped a tear from his cheek. "You were right."

"I know." She slid to the ground and gave him a soft smile that settled in his soul. "And I forgive you."

He stepped forward, dropped his gloves. Beth was standing in front of him. In Oregon.

"I would have been here sooner, but my first flight got canceled."

"You flew to get here?"

She gave a shy smile. "They even gave me wings for my first flight." She flipped the ends of the reins in her fingers. "I don't recommend a connection in Salt Lake, though. A wee bit bumpy."

He nodded and took a step closer. "I've heard that."

"But I checked it off my list." She took another step.

Her lips curved in a smile that made his heart flip-flop.

"And you rode Daisy all the way out here?"

"Yes. The woman at the house—Rose?—grabbed the only horse in the barn, pointed me this direction, and told Daisy here to go find you and Vincent." Her smile turned coy. She rubbed the horse's neck and wrinkled her nose. "It took a while, though—she only walks."

"I know. She's twenty-eight and has arthritis in her hocks." He stepped closer. "But you're here—and I can't even believe you're here." He reached out and tucked a loose lock behind her ear. She was a whisper away from him. "I tried to call you. To tell you what a jerk I was...to ask you to come."

Trust Him.

"And here I am." She closed the gap that remained until he could smell her coconut and orange blossoms and see the freckles on her nose and the gold sparks in her eyes. "Vivien scorched me."

"Oh?"

She nodded. "I've hidden behind a lot of fear excuses—so has my dad."

"It's understandable the two of you would lean into each other. Be a little cautious about the world."

She pressed her hands against his chest. Looked up at him. "I didn't understand why God would allow you to walk away." She worried her lower lip. "Then Vivien...well, let's just say that she pointed out I might have been looking at things backward."

"Oh yeah?" He let his fingers skim across her cheek. "I'll be sure to thank her." He studied her. "You came all this way to tell me that?"

She shook her head. "I came to stay. If you want me here."

Everything in his head screamed yes.

Oh, good and gracious God.

He held himself together. Barely. "Are you sure?"

She nodded, fierce confidence in her eyes. "Dad's been afraid to let go as much as I have. He probably needed a little nudge too. We aren't losing each other." She waggled her brow. "He's signed up for that river cruise with several of his classmates from high school. Did you know he and Janet have been dating? Well, he doesn't want to call it that, but that's exactly what it is."

He lifted a shoulder. "I had my suspicions." He squeezed her hand. "But what about Trinity? Your job?"

"Something's happened." She dug in her pocket and pulled out a printed page. "Look at this."

He skimmed the page—an email she'd printed. Stolen quarter horse...lost trail...civil case...reward. He squinted at the photo of a horse embedded in the email. "Is that...Maverick?"

"Yeah. He's from some famous horse's line. He'd been leased for showing and ranch work, then stolen." She looked up at him. "The owner's been searching for him for four years. The person who'd leased him disappeared with him and some other high-value horses. Four—can you believe that?"

Grayson knew of similar situations—though no, not quite like this.

"Did you get to the important part?"

"Which part is that?"

"Okay, it's all important—reuniting a horse and human. I meant this." She turned the page toward herself and pointed. "'I've issued a reward check in the name you provided.'"

He looked at the dollar figure and his jaw went slack. "That's a lot of zeroes for a gelding. He can't be used for breeding."

"He was the last colt out of his mom's favorite mare." Her voice dropped. "His mom passed away three years ago."

Connection. He swallowed.

"He came to see him in person and brought the registration papers. Verified it with his own eyes. Maverick even recognized him, I think—whinnied when he heard the man's voice." She tucked a lock of hair behind her ear. "Of course, Noah offered him back. He's finally home."

"Good work."

"Thank you." Beth pulled an envelope from her back pocket. "This is yours." She opened it and handed him a check.

A check with his name on it.

Man, that was a lot of zeroes. "But—you're the one who found out who he belonged to. Noah bought the horse."

Beth held up her hands. "The sale of the lot has more than covered Noah's needs. This is yours."

Trust.

"It's enough, isn't it?" She looked up at him, her green eyes clear and bright and filled with hope. "Enough to buy this place?"

He stared at the check, the words and numbers blurring. All he could do was nod.

She laughed. "I love you, Grayson Fox."

"I love you, Bookworm Bethy."

He drew her to himself, wrapped his arms around her, and let his lips meet hers. Sweet and tender and whole.

epilogue

. . .

"S<small>ERIOUSLY, WHERE ARE WE GOING</small>?" B<small>ETH LOOKED OUT THE TRUCK</small> windows, watching the lush green blur of forests and meadows. Oregon's mid-August sunshine had turned the land into an outdoor paradise.

Miles passed beneath the deep blue skies.

Oh, how she enjoyed the view from the middle seat, with Grayson next to her, the world ahead of them.

"You'll see," Grayson answered and wrapped his hand around hers. He gave her a wink, then turned back to the road.

He'd packed up the horse trailer the day before and they'd headed west. They'd driven through the mountains and halfway across the Willamette Valley. The scenery had changed from high desert to Douglas fir forests, which made way for the rolling hills and farmlands punctuated by small towns.

He had a silly smile. They'd stopped overnight in a little town named St. Paul. He'd dropped her off at a cute little farmhouse bed and breakfast, then overnighted with the horses at the rodeo grounds.

He'd picked her up as the sun peeked out from behind Mount Hood, then took Highway 219 to 99W.

They passed farms, dairies, plant nurseries. Such a different landscape from Sisters.

He slowed the rig for a traffic light ahead.

"Dad called this morning before you picked me up." He'd called early due to the nine-hour time difference from Germany, something he still had trouble calculating.

"Oh?"

"He said he'd spent the day at Marksburg Castle. Tomorrow's stop is a town with cobblestone streets."

"Quite the world traveler, huh?"

Beth scrunched up her face. "Yeah, right?" She leaned against him. A girl could get used to living like this.

"I had a call this morning too—not as early as yours, though. Noah said Jesse's back on the job now, and everyone keeps asking about the overnight trail rides."

"Even after that disaster?"

"A wise person once told me God can use even the disasters in our lives for good."

He turned the truck and trailer west, merging onto Highway 18, eventually climbing into the western mountains before descending again.

His phone rang and he hit his hands-free button. "Hey, Robin."

"Hi, Robin," Beth said.

"Hey—I won't keep you long since it sounds like you're driving. Just something to think about. I have this idea for an anniversary party for Grandma and Grandpa. Will you guys be up for a fall trip to Deep Haven?"

"Sure," Grayson said.

"Perfect. I'll get you more info as it comes together."

"Sounds good."

"I'll be in touch. Bye."

He clicked off the call. "Sounds like we might have a trip back to Deep Haven in our future. Their anniversary is in October."

"You know I'm game."

"I figured you would be." He glanced over at her. "So, speaking of the future, I have this crazy idea for my new property."

Beth rubbed her hands together. "Like remodeling the farmhouse?" Grayson's new property held a 1950s farmhouse, complete with a saggy front porch and stairs that squeaked. "I think you should do an apron sink and a gas stove."

He laughed. "Clearly, you have a vision for the place—that's good." He winked. "But I was actually thinking about the business side of it."

The little ranch sat at the end of a long dirt road with scrubby sage and tall pine trees, through which the peaks of the Three Sisters could be seen. The irrigated pasture was an oasis of green. Her favorite part, though, was that it backed up to federal lands, and they could ride for days straight out his back gate. Of course, the barn needed work, the fencing was in terrible condition, and the tractor that came with it had died five hours into clearing brush from the intended arena.

And she never tired of seeing Tally out in the paddock. The buckskin nickered and met Beth at the gate every day. She'd come a long way in rebuilding trust, and Grayson had even taken a few short rides on her.

"Business?"

"I'm going to need a partner to help me run this camp."

"Really?" Her heart gave a little flutter.

"Someone who knows how to write grant proposals. Organize waivers and payments and advertising."

"Right. She should know how to ride too."

He looked over at her, a smile in his eyes. "Yes, for sure."

She quirked a brow at him. "Where are you going to find a girl like that?"

"Hmm...I was actually wondering if you might like that job. We could run the camp together. Just like Trinity."

"We?"

He took her hand, wove his fingers through hers. "Yeah. We."

"I think that would be amazing."

He squeezed her hand, a silly smile slapped across his face.

He slowed the truck and turned off the highway. They drove alongside a swampy area with driftwood and dead trees.

"Where are we?" she asked.

He winked at her and kept driving.

They rolled into a small town. Wind-worn signs greeted them with offerings of fresh fish, kites, and dory charters.

"What's a dory?" All she could imagine was a blue-and-yellow fish with memory issues.

"So many questions." He grinned. "It's a flat-bottomed fishing boat." He put down the windows, letting salty, briny air whip through the truck. They crossed a bridge, and a flock of seagulls cried along the river's edge. "The dories launch straight off the beach."

"Oh, we aren't."

"We are."

"It's really the ocean?"

He nodded.

Her first time seeing the ocean. And it would be on horseback.

She palmed her chest, hoping to calm her racing heart. A ride on the beach? And she'd thought her acceptance into Oregon State University's outdoor recreation program and the cute little rental cabin in Sisters was her big news.

Wait until Vivie and Courtney heard about this.

"You're okay with this? Riding on the beach?"

She nodded. Her feet bounced against the truck seat with excitement. "Yes. Oh yes." Riding on the beach? Every nerve in her body electrified.

He laughed, the warm timbre filling her heart. "The girl I scooped off the sidewalk back in May would have called this crazy." He turned his head toward her and whispered against her ear. "What's changed?"

"I don't know." She giggled. Turned her face away. "That's not true." This time, she looked up at him, met his clear green eyes when they rolled up to a stop sign. "It's your love."

"Oh, Beth. I do love you." He pressed her hand to his lips, and she settled back against him.

He took a left and then a second left, pulling into a large lot. Only two other trailers were parked in the long spaces. Thin veils of low clouds revealed a bright blue sky beyond.

Grayson parked the trailer and they unloaded the horses. "I'm going to let you ride Rio. He's an old pro at this."

She laughed. "Yeah, you can ride Jet." The chocolate-brown gelding from Klamath Falls was known to have a bit of a hot streak. Riding him around Grayson's ranch during her off time was one thing—but the ocean? Not today.

"You're going to have a blast."

"I'm still in shock. Like, pinch-me shock."

She tugged on his belt and he turned. Smiled down at her. She wrapped her arms around his neck and her lips met his. He tasted like coffee, and she leaned into the warm, masculine smell of him.

Oh, how she loved this man.

She released him. "Thank you. For everything."

"Of course," he said, that crooked smile turning her to mush.

They made quick work of saddling. Her fingers trembled with excitement when she slid the bit into Rio's mouth. She adjusted the brow band and then the stirrups.

"Ready?"

"Yeah. I think." Her heartbeat thumped a million miles an hour.

Grayson gave her a leg up, then hopped up on Jet.

They rode across the parking lot, the hooves clip-clopping on the asphalt until they reached the trailhead.

The sandy track wound through stunted fir and tall clumps of grasses.

"That's called Nestucca Spit." He pointed to the body of water to their left. "It reaches the ocean up ahead."

The thunder of surf swelled, the tide swirling in and spraying against the cliff. Several seals sunned themselves on the rocks.

They crested the final dune and she met the ocean. Nothing could have prepared her for the sense of greatness and smallness. Both a roar and a whisper as the breakers crashed onto the sandy shore.

The endless green-blue waves rising, peaking, and tumbling over, rushing across the sand.

The wind lifted Rio's mane, and Beth could taste the salt on her lips. The twenty-minute ride along the windy trails had warmed up the horse, and she could feel Rio's body tightening beneath her.

She shortened her reins.

"You good?"

"Yeah. We're good. He's excited."

"What if next time we can bring Tally?"

She grinned. "You think she'll be ready?"

"I do. She's got a big and forgiving heart, like someone else I know."

"I'd like that."

He pressed his hat down. "Rio's been here before and is comfortable even in the waves. I'll be right beside you." Grayson circled Jet around. "You set the pace. Rio will respond."

He settled Jet next to them and reached down to pat Rio's neck. "Be careful."

"I will."

He gave her his crooked smile. "I wasn't talking to you."

Oh. Right. Rio. And the realization nearly unraveled her. She wasn't the only one who'd faced fears. Even the most solid of horses were still horses. Things could happen and she knew what it took for Grayson to take this risk. To release his own fears. To trust God.

For both of them. She held out her hand to him, and he

placed his in hers. She drew it to her lips, kissed it, and released it. "We'll be okay."

He nodded. "You ready to run?"

Yeah. Oh yeah.

All she could do was nod, grin, and let Rio launch beside Grayson's gelding, taking a long gallop in the smooth sand above the water line. The spray of water and wind brought tears to her eyes, and the pounding of hooves aligned with the rhythm of her pulse.

Alive.

And unafraid.

THANK YOU FOR READING *IT'S YOUR LOVE*! TURN THE PAGE TO learn what's next for the Fox Family . . .

Oliver Fox reluctantly returns to Deep Haven in a captivating story of healing, forgiveness, and the transformative power of second chances in *The Way You Love Me* by Michelle Sass Aleckson.

Oliver Fox never thought he'd step foot in Deep Haven again—not with the ghosts he left behind. But when the custody battle for his beloved daughter hinges on his ability to face his past, he returns to Deep Haven and dives back into the fray of his mistakes...starting with the girl next door.

Veterinarian Lena Larson has her hands full with the town's pets, including a shelter for lost animals. The last thing she needs is the arrival of the man who once shattered her heart. But back he is, and with an adorable daughter...and the need to start over. She has no intention of letting him back into her life. But when her shelter is destroyed, Lena finds herself with a garage full of homeless animals—and an unlikely ally in Oliver. Together, they embark on a mission to find homes for the abandoned animals, and help Oliver make peace with his past.

But it's not easy to come home. Not everyone believes Oliver has changed, and their doubt could keep him from retaining custody of his daughter. More, Lena has ghosts of her own, and they've returned to haunt her. If she isn't careful, they might even have the power to destroy the surprising happy ending she never saw coming.

LOOKING FOR MORE SWEET ROMANCE IN DEEP HAVEN? CONTINUE YOUR DEEP HAVEN JOURNEY WITH RACHEL D. RUSSELL

It's never too late to finish a love story…

Former Army Ranger Cole Barrett has a new mission objective—sell his grandfather's house in Deep Haven, and leave the town that contains his childhood hurts for good. Unfortunately, the tenant in the garage apartment refuses to move. Even worse? It's his childhood crush, Megan Carter, and her son.

Wedding planner and single mom Megan Carter loves Deep Haven. To her, it's the place where she makes dreams come true—at least, everyone else's. Hoping to purchase a local B & B and turn it into a premier event venue, she's oh, so close to her down payment…until Cole Barrett returns to Deep Haven. Even if he's not back to fulfill a silly childhood promise to marry her, she never expected him to evict her!

When a blizzard strikes Deep Haven, and Megan is overrun with wedding catastrophes, it takes a former Ranger to step in and help. Besides, the more he comes to her rescue, the sooner she'll be able to move out…and he can move on. And that's what they both want, right?

Return to Deep Haven with this magical tale about the one who got away…and came back.

Start this sweet contemporary romance today!

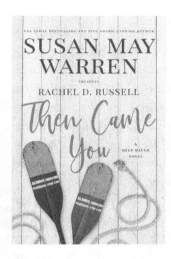

He's in Deep Haven to relax.

Detective Daniel "Boone" Buckam is more than burned out. After fourteen stellar years on the job, one bad judgment call—and, fine, a whole lot of cynicism—has forced him into a mandatory vacation. If he can get his head on straight, there's a job as Police Chief waiting for him back in his Minneapolis suburb.

But then he meets Vivien.

Actress **Vivien Calhoun** isn't really a drama queen. Sure, she gets swept up in the emotions of life—but please, she's an actress. Or, um, was until a stalker made her flee the bright lights of Broadway. Now, she's passionate about directing her local theater production. But when she accidentally ropes an uptight police detective on vacation into her cast, she can't help but wonder if he might be the leading man she's always longed for.

Of course, she's in trouble.

Boone can't help but like Vivien. He might even have a type—vivacious and bubbly, with a penchant for attracting danger. He can smell trouble even if she can't, and is pretty sure her stalker has hunted her all the way to Deep Haven. He'll have to stay by her side—even if it means being in her silly play—to keep her safe. But Vivien is more than he expected as she helps him discover a part of him he's locked away…the part that said he could never love again.

So much for relaxing.

It's summertime in Deep Haven, and the fun is heating up in this laugh-out-loud, charming story.

Get your copy now!

Join USA Today best-selling author Susan May Warren, award-winning author, Rachel D. Russell, and best-selling Minnesota authors Michelle Sass Aleckson and Andrea Christenson in this delightful twist on Bing Crosby's holiday favorite song, Winter Wonderland.

A Deep Haven wedding at Christmas? With snow glistening in the lane, sleigh bells ringing, and all the world a winter wonderland—magical, right?

Or maybe not, because the snowstorm of the century has buried their small town, and as Vivien Calhoun and Boone Buckam fight the sleet, snow, and ice, just about everything can—and does—happen to skid their big day into the ditch. It'll take all their friends—and a few strangers—to turn this Christmas wedding from a blizzard to a beautiful sight in this charming collection of novellas.

Discover four enchanting stories featuring old friends, and new, who discover that there just might be a happy ending waiting in this winter wonderland—if only they can shovel their way out of trouble.

Available now!

acknowledgments

Thank you to Sunrise Publishing, especially Susie and Lindsay, who walked with me through some tough times and personal loss during the writing of this novel. Thank you for believing in me and the story I had to tell. Susie—once again, thank you for sharing the beloved town of Deep Haven with me. Thank you, Barbara, for helping me polish this story through your editing.

My Deep Haven sisters, Michelle and Andrea. Ladies, I can never thank you enough. Through laughter and tears, video calls, and a lot of gifs, I'm grateful for your friendship and prayers. I'm so proud to be a part of this journey with you.

My Novel Academy huddle members— Jenni, Barbara, Suzy, and Nancy. Thank you for the prayers and encouragement. I've learned so much from each of you and am humbled by your belief in me.

Thank you, Mandy and Tari, who never ignored my SOS phone calls and texts, as well as Deanna and Heidi who prayed for and encouraged me without fail.

My local writing group, who truly are encouragers, thank you.

Thank you, Kim, for your continued support, friendship, and willingness to read my writing are deeply appreciated.

I can't even tell you how excited I was to write a story that brought my passion for horses to Deep Haven and introduced my beautiful state of Oregon. After my first draft, I might have been told by a certain mentor, "Less horse." It was a lot harder than I expected to put the horse-related details on the page that would make sense to non-horse people without overwhelming them, but also cover the bases for all my fellow equestrians. There was a lot of deleting and rewriting that happened after that conversation. I hope I found that balance for readers and that you'll grant me grace anywhere I fell short.

While the horses in this novel are fictional, they are a reflection of the many horses I've known. My dear, sweet quarter horse—who once suffered an injury similar to Tally's, only much more dire—has often been referred to as a puppy-dog. She's what is referred to as my "heart horse." The final scene takes place in Pacific City, Oregon, at my favorite riding beach. I'll never forget that first beach ride, and I tried to capture it in Beth's experience.

Of course, I don't know that anyone goes through decades of riding many different horses without having some significant accidents and injuries. Those horses from my past gave me great fodder for the riding accidents that befell Beth in her youth and on these pages. While I took the liberty of putting Beth in a Stetson, this cowgirl wears a helmet.

For my husband and children, thank you. Thank you for your love, your belief in me, and your support. For every meal and hug and word of encouragement. Thank you for not only supported my writing career, buy my passion for horses. You bless me daily and I'm so very grateful for you.

Thank you to my mom. I know you would have stayed to see this story to completion if you could have, but God called you home in His right timing. I'm forever grateful for all your belief in me—how you knew I could write stories long before I believed I could. Thank you for being a champion to my career, sharing with everyone you met the novels I've written. For being the one who so often shared Deuteronomy 31:6-8.

And, my Lord, who has been with me in my grief, in my struggles. He has never abandoned or forsaken me. May my work be an offering to You.

connect with sunrise

Thank you so much for reading *It's Your Love*. We hope you enjoyed the story. If you did, would you be willing to do us a favor and leave a review? It doesn't have to be long—just a few words to help other readers know what they're getting. (But no spoilers! We don't want to wreck the fun!) Thank you again for reading!

We'd love to hear from you—not only about this story, but about any characters or stories you'd like to read in the future. Contact us at www.sunrisepublishing.com/contact.

We also have weekly updates that contains sneak peeks, reviews, upcoming releases, and fun stuff for our reader friends. Sign up at www.sunrisepublishing.com or scan our QR code.

about rachel d. russell

Award-winning author **Rachel D. Russell** writes contemporary inspirational romance focused on forgiveness, redemption, and grace. She's a country girl living in the suburbs, whose resume includes presenting live-animal reptile programs, being a park ranger, a reserve police officer, and a stint in federal prison (where she worked, not lived). She makes wild attempts to balance writing under publisher deadlines with her full-time career with the federal government. When Rachel's not cantering her horse down the Oregon beaches, she's probably interrogating her husband on his own military and law enforcement experience to craft believable heroes in uniform. The rest of her time is spent enjoying her active family, including two college-age sons and three keyboard-hogging cats.

facebook.com / RachelDRussellFiction

instagram.com / racheldrussellwrites

twitter.com / RDRussellWrites

bookbub.com / authors / rachel-d-russell

amazon.com / stores / Rachel-D.-Russell / author / B01APTDXUY

other deep haven novels

Fox Family Series

How Sweet It Is

It's Your Love

The Way You Love Me

Deep Haven Collection

Only You

Still the One

Can't Buy Me Love

Crazy for You

Then Came You

Hangin' by a Moment

Right Here Waiting

Once Upon a Winter Wonderland

Deep Haven Series by Susan May Warren

Happily Ever After

Tying the Knot

The Perfect Match

My Foolish Heart

Hook, Line, & Sinker

The Shadow of Your Smile

You Don't Know Me

Christiansen Family Series

I Really Do Miss Your Smile (novella prequel)

Take a Chance on Me

It Had to Be You

When I Fall in Love

Evergreen (Christmas novella)

Always on My Mind

The Wonder of You

You're the One That I Want

Have Yourself a Christiansen Christmas

It's Your Love: A Deep Haven Novel
Fox Family Series, Book 2
Published by Sunrise Media Group LLC
Copyright © 2023 by Sunrise Media Group LLC
Print ISBN: 978-1-953783-58-5
Ebook: ISBN: 978-1-953783-61-5

For more information about Rachel Russell, please access the author's website at the following address: https://racheldrussell.com/.

Published in the United States of America.
Cover Design: Jenny Zemanek, jennyzemanek.com
Editing: Susan May Warren and Barbara Curtis

Printed in the USA
CPSIA information can be obtained
at www.ICGtesting.com
LVHW041548041123
762973LV00047B/506